Daughter of the

Overking

ALSO BY
ASHLEY YORK

The Warrior Kings series

Curse of the Healer

Eyes of the Seer

Daughter of the Overking

The Norman Conquest series

The Saxon Bride

The Gentle Knight

The Irish Warrior

The Seventh Son

The Order of The Scottish Thistle series

The Bruised Thistle

Daughter of the

Overking

Ashley York

Daughter of the Overking was previously published as
Daughter of the king.

DEDICATION

To Jack.
Look into my eyes
you will see
what you mean to me

AUTHOR'S NOTE

Despite their difficult struggle for survival, the ancient people of Ireland had a very structured way of life. Kingship came not from a single, royal family, but from the line of previous kings who had proven themselves in battle. This was their nobility, and the fictitious heroes and heroines you meet in The Warrior Kings Series come from the line of the High King, *árd rí*, Brian Boru.

Their strong oral tradition kept their histories alive by the telling and retelling of events. That is not to say they were illiterate, just great storytellers. The Dark Ages may have cast a long shadow over most of Europe, but Ireland ensured the survival of many ancient texts by transcribing and rewriting them during this period. The actual treaty uniting my characters, however, is a work of fiction.

I've used authentic names and an occasional crude reference to convey the ancient and unrefined flavor of the times. A pronunciation key can be found at the back of this book along with a glossary for the levels of kingship and explanations for certain words.

Ashley

Prologue

"Can. Ye. Shut. Yer. Mouth?"

The small fire cast enough light that Darragh of Clan MacNaughton, hidden atop his mount in the trees behind the clearing, could make out the lads' expressions. Three silent, grim-faced figures sat around the small fire while their horses grazed nearby. The two who were speaking stood beside a familiar black destrier. The angry voice belonged to Lachlann, the younger brother of Darragh's betrothed.

"I do not see any stone, so why is the beast favoring her leg?" The speaker, a wiry red-headed lad was met with a glare from Lachlann.

Darragh shook his head, unseen in the darkness.

1

After catching wind of Lachlann's plan to sneak away from the festivities with friends, Darragh had decided to follow them. The lads had been practicing a harmless version of raiding on their neighbors, riding like the wind along rutted trails in the dark, spooking the cattle. He suspected they'd been motivated by Lachlann's Uncle Niall, who was visiting from Alba. The big Scot told stories of his own exploits at every meal, and he'd no doubt ignited the lads' imaginations.

Enough for them to borrow the man's prized courser in order to ride faster.

Now that Darragh had proof, it was time to confront them. While his future father-in-law, Sean, should appreciate the intervention, the man always acted as if Darragh would never be worthy of his daughter.

One of the small lads beside the fire held a thumb to his mouth, nibbling at the nail between darting glances at the injured horse and Lachlann.

"We're in it now," he said, his gentle voice carrying the sting of condemnation.

Lachlann didn't hold back his own angst when he responded, pinning the small figure with his gaze. "And what would ye have me do? I find nothing wrong with her."

Darragh winced at the lad's angry tone and dismounted without a sound, a mere stone's throw away from the fire. Lachlann was not usually one to lose his patience, unlike his sister. Brighit's temper was easily ignited, simmering like an iron pot too close to the fire. No doubt Lachlann was feeling the weight of how badly their 'adventure' had gone awry.

"Uncle Niall will have yer head!"

Uncle? All of Brighit's brothers were nearly a head taller than this smaller figure…

Inching a bit closer, Darragh paused again to search their faces, each one smudged with ashes, giving their features a ghostly appearance. The nail biter dropped his hand and turned toward him, searching the darkness with narrowed eyes. Darragh held his breath, his suspicions growing.

When the nail biter stood, the long, dark hair clubbed at the back confirmed Darragh's fear. It was indeed his betrothed, Brighit, dressed in trews and a tunic and looking like one of the younger lads. How had she hidden all her burgeoning curves?

Stepping soundlessly over to Lachlann, she spoke in a tone too hushed for Darragh to hear, but the others turned as one toward his location. He was surprised to feel a slight rush of pride that she'd been the one to hear him since she seemed to be of the same mind as her father, finding Darragh lacking in all ways.

"It took ye long enough." Darragh spoke in a strong voice, crossing the distance to the fire in a few long strides.

The mad dash for weapons ended as quickly as it had begun when they recognized his voice.

"What are ye about? Have ye gone and damaged yer Uncle Niall's horse?" he asked, his sardonic tone raising a few eyebrows.

Lachlann blew out a breath, stepped away from the horse, and turned his pained expression on Darragh. "She's got nothing wrong with her foot but continues to favor it."

Darragh frowned at the dark-haired man, watching from the corner of his eye as Brighit sidled her way to the back of the group and the lads drew together to shield her from him. Lachlann ran his hand down the horse's leg, squeezing above the ankle for it to lift its hoof.

"Clean." The lad made the pronouncement with about as much irritation as Darragh had ever heard him display. That Lachlann recognized the extent of the trouble he could be in made Darragh feel some sympathy for him but not much.

Stepping closer, Darragh slid his hand along the beast's side, patting its rump to calm any fears. His way with animals was no secret. "Easy now."

The answering whinny made him smile. He brushed a hand over the beast's hoof. "Are ye familiar with these iron shoes?"

Lachlann's shrug was his only answer.

"She's only recently been shod. It looks as though they may have trimmed this one a bit too much." Darragh adjusted his hold so Lachlann could also see and then released the sore leg.

Brushing the dirt from his hands before speaking again, Darragh allowed his gaze to take in each of the lads around him, noting the way they kept Brighit hidden. Her head popped up from between their shoulders. Even with ash smudged across her fair features, she was still a beauty. A very feminine lad indeed.

"I'm thinking Niall did not expect his prized animal to be taken on such a ride as ye've given her this night. Her lameness will disappear once she's rested, but I suggest ye walk her back."

"Walk her back?" Lachlann all but whined and the rest of the lads quickly joined in, voicing their own objections to dragging out the return journey.

Darragh raised his hands, ceasing the complaints. "Only a suggestion, but if ye force her to bear the weight of a rider on that sore hoof, she may take longer to recover. I'm not sure how yer uncle will feel about trusting ye again."

The grumbling started right back up as the lads tossed ideas back and forth. Darragh remained calm, keeping his face relaxed and his bride-to-be within sight. She remained silent, again nibbling at her thumbnail.

"Or—" the lads' discussion ceased and Darragh continued. "—ye could allow me to take my betrothed upon my own horse while ye lead the lame horse home."

The men separated like Moses parting the Red Sea, all eyes on Brighit's shocked expression.

"Ye've been caught," Lachlann said.

Brighit finally closed her gaping mouth to give her brother a fierce scowl. She then turned that same expression on Darragh, closing the distance until she stood directly in front of him. Her small body heaved with indignation.

"Are ye not the sneaky one? Pretending not to see me."

"Pretending not to see ye?" Darragh forced an even tone. He found her pursed lips and narrowed eyes intriguing, but he wasn't ready for her to know that. She was unlike any other lass, and this close proximity to her and her family was providing quite a bit of insight into her true nature. That she would go off playing lad, however, had been no more than a sneaking suspicion until this night. "And when was this?"

"This whole time." she huffed.

With dramatic flair, he glanced at Lachlann and his friends with wide, innocent eyes, arms open in supplication. "Did I ever say that my betrothed was certainly not here?"

The others averted their eyes, their quiet chuckles receiving the same unrepentant glare from Brighit.

"Or that the daughter of one of the most powerful *ri túath* would certainly not be dressing up as a lad to race across the countryside in the dark of night." His easy tone ended in a combative declaration.

"Ye did not call me out!"

"And why would I be doing that?" Darragh stood tall and crossed his arms, setting his lips to curl before he spoke again in a much quieter tone. "These lads certainly knew ye were here. As did I. There was no pretending involved."

Shifting uneasily, Brighit glanced around, her proud demeanor slipping away with her obvious distress. There was no help for it. Her father had trained her alongside her brothers since they were young, but it was time to set aside such foolishness.

Darragh glanced about at the lads. Men, really, about the same age as he was. Why wasn't someone curbing her behavior? Protecting her? They were doing the opposite by aiding her in the deception.

Surely they realized they were playing with fire to have the only daughter of their king ride with them, dressed as a warrior. What if she were hurt? What if they were attacked?

Turning his ire on them, Darragh said, "Lachlann, what were ye—"

"*I* told her not to come. *She* doesn't listen."

"Aye, she doesn't listen," Darragh agreed.

Brighit glowered.

Glancing over her attire, he continued, "But are those not *yer* trews? I recognize the stain on the arse." He pointed, and all eyes were suddenly on her derrière. Darragh stepped forward to block the view, irritated with himself at the sudden urge to strangle them one by one for turning their eyes to her. Heaving a heavy sigh, he swung an arm under her knees and grasped her shoulders to pick her up in one fell swoop.

"Put me down, ye oaf!" Brighit punched at his chest—surprisingly strong punches—and came damn close to heaving herself right out of his arms.

He tossed her astride his own mount, leaping up behind her before she could escape. With a strong arm wrapped around her waist, he yanked the reins with his free hand.

"Ye can continue to argue amongst yerselves, but *I* will see the daughter of the overking safely returned myself."

The only objection was the unexpected elbow to his side. He *oomphed* and tightened his hold on her.

"Behave, or I'll take ye over my knee." He spoke under his breath, loud enough only for her to hear, and urged the horse into a trot, away from the others and the wider path they would have to use.

"Ye and whose clan?"

He couldn't be certain he'd heard her correctly. Once they were far enough for privacy, Darragh reined in his horse.

"Ye think I need help subduing my own wife?" He allowed his gaze to wander the length of her, a self-assured smile turning up his lips. "I think not."

"Subduing? And won't that be the way of it?" She snorted. "Forcing me to obey yer every command."

Her words shouldn't surprise him since she showed the same willfulness with her family. And just like with his own clan's teachings, she'd probably been told the only reason a man took a wife was to have his needs seen to: food, children, intimacy.

7

"Ye'll be an obedient wife." His tone was even, his words untroubled.

"I'll fight ye at every turn." Her voice cracked with indignation, her body rigid before him.

Her determination set something off inside of him. "Ye'll lose."

Her eyes widened, and she nearly succeeded in leaping from his horse, but he was able to halt her movements.

"Settle yerself." He kept a tight hold round her while her legs flailed, until she stopped struggling against him. "Does yer father know of these midnight jaunts?"

Turning to give him that tolerant expression he knew so well, she said, "Of course he does. I always have his blessing."

And she lied. Brighit enjoyed treating him as if he lacked any intelligence, as if she thought him incapable of understanding anything beyond battle tactics. Mayhap not even that.

Her condescension had sparked his temper at first, but only until he noticed how irritated she became when he didn't attempt to defend himself. When he answered in a calm tone, his demeanor remaining relaxed, she would scowl. And when he didn't answer at all, she appeared about ready to scream.

In truth, why should he defend himself with any of them? The bards and *fili* sang of his abilities as a warrior even now, not to mention his schooling in numbers and letters. He served as warrior, clerk, and *brithem* to his ambitious father. If not for his sire's expectations for him, Darragh would have been happy leading a quiet life, raising a family with a woman who loved and wanted him. But *he* had no intention of

8

dishonoring his parents by breaking the betrothal, no matter how she behaved.

"Tsk. Tsk. Sneaking behind his back after he's given ye more freedom than any other lass is not the best way to repay his generosity."

Her eyes widened. "And *ye* know nothing about it."

Darragh gave a shrug.

Her expression relaxed into clear gloating.

A sudden desire to keep her engaged pushed him to say more. "Explain it. Explain to me why ye're off with the lads getting into mischief instead of safe in yer bed with the other maidens?"

"The other maidens." She scoffed. "'Tis no concern of yers."

"Ah, but it would give me great pleasure to know of ye." He smiled at his own choice of words. "And soon I will be yer husband."

In the flick of an eye, she was nose to nose with him, her chin jutting out. "Not. Of. My. Choosing."

Facing front again, Brighit was stiff before him. Was there someone else she preferred to marry? She'd shown no partiality to anyone else that he'd witnessed. He'd watch more closely now. Not that it mattered overmuch. They were already as good as wed.

"Our betrothal is not up for debate."

She remained unyielding.

"Mayhap 'twould be best for ye to remain with my clan."

She glared at him.

"Getting to know the clan that will soon be yers will no doubt ease any concerns ye may have about our joining."

"I'm not afraid of ye."

"Brave words from a lass untried."

Even in a loveless marriage, attraction went a long way to smooth the rough edges, and he definitely liked that flush of passion he saw in her when she verbally sparred with him. Passion was passion as far as he was concerned. Anger. Lust. Her willfulness, however, could put them both in a bad situation.

"We'll see." The declaration, delivered with her nose in the air, did not sit well with him.

"Take heed, Brighit. Yer father's disapproval over yer behavior will not compare to my wrath if I find ye have dallied with another."

Her wide eyes quickly narrowed. "And until we are wed, ye will understand if I give yer concerns the attention they deserve. None."

That last word, spoken with such finality, felt like a call to arms. The excitement coursing through him was undeniable. So be it.

"Well then, ye will understand if our wedding night is not everything a young lass might hope for."

Her mocking smile said it all, and he was surprised to find she could indeed still anger him. Darragh squeezed the beast into a gallop so fast, Brighit had to grab him to keep from falling off since he resisted the urge to give assistance.

The battle lines drawn, he settled himself with a deep breath. No, being married to Brighit would never be dull. And he looked forward to it with relish.

Chapter One

One year later

Betrothed since birth.

That pronouncement had hung over Brighit for eighteen long years, and now that her wedding was on the horizon, the days she had left to see to her own pleasure were quickly coming to an end. She needed to take every opportunity she could to indulge herself. Heaven knew, there'd be none of that with Darragh as her husband. He'd require her constant attention, no doubt.

So Brighit decided to stay abed as long as she could... only to have her efforts thwarted by her mother. Thomasina, small though she was, managed to rip the covers from around her toasty warm body in one strong tug.

"Out of the bed this instant, or I'll be calling yer father."

Brighit sat up but refused to get off the pallet. "That's yer threat?"

Thomasina's usually beautiful face squeezed into a scowl. "Do not tempt me, Brighit. Ye'll not like the outcome."

Her mother was like a dog without teeth, but she was clearly piqued about something. Something to do about Clan MacNaughton, more likely than not. And it was Brighit's fault that they were here. If she had married Darragh before now instead of dragging out the betrothal in the hopes she could get out of it, her mother would have peace.

"If I am out of the bed, will ye feel better?"

Her mother's stern expression was the only reason she relented, raising her hands in a show of submission.

Brighit continued, "As ye say. I am a good daughter—"

"I said no such thing."

"—and I would not want to add to yer burdens this day."

"Aren't ye the thoughtful one?" Her tone indicated her disbelief.

She did love her mother even when she was in a foul mood. Thomasina huffed, shook her head as she glanced heavenward, and left Brighit to her ablutions.

Dipping a cloth in the cold water, Brighit scrubbed at her face and neck. Calling on her father to ensure she did as she was told? Given that her father was wrapped around her finger like a strand of thread, that was no threat at all. Her betrothed, however, was a different matter.

Brighit yanked the well-worn gown over her thin shift and tucked her feet into her slippers, foregoing any stockings. No one would know.

What did it matter that the great MacNaughton *ri túath* was here? He was only Tadhg and his wife was only Tisa. And their son, Darragh. *He* was a thorn in her side. Catering to him this day was something she'd rather not do and he did so love to provoke her by asking her to do things for him, things he should be able to do himself. And if she resisted his unreasonable request, both Tisa and her own mother would be giving her that expression of disappointment.

It wasn't until shortly after they broke their fast that Brighit had the opportunity to slip away. The day was perfect for a soak—the sky a clear blue without so much as one wispy cloud to mar its beauty. The lough was a wee bit cold, but Brighit minded not at all. The weightless floating was a welcome respite from her mother's irritation. It was freeing to do as she pleased... except she found herself thinking of Darragh.

The distance between the two clans was great enough that she'd only seen him on occasion in her youth and he'd kept to his father's side. She'd thought he was the most handsome lad she'd ever seen. When her mother told her that he would look out for her, Brighit had immediately thought of the boys who'd run away after pushing her in the mud. She had no older brothers to defend her and the idea that *he* could put them in their place for her? Well, that had made him even more appealing. His disinterest in Brighit had angered her. She'd wanted to get to know him. Not anymore. Now the distance suited her fine. The more distant he remained, the better she liked it.

As Brighit grew older, she had learned being

betrothed to someone from another clan meant she had no lad's attention at home. No one would dare look at her, or even compliment her. Not as a lass. But when she donned her brother's trews and tunic, they'd pat her on the back and treat her as one of their own. She'd prefer that behavior to the drooling she'd witnessed from those same lads—including her own brothers—over the dainty lasses with their pretty hair and flirty smiles. Dumbstruck more often than not. Much better to earn their respect and companionship.

Many a time the lads would forget her presence and remark on the size of this lass's bosom or the roundness of that one's bottom. She would try not to laugh at their embarrassed expressions when they'd turn and see her listening to every word.

"Do not be looking at me," she'd say. "I have my own and no interest in theirs."

"And ye should not be talking so," her brother Lachlann had said to her once. "'Tis not ladylike."

"And what do ye know about being ladylike?"

"More than ye." His face had turned nearly crimson enough to hide his freckles. "Ye should not even be here."

His censorship had seemed like a betrayal. They had always been so close, training side by side. Though younger, he was her eldest brother. Her closest friend. That had set her off something fierce.

"Lachlann, ye have no right to be telling me what I should be saying or how I should be spending my time."

He'd leaned over her, intimidating her with his size. Up until his latest growth spurt, he'd only been a bit taller. His new height dwarfed her small stature. "And if that is so, how would ye feel about me telling

14

Ma and Da where ye been sneaking off to?"

Neither of her parents would be any happier about her escapades than Darragh had been, and well her brother knew it. Her father had been proud of her accomplishments, fighting and hunting right along with the other boys… right up until her menses had started while they were out hunting for the winter and far from home. Her da had been shocked speechless by the blood, but her cousin, Aednat, had been there as well. She was like a big sister, older and wiser, and she'd helped her.

Truth to tell, Brighit had not been well pleased herself. Neither with the inconvenience of the whole experience, nor with the way she was now kept close to home and forbidden to go off with the boys. Sean had refused to listen to reason and his whole demeanor toward her had changed. He'd demanded she start wearing the longer, traditional *léines* and agreed with her mother's assessment that it was time to put away childish things.

That was when she started to sneak off.

The lads she'd ridden with had been sworn to secrecy, and it had worked out fine. Darragh's threat a year earlier had not failed to make its mark, giving her even more reasons to dislike the overbearing man. Her brother had toughened his stance since then. He'd insisted that he only wanted what was best for her—which now meant being safely tucked away with the other lasses. Lasses who had no use for her. Lasses who laughed at her lack of "ability." Lasses who called her strange, stopping just short of saying she should have been born a boy.

She couldn't ride with the lads anymore and Darragh was surely to blame. He'd taken away her freedom. That's what the lads had, what they took for granted. And the lasses? They had to stay behind with their sewing and their gossip and their viciousness. What a waste.

The sound of men approaching jerked her back to reality. If she were caught here unguarded, it wouldn't go well. Her father had warned her to take at least three men with her if she went through the woods and here she was with not a one. How many men would he have insisted she bring had he known she'd be floating naked in the lough?

The dark green bushes to her left, intertwined with delicate honeysuckle, were thick with branches hanging close to the water, providing her with a chance to go unnoticed. Unfortunately, her gown was out in the open, but there was nothing she could do for it now.

"And so ye have the right of it."

Darragh's voice. Brighit gasped and ducked below the water, shoving off the bank toward the bushes.

Chapter Two

"Did ye hear that?" Darragh's eyes scanned the water of the lough, easily finding the ripples marring the lough's flat surface. He lowered his voice and quirked a brow. "Someone's gotten here afore us."

His companions grumbled behind him like they'd grumbled when he'd offered their help with the work Sean needed done. The promise of a refreshing dip had made the hard work of rebuilding one side of the ring fort go much easier. His own disappointment was as keen.

"Mayhap they'll not mind our joining them." It was Terrence who spoke. He usually spoke without thinking and Darragh decided against pointing out the small size of the lough, the number in their group, and the fact that they were not well known here. Instead, he signaled them to wait and moved closer.

Once alongside the water, Darragh noticed the gown and slippers laid out on the boulder. His heart skipped a beat. A lass. He dropped to a squat and turned to his men, pressing his finger to his lips and then pointing at the garments. They remained huddled close together, intent on him. When they caught his message, their eager nods encouraged him and they exchanged goofy smiles. Mayhap they would get a glimpse of a comely lass.

The green color of the material seemed vaguely familiar, but it could not hold his attention. His eyes were on the lough. The brightness of the lass's chemise would be unmistakable against the darkness of the lough floor if she glided past them.

Darragh fingered the gown, a fine material and still warm from her body. He wetted his lips, exhaling a slow breath as anticipation coursed through his veins, but then he heard his father's voice.

This is childishness.

Darragh should not wait here in hiding to watch her. He should lead his men away, set a good example, and above all *not* encourage foolish behavior.

"Is it a lass?"

Darragh turned a scowl on Terrence, signaled the other men to back up, and jerked his finger back to his lips. Their eager faces decided it. He needed to leave. His eyes found the gown again and his stomach sunk all the way to the soles of his feet. He knew where he'd seen it before. On his betrothed. It was Brighit's.

With narrowed eyes, he scanned the banks and the woods around them. She'd come with no protection at all to a place far enough from the village that no one would hear her if she screamed for help. She could easily be discovered by undesirables waiting to catch her unawares.

His face heated.

Undesirables worse than him and his friends?

He stood to face Terrence. "Return to the village. I will be there anon."

They did not question his command, but Terrence's skeptical glance warmed his cheeks even more. The man clearly thought the worst of his intentions. As soon as the others were gone, Darragh strode toward the bush, the gown clasped in his hand.

When Brighit broke the surface, she dragged in air as quickly as her lungs were able. He tamped down a rush of concern for her. It was obvious she'd heard their approach and hidden from them. Her choice to do so under water deserved no sympathy.

"What d'ye here, Brighit?" Darragh stood tall over her where she trembled in the water. "I do not see the men yer father insisted ye take with ye. Just. This. Morning." He turned about, even opening his arms, pretending to look for them. "Where have they gone off to? Surely they should be whipped for such disobedience."

Her wet shift and long brown hair were plastered against her skin. She looked so innocent and vulnerable. The thought of what could have happened to her cooled any sympathy for her condition. "Did ye leave with no one to protect ye? Ye *are* a foolish lass."

Her eyes flashed and before he could stop her, she was climbing out of the lough.

"I do not need to be guarded! My father is overprotective."

He sucked in a breath, backing away as if he'd

been struck. Her brazen move left him speechless and fighting, without success, to not take in every inch of her unabashedly displayed body. A fine body it was with long, shapely legs, and a narrow waist, no wider than the span of both of his hands.

"Wh-what are ye about now?" he asked, irritated with himself for revealing his own uncertainty, but she showed no indication she'd noticed it.

"I'm leaving. Isn't that what ye're suggesting? That I return to the village, where I will be well protected?"

When she stilled, his eyes widened in an effort to remain on her face, the angry slash of her brows and her wide, demanding gaze, and *not* the erect nipples atop her glorious, full breasts or the dark patch betwixt her thighs.

"Well?"

Her tone was demanding, and he struggled to focus on what she had asked. When he finally did, he tightened his jaw and narrowed his gaze right back at her.

"I'm not *suggesting* anything. Ye've no business being out here alone, Brighit, and well ye know it. 'Tis not the time to be sneaking off. There are dangerous men about that could easily take advantage of an unprotected lass."

Brighit shoved past him, ripping her gown from his loose grasp, leaving the scent of ever greens and honeysuckle in her wake.

"Ye know nothing about it, *Lord* Darragh."

She'd taken to using the title for the sole purpose of irritating him ever since her family's visit to Alba where her uncle lived. They'd been visited by Norman knights, friends of her parents. The deference paid to them as landed warriors was a stark contrast to their own system of nobility.

She continued, "*Ye've* not been here long."

When she faced him, he gave up the fight. The air in his lungs expelled as he finally gave in to the urge to let his gaze travel along each enticing curve. He took a step toward her, then halted when Brighit's eyes flashed, in surprise or fear, he couldn't be certain which. She dragged the gown over her head and then hugged herself, covering her breasts, admittedly the area his gaze had lingered the longest—they were exquisite breasts. Her expression remained defiant even as her teeth began to chatter. Darragh pulled the fur-lined *brait* from his shoulders to drape it around her and her sweet scent drifted to him, enticing him to linger near.

"Anyone could have come upon ye. Anyone." He kept a firm tone despite the leanings of his imagination.

"But it was ye." Irritation seethed from her. She tilted her head to pull her long, dark hair out from beneath the covering. The curve of her elegant neck beckoned him nearer still. The only thing that stopped him from lowering his lips to her soft flesh was the decision that this—her neck—was where his assault of her senses would begin on their wedding night.

"I'll see ye to yer father now and tell him what ye've done."

"Do not." Her plea brought her hand up, just short of actually touching him. "I beg ye, Darragh."

The quiet words hung between them. The first time his name had been uttered by her with no hint of derision or sarcasm since his clan's arrival a week earlier. He took a breath, ready to reply, but halted. Her eyes were rounded a little too much. Her brows raised that perfect amount. The lass was working her wiles on him, damn if she wasn't.

He'd almost reassured her that he would stay silent as long as she would promise never to do it again. And he would have been the worst of fools. She *would* do it again. Brighit would always do as she pleased. Only now, instead of being forthright, she was being sneaky. Instead of verbally sparring, she was trying to charm him. That was something the other lasses did, but hadn't she shown him a thousand different ways that she was not like other lasses?

He paused before he gave her his reply. "As ye wish. I will not tell Sean."

Her face immediately relaxed, and she dropped her gaze. He'd swear there was a hint of smile on her lips.

Darragh crossed his arms about his chest. "*He* is only yer father."

Her gaze flew back to him and she narrowed her eyes.

"A father sees to a lass only until she is wed." He smiled. "*I* am the one ye need to worry about."

Her brows slashed down. "Ye have no say over me."

"*I* will control everything about ye."

Her eyes clouded in that thoughtful way she had.

So he continued, "*I* will decide yer punishments."

"Not yet." She spoke through gritted teeth, having dropped all attempts at coercion. "And not ever if I can help it."

"There is no help for it, but I see ye're still struggling with that fact. Whoever else we might have preferred, it is ye and I who have been betrothed. Even now they discuss *when* it will be seen to."

"My father will not force me."

"Is that the game ye've been playing at?" Darragh shook his head, chiding her with his expression. "Sean is beside himself with how best to handle ye. And last fall when he left ye with my clan? It was so ye could get accustomed to our ways and lose yer aversion to marrying, but instead ye snuck off alone to follow him to the Meic Murchadha—"

"I did not go as far as that."

"Ye should go nowhere *alone* and unprotected." Darragh's anger was getting the best of him. He hesitated, struggling for control, but all his emotions were riding him hard.

"My father *loves* me. He does not wish to see me married to a brute of a man."

A brute of a man? Hardly. "But yer behavior has not worked out as ye'd hoped. Ye've merely demonstrated ye need someone to look after ye *now*."

"I do not!" Her nostrils flared. "And yer arrogance is intolerable."

"Arrogance? So ye question my ability to protect ye?"

"And ye question my ability to protect myself." She dropped her arms to press her chest out. Intended as a defiant gesture, it gave him a pleasant eyeful instead.

Her eyes clouded over again. "I've sparred with all the lads. I've proved myself a worthy opponent."

"When were ye forced to defend yerself against a stranger? A man ye didn't know?"

"I'm ready for battle, do not doubt it."

"That, dear Bright, is arrogance." He shook his head, recognizing the uselessness of the argument even as he made it. "Yer father is correct. Ye need to be taken in hand."

Her gasp gave him great satisfaction. "He would never say such a thing."

Darragh merely shrugged. "The wedding can happen in a fortnight, or it can take place this very night."

He was pushing it a bit. His mother had expressed a desire for the priest to be present and he was at least a two-day journey away.

Wetting his lips, he gave her his most charming smile. "I believe it should be this very night that I take ye to my bed."

"Ugh!" Brighit rolled her eyes. "Ye want this even less than me."

That was a bit of a surprise. In truth, he was the envy of all the lads, both in his clan and her own. Brighit was a beautiful, feisty woman. He wasn't sure how to reply.

"So? What is it ye want?" Brighit's expression revealed nothing. "I promise I'll not leave—"

"Yer promise means nothing." Darragh raised a hand when she opened her mouth to protest. "A display of how insulted ye are will not change my mind. I know ye better than that. Instead, let us have a truce."

She remained silent, her lips tightly sealed.

"Ye will *not* misbehave again—and I will agree to wait to take ye to wife."

"Until next summer?"

"Oh no. No one will agree to waiting another year. Yer behavior demands ye be taken to wife now."

"Then how long will ye give me?"

"A fortnight is all." Admittedly, her enthusiasm for putting off the inevitable stung a bit. "But *any* disobedience will result in the truce immediately being

24

set aside."

Her skeptical expression was almost comical. Almost.

"This can no longer be avoided, and they are not inclined to break the betrothal. Yer father is eager to see us wed."

Her eyes rounded. Brighit's love for Sean ran deep, and if she'd been given an opportunity to find a man she could love, no doubt that man would have known that same depth of feeling. He tapped down the regret that clawed at him.

"Ye'll be in good hands. Everyone knows that." It seemed irrelevant that Sean also found him lacking.

"Hah!"

In a flash he grabbed both of her wrists and drew her flush against him. A scowl on his face, he said, "Yer defiance will be the death of ye."

She immediately began to struggle against his greater strength. A futile waste of her energy.

"Let me loose, *Lord* Darragh."

"And ye'll not use that insulting term again."

"I am not yers to command yet."

He smiled at her winded tone. "I need only say the word."

She ceased her struggle, and he loosened his hold.

"Did ye never learn in all yer training that the protection of a village against attack is of primary importance? Yer ridiculous attempts at stalling show ye are no true warrior, no matter how many lads ye've bested. Our parents may have decided on this betrothal when times were better, but there is trouble brewing now. The joining of our clans is imperative for everyone's protection."

He hadn't expected her eyes to dampen and the

irritated way she brushed the tears aside convinced him they were genuine. An overpowering need to soften his words took hold. "I speak to ye as I would to any of the men under my command and not to upset ye."

"I am not upset. Yer spittle went in my eye."

He bit his lip to keep from smiling at the obvious lie. "If ye agree to wed as soon as it can be arranged, we can return and see this done. 'Twould be best for all."

"No."

"No?" Darragh was beside himself. "Ye still wish to act the spoiled child with no regard for—"

"I want the fortnight." She swallowed again. "Please."

That last word cost her. It was there in her eyes—that and her sincerity. He had a sneaking suspicion she would still fight the inevitable, although he'd swear she felt guilty now for making such a fuss. Was Sean so very protective of her that she'd had no idea of the troubles?

It would certainly be easier to proceed if she could offer some sort of concession, mayhap even apologize for the way she'd been behaving to show she'd had a change of heart. Darragh snorted. That would never happen.

"Well?" she asked. Her face was tight, as if she was ashamed of having shown any emotion at all.

"Convince me of yer sincerity," Darragh said.

"I *am* sincere."

"Then show me ye've accepted the inevitable, that ye're willing to become my wife."

Her eyes widened in irritation. "I am."

"That's the problem with prevarication."

"Prevarication? When did I ever lie to ye?"

"When ye flashed yer lashes and begged me not to tell yer father."

"It works for the other lasses, why not me? They get whatever they want. All the lads begging at their feet, telling them how beautiful they are—" She averted her gaze. "—and they're not so very beautiful."

A telling statement of how she viewed herself, but he resisted the urge to reassure her that not one of those lasses compared to her in looks or intelligence.

When she finally turned back, her expression had softened. "I do not normally prevaricate."

He crossed his arms about his chest. "If ye say so."

"I do say so. Ugh!" She blew an irritated breath. "I canna convince ye when ye won't believe what I say."

Brighit's nose flared in irritation just before she shook her head in a most defeated way. The idea came to him in a flash, and Darragh smiled at his own thought before sharing it.

"A kiss. A kiss will convince me." He half expected her to slap his face for even suggesting such a thing.

Only she didn't. Her eyes widened, and she glanced at his lips before wetting her own. She was excited by the idea. Could it be she'd never been kissed before? He'd bet his favorite horse she had not, not with Sean as her father.

"Ye are willing then?" Her look told him she was not only willing but eager. With the slightest movement, he slipped his hands beneath the mantle to graze his open palms up her arms until they rested on her shoulders. Her lips glistened and the vein in her neck throbbed. With a low voice, he asked, "Would ye seal our agreement with a kiss?"

27

The sharpest tip of her head, barely a nod at all, but Darragh would not quibble. He slid a hand from beneath the heavy material to tunnel it under her thick, silky hair and cup her neck, the skin there still cool from her swim.

She leaned in, meeting him halfway. His mouth slanted across hers, a gentle caress, before he slipped his tongue between her parted lips. She gave as good as she got, deepening the kiss to where he was no longer certain who was doing the kissing. He was glad he hadn't wagered his horse on her inexperience, though mayhap she was simply an extremely fast learner.

Without warning, she released him and backed out of his hold, wiping the back of her hand over her mouth. Her heaving chest matched his own.

He reached for her. "Brighit, I—"

She raised a hand, shaking her head, and put more distance between them. It was a long time before she spoke again. "We will wait the fortnight."

Darragh tipped his head, blowing out a breath to slow his racing heart, and said, "Of course… and ye must promise to obey and get into no more trouble."

"I do promise."

Darragh closed his eyes, struggling to quell his throbbing desire. He'd had no expectation of how she would feel in his arms—like she belonged there. Total madness. More likely than not it was his own abstinence that made him so needy.

Brighit walked past him and he took a deep, cleansing breath, adjusting the tightness in his trews before turning toward her. When she mounted, he stiffened, half expecting her to take off at a gallop back through the woods, leaving him to chase after her. That would give him the perfect excuse to lay hands on her, although for what purpose he couldn't be certain.

Instead, she stood tall in her saddle and said, "Would ye be so kind as to escort me back to my father?"

"At once."

Retrieving his mount, he led the way back toward her village, her horse close to hand.

Neither of them spoke.

Chapter Three

Clan MacNaughton, Drogheda

It was a lovely sunny day with a deep blue sky. The kind of day that made a lass want to lie back and watch those wispy clouds as they drifted overhead. At least that was what Brighit would have been doing had she been home, but the fortnight was nearly over. The decision that the betrothed couple would be wed at Darragh's home had come as a surprise. Something about one particular priest's blessing and some local unrest.

It was such an obvious attempt to get her accustomed to her new clan before dumping her there. Even wee Lorcánn had rolled his eyes when their mother had mentioned yet again how happy Brighit would be when she married. Of course, they had all abandoned her once they'd arrived, finding everything else much more interesting than helping her become "accustomed." Over the past few days, she'd seen little of her family except in the great hall of this cold stone castle left from the days of Brian Boru, the High King of Éire.

And now she was to be escorted on an official tour of the *túath* of Clan MacNaughton, the clan of her husband, *her* new clan, by none other than her future husband and his parents. She felt sick to her stomach.

"Are ye certain ye prefer to ride?" Darragh's mother was more than gracious, never failing to show her that supportive little smile as if to say, "Now, now, Brighit, ye know ye can do this fine."

Tisa was right. Brighit could definitely do this. Move here to live among these strangers, see to her husband's needs, bear his children and provide a peaceful place for him to return to after battles at some far off place. Oh yes. She could definitely do this. She just didn't want to. What she wanted most was to be at those battles. To use her training and her weapons. To catch the enemy unawares and then—SPLAT. She'd crush them like a bug.

Only lasses didn't do such things... or so she'd been told again and again.

"Is ought amiss, dear?" Tisa's concerned expression brought Brighit back to the present.

"Nothing. Thank ye, Tisa."

"*Mamaídh.* Please, call me *Mamaídh.* I insist."

Brighit managed to return the woman's smile. "*Mamaídh.*"

"And d'ye not prefer a carriage?"

A carriage? "Many thanks for yer kind offer. I

31

prefer to ride."

Brighit definitely did, but when the horse was brought to her, saddled and ready, Tisa's eyes widened. "Ye aren't going to sit astride the beast, are ye?" she asked.

Brighit actually had to grip her hands to stop from yanking up her gown and showing the woman the leggings she wore beneath. Of course, Darragh's mother would never wear anything so manly as hose or trews. She was ever the feminine beauty at her strong-as-an-ox husband's side.

"Of course not." The words were forced out of Brighit through clenched teeth.

"Good." Tisa turned to the stable lad. "Please see to the saddle."

Darragh and his father were conversing in low tones, something about a treaty violation. Despite their apparent disinterest in her, she was certain today's tour of their land had been suggested as a chance for her and Darragh to spend even more time together. Her husband-to-be did not seem so inclined, staying as aloof as ever.

"*A thighearna?*" A brawny man dressed in mail approached the group.

For the first time, Brighit noticed that all the men traveling with them were dressed that way. As if they were ready for defense. And the sheer number of warriors seemed extreme. She'd thought they were trying to impress her with the number of guards accompanying them across their own land. Now she was having second thoughts. Darragh *had* mentioned some trouble...

"Is there a problem?" Tadhg's expression matched the concern in his tone and right alongside him, wearing the exact same look, was her ever-stoic betrothed, Darragh.

"They've found another carcass left to rot."

Tadhg glanced toward them. "Not in front of the ladies."

Brighit stopped just short of rolling her eyes. He was like every other man, believing a woman's only purpose was to birth children and be at the beck and call of her husband.

Despite Tadhg giving her his back, she heard his next words clearly. "Has it been seen to?"

"Of course, *a thighearna.*"

"Very good."

There was more discussion meant only for the men's ears, but it was lost on Brighit as Tisa saw her properly mounted, her legs together, hanging on one side of the horse.

Tisa, assisted by the stable boy, mounted the same way. Pulling her riding gloves tightly over her perfectly feminine hands, her eyes downcast, she said. "I hope to show ye our loughs. One is quite deep and very private."

Brighit's mind immediately went back to the day Darragh had caught her swimming in her own lough. She felt certain that episode was the reason they'd come to Drogheda. Had he shared the story with his mother?

"I think ye will find the place quite peaceful when the weather permits," Tisa said, a quiet smile on her beautiful face.

Brighit's cheeks grew hot at the betrayal and she shot a scowl at Darragh. He was deep in conversation, paying her no attention. How could he? Why would he share such information with his own mother? Had they laughed over the incident?

"I look forward to seeing all that ye have to show me," Brighit said.

Tisa beamed. "Tadhg. For what do we wait?"

"Nothing of importance, *a ghráidh*. Let us be off."

The guards went first down the narrow path leading away from the aging dark castle. Two riders ahead, three along either side of their group, and two in the rear. Brighit glanced around as if to enjoy the scenery, but her attention was on the guards. Just as she'd suspected, each man had a bow at hand and the keen alertness of one expecting trouble.

"D'ye see the lovely pennyroyal? Oh, and over there," Tisa pointed deeper into the forest they passed. "Ye can find a great variety of Motherwort and yarrow. I do keep my own garden, but there are times when knowing where to find more herbs is worthwhile. D'ye know any of the healing arts?"

Brighit's tight smile was the best she could manage for the lie she was about to tell. "Certainly. My mother took great pains to teach me all that I would need to know as Darragh's wife."

Thomasina had indeed *tried* to teach her about the plants, but that was the day Bright had been working on a small bow for her own use, made from a perfectly supple branch. She'd insisted that she had no time for such foolishness. Besides, Aednat was a great healer and more than willing to teach her anything she actually needed to know. Now Brighit wished she'd taken the time to listen to her friend.

"My *mamaidh* always said I was a fast learner. I will be a good wife."

"I have no doubt of that."

Tisa's knowing smile grated on Brighit's nerves

34

since Darragh's mother knew her not at all. She was glad when the woman finally fell silent and faced front. Left to her own thoughts, Brighit was confronted by the fact that she would actually make a terrible wife. Despite the promise she'd made to Darragh, she cared nothing for wifely duties, though she didn't mind overmuch bossing others around. Truth be told, she was quite good at that.

A rustling on her left attracted her attention. Two birds of some sort. She searched out the pheasant or quail in the underbrush, wishing she'd thought to bring her bow. Distracted by pleasant imaginings about the appalled look her mother-in-law would give her if she supplied the meat for their upcoming feast, she didn't immediately realize the trail had narrowed and the group had fallen into single file. Nor that they had stopped. Suddenly, Darragh was in front of her on horseback, holding her reins to keep her from colliding with Tisa's horse, which had gone ahead. He searched Brighit's face as if to discern her thoughts, his own expression revealing nothing. No one else seemed to notice she'd been distracted.

"*A thighearna,*" the lead guard was speaking, "'twould be safer to return rather than continue on this path." She heard some further whispers, including something about the MacCochlain.

Brighit ignored Darragh, instead stretching her neck to see what dangers lay ahead. The path didn't seem unsafe to her eyes—a simple passage between two high cliffs—but the guard was pressing them back. Darragh stayed with her after helping her turn her mount about, her horse's lead in his hand. The pheasants burst out from the undergrowth to their right in a flutter of feathers. There were two, just like she'd thought. Plump birds with beautiful brown plumage. What a wonderful addition they would have made to their wedding feast.

Darragh turned to her. "Ye have a good eye."

She'd not mentioned the birds, so mayhap he was paying closer attention to her than she'd thought. "I have many abilities ye know nothing about."

His already broad chest seemed to expand even more beneath the tight green tunic he wore adorned with a gold-threaded design at the neck and wrists. His bright eyes were suddenly filled with amusement. "I look forward to learning about them all."

She was certain he was laughing at her and locked her jaw to keep the words she wanted to say from escaping, words that would reveal her true sentiments about this whole ride.

His smile widened as if he recognized her inner struggle.

"Are ye enjoying my mother's companionship?" he asked.

"She is charming." Nothing to be inspired by, in her opinion. "But most women do not find *me* very... acceptable."

"Have ye offended her as well?"

"As well?" Brighit's mouth dropped open. "Who have I—"

Darragh pulled her horse to the side, and although three vigilant guards remained a discreet distance from them, the rest of their party moved past them.

She waited patiently for Darragh to explain himself, but he did not seem inclined to do so.

"Well?" Her throat was tight.

He tipped his head. "Well, what?"

"Who have I offended?"

36

"Dear Brighit." His defeated expression matched his tone. "Yer unhappiness does not go unnoticed."

That caught her off-guard since she had been trying to put on a happy face for everyone. Had she failed so miserably? No. She tightened her lips.

"Ye're being intentionally cruel. I have not broken our agreement."

"And yet ye have not demonstrated yerself a willing bride either. Yer father is worried for ye, believing ye may never smile again."

"Why would he believe such things? I fit in so well here." Brighit tapped her finger to her lips as if in deep thought. "Could it be because yer mother chooses not to control her own horse, and she apparently expects the same of me?" Irritation was riding her hard. "I will confess to ye now. I know nothing about plants and healing and even less about preparing the pheasants after I've bagged one or two—but I *am* quite good at that."

Darragh threw back his head and laughed. Brighit immediately regretted sharing that last bit. The guards seemed perplexed at the outburst, though none dared approach them.

"At every turn I find ye are like no other woman of my acquaintance."

She prayed he wouldn't notice the redness creeping up her face. If the prospect of having a wife 'like no other' resulted in him setting her aside now, her parents would be furious. Especially if he was correct about the importance of the union between the two clans. She had questioned some of the warriors, but none seemed willing to give her any information.

"So ye do not wish to be a wife?" Darragh's expression had softened considerably, but his intent gaze set her heart to fluttering, that kiss immediately coming to mind. It had been nothing like the tight-lipped peck her brother's friend had "stolen." That one had left her wondering what the fuss was all about.

"I… did not say that… exactly."

"No. Ye did not." He urged his horse nearer, close enough to touch, and covered her hand with his own. Darragh continued. "Instead, ye tell me ye believe I want a woman like my mother for a wife."

Had she said that? "She is the perfect wife. Why would ye desire less?"

Darragh's heated gaze swept along her length, making her heart race again.

When he faced her, his words confirmed what she'd seen in his eyes. "Desire is a strange thing."

She wrestled with a response, something light and witty, but her mind was blank. Her body, however, became acutely attuned to him when he leaned in closer, the musky scent of him drifting to her.

"Listen closely. I have *never* said I wished to wed a woman like my mother." His low voice soothed her as did his palm, sliding up her arm to slip beneath the heavy weight of her hair. His skin hot against hers. "Never."

With a gentle tug, Darragh pulled her toward him, meeting her halfway. His lips were persistent, his tongue sweeping out to dampen her own, making the sensation even more intense. The urgency of it stole her breath away. This was the kissing she remembered. The kissing she'd thought about while alone in her bed, the other lasses snoring quietly around her. When he stopped, it took her a moment to get her senses back, to open her eyes.

"I promise ye, Brighit." he spoke the words in the

tiny space between their mouths. "*My* desire is for more. Much more. And I promise I will *not* settle for less."

His words and his heated gaze confirmed it. He desired her. Her! He drew her onto his lap and then slipped his hands along her sides, caressing her, and he deepened their kiss until his tongue was sparring with her own. His desire sparked an answering fire inside her. A need she couldn't name. A need she wanted him to see to.

When he finally broke the intoxicating kiss, he was breathing hard. "Oh Brighit. Never believe I would compare ye to another. Ye will not be found lacking because *I* will teach ye the only things ye need to know."

"*Ye* will teach me?" Memories of the other lasses flashed in her mind. Their disdainful expressions and the condescending comments they'd made about her attempts to clean the fall vegetables—those darn leeks. All she'd managed to do was mutilate them.

He smiled, his gaze gliding over her face and his hand caressing her cheek. "I will take great pleasure in teaching ye."

His touch was gentle, and her eyes drifted closed before they widened when she realized what he'd said. She doubted there were any womanly chores she would find pleasant. Better she admits her shortcomings now. "I confess I never cared to learn what other woman so enjoy doing."

"I will see that ye enjoy what I teach ye." He nuzzled her neck, sending goose bumps along her arm. "I promise ye much enjoyment."

Darragh pulled away and heaved a great sigh. His confident tone settled her somewhat, although she would have liked to continue with the kissing. And the touching. She didn't like this feeling of restlessness he'd sparked in her. The guards around them had their backs respectfully turned.

"I am a good learner." For some reason she felt the need to reassure him of this.

"Oh, I believe ye, dear Brighit."

Brighit had the distinct impression he was truly pleased with her, barely able to contain his joy, she'd venture. But something gnawed at her.

I will teach ye the only things ye need to know.

Her hackles raised, she said, "Ye misunderstand me."

A quirk of his brow. An expression of warning. She ignored it and pushed on.

"I do not come to ye without skills. I come without the skills of other wives. I have been well trained in hunting and trapping, in battle strategy and combat. When ye leave our *túath*, ye will not leave yer clan unprotected."

"I may never be king. I may never have my own *túath*."

"That is of no consequence."

"And I would never leave what I value unprotected." His face darkened. "I cannot promise *ye* will be that protection."

Brighit shrugged nonchalantly despite the feeling of having been slapped in the face. "Ye may leave who ye wish in charge, but I will not accept their protection over my own."

"Explain."

His angry tone forced her to swallow down her fear. She found an irritated Darragh was extremely intimidating. The guards' darting glances assured her she was not being overly sensitive.

"If I believe one strategy is more prudent than another, I expect their obedience." Her father was an amazing leader and he'd shared what he knew with each of his children.

"Strategy? If there is a battle to fight, my presence will not be found lacking. I command my own men."

"But if we are attacked while ye are away, I will take the command."

"By whose order?"

"As yer wife, they will take orders from me."

"So ye are declaring if the warrior I leave in charge gives orders for ye to take cover, ye will refuse him?"

"If my presence will be better served by staying and fighting, then I will refuse him."

"And if ye are with child?"

Brighit hadn't considered that, but why should that make any difference? Unless she was too unwieldy and cumbersome to be effective in fighting. "I will approach each instance on its own merit."

Having spoken her mind, she felt a definite sense of peace. Mayhap it would not be so very bad to be married to this man. If he understood she would never be satisfied doing the things his mother did, wasn't it better for him to know what she could offer instead? That his dark expression persisted gave her pause. He didn't seem inclined to either move on or say anything in response. Discomfort nipped at her heels, but she squared her shoulders and avoided looking directly at him.

"We best join the others," she said, then cleared her throat, waiting for the awkward moment to pass. "D'ye not agree?"

"Oh, are ye asking for my opinion now?"

"Well, I—"

"So 'tis only certain decisions ye plan to make without me?"

Brighit's thoughts whirled like a dry leaf caught in the wind, but no response came to her.

His broad chest widened even more, and his nostrils flared. "And ye have nothing to say now?"

She tipped her nose up. "I have said my peace."

"Yer peace?" He slapped the rump of the courser she'd been riding, and the horse headed off into the woods, following the others. The guards around them were immediately alert, but they settled when Darragh raised a commanding arm.

"Wh-what are ye about?"

"Mayhap ye need a taste of what relying on me looks like."

"I do not believe—"

"Hold tight." Darragh's command sounded more like a growl. He snapped the reins on either side of her so hard, the horse's responding gallop slammed her against his solid chest. The guards scrambled to catch up.

Unlike the last time she'd ridden with Darragh, he wrapped a firm arm about her waist, tucking her against him, so that they rose and fell as one with each gallop across the open field. His own solid legs firm against hers. He had total command even at top speed. Breathtaking. They were quickly heated by the ride— and so was the horse. When Darragh finally slowed and signaled the guards to stay back, Brighit had a strong sense of trepidation, but she couldn't deny her excitement. It had been exhilarating to be crushed against his powerful body, feeling his great strength surrounding her. All her senses were fully aroused.

They were pressed so closely together, she could feel his heart slow as hers did the same.

He blew out a breath and said, "I will think on what ye've shared with me, but know this, I will not jeopardize what I've been given to protect even to appease ye."

Brighit's spirit soared with those first few words, then dropped just as quickly. "I do not look to be appeased."

Raising his brow in that irritating way, Darragh indicated he'd said all he was going to say on the matter. How quickly she was learning his style of command. And his style of command was extremely irritating.

Chapter Four

As the sun lowered in the sky the next day, the level of excitement reached a crescendo. The long-awaited wedding would finally take place in Drogheda on the morrow, and tension hung in the air. Even as they encouraged the guests to relax and imbibe in a heavy amount of mead, cider, and ale, the parents of both bride and groom seemed near giddy with anticipation. The event had been postponed many times for one reason or another.

Darragh removed himself from the goings on before the music and dancing started, wanting some quiet time to think. As he side-stepped his father and Sean, something in Tadhg's voice called his attention.

"It appears the time is at hand, my friend. How fare ye?" Tadhg was enjoying the warm ale, his lips puckering in the way they always did when he savored the bitterness of the drink. Darragh smiled. His father was most predictable.

The wide-eyed look of astonishment Sean turned on Tadhg made the overbearing man seem somewhat less foreboding. "D'ye seriously ask me that?"

His fear was ridiculous and unreasonable. Darragh and Brighit were both here. There'd be no turning back now. Tadhg, on the other hand, merely smiled. Darragh accepted that as his father's show of confidence in the inevitable.

Sean demonstrated no such contentment. Instead, his expression shifted to concern, worry lines etching his face. "If I'd known the problems we'd have wedding these two, I admit I'd have found another husband for my precious daughter."

Tadhg did laugh at that, but Darragh seethed. It wasn't the first time Sean had voiced his concerns about how his daughter would be treated in the marriage. Did the man think he'd take a strap to her? Admittedly, she needed to be taken in hand since Sean had shown no inclination to do so, but Darragh would never choose to break her spirit. Her feisty nature excited him—it was like standing out in the rain with the lightning striking all around.

Sean had lived here in Drogheda until he was named *ri* to his mother's tribe. Darragh's father considered him a brother, which meant Sean could probably say things to him that no one else would get away with. Darragh knew he should stop listening and moved to do so.

"Mayhap someone older? More experienced? More commanding?"

Darragh froze in his step. What was his father

saying? Brighit would be crushed by marriage to a man more sedate and stuck in his ways, but Sean nodded his head.

Opening his mouth to voice his objection even if it revealed his presence, Darragh paused when Sean suddenly jolted as if coming awake. "Older? Why am I nodding? Ye've tricked me."

Tadhg laughed. "We've never thought a man advanced in age should have the pleasure of touching a young lass."

Sean dropped his face to his palm. "I am beside myself with emotion."

"And now with all these clans assembled to witness the joining of our clans, ye are concerned. I understand. The other clans are here for purely practical reasons. When they see we are united in *all* ways, they will cease to try to break us apart by coercion and intimidation. As for yer daughter being taken to wife." Tadhg patted his friend's shoulder, "Ye've a comely lass and great expectations for their joining. She will be well cared for by my son with many strong sons and daughters to come, of that I'm certain."

Darragh's chest swelled with his father's words. Tadhg was not one to be overly complimentary. As a matter of fact, he couldn't remember the last time his father ever patted him on the back for a job well done.

"As am I." Sean raised his head to impale Tadhg with his gaze.

Tadhg stilled the patting. "Quite a menacing tone."

Tipping his head to the side and raising one heavy brow, Sean clearly indicated the tone had been intentional.

Tadhg removed his hand. "Ye believe ye need to

threaten me or my son for yer daughter to get the proper treatment?"

Darragh couldn't say he was surprised. He'd encouraged the shift of location for their wedding for this very reason. Sean's insinuations that Darragh was lacking in some way did not sit well with him. It was unfounded.

"'Tis understandable that ye're overcome with emotion."

Sean glanced skyward, his lips tight, as if searching for control. "I *am* concerned. I am concerned that my lass be treated with the utmost care."

"She. Will. Be. And *not* because we're afraid of any retribution from ye, but because we all treasure her. My son included." Tadhg finished his drink and stood. "Besides, ye're not that intimidating."

Sean barked a laugh at Tadhg as he walked away. Darragh was speechless, shocked that his father had stood up for him so adamantly. And yet there was no denying everything his father had said was true. He'd be a good husband and provider. Brighit was a handful but well worth the effort.

"Did ye hear enough?" Tadhg passed Darragh without stopping.

His face heated. "I hadn't meant to—"

"I can't say why Sean's behaving like an arse or why his wife is insisting on so much tradition, like the bedding ceremony."

Darragh had also heard Thomasina wanted the bedding witnessed. "It does not appear that the woman has any sensitivity to Brighit's own wishes."

Tadhg stopped at that, turning to his son. "She has confided in ye?"

"She does not need to confide in me. I know 'tis

not what she wants."

A flash of something in Tadhg's expression surprised Darragh, but then his father smiled and slung an arm around his shoulder. "I am surprised when I see ye are indeed much like yer mother."

Now his confusion was complete. "How so?"

They passed Niall, who was regaling the lads with more tales of his midnight raids back in Alba.

"I am inclined to action, whereas yer mother is more thoughtful."

Darragh wasn't certain how to take that last bit. When he noticed Brighit off to the side of the group, awkwardly hunkered down beside the garden as if she were weeding, he gave it no more thought. From her flushed face and the way her hand was barely moving over the tops of the plants, Darragh knew she was listening to Niall's tales.

Everyone enjoyed Niall's stories, each more exciting—and exaggerated—than the last. The young warriors especially enjoyed the entertainment, always asking for more. And Niall enjoyed keeping their eyes, wide with awe and wonder, stuck on him. Surely there would be no harm in such worship of a man they barely saw. One who would be leaving soon. No harm at all.

"When they chased after us, their swords high in the air and ready to attack," Niall said, "they lost us at the first bend in the road."

"But, Uncle, how were ye able to lose them so quick?"

"Have ye not been listening, Lachlann? That was

where the trail started. We had ducked onto it, disappearing before they made it past the first boulder that shielded us from them."

Lachlann slapped his leg and guffawed. His amazement at Uncle Niall's stories was shared by all present, including Brighit. She'd stepped away from the others upon catching sight of her father and Tadhg, their heads tilted together in conversation. Tisa had sent her over to gather some dandelions from the garden, a task she'd neglected in favor of joining the group of lads listening to her uncle. Scooting down beside the garden, she picked the dandelions half-heartedly, her ears perked toward her uncle.

Her skin tingled as Niall re-told the story of his near capture. Her breath caught as he spoke of his captors pressing a knife to his neck. She edged closer, abandoning the dandelions.

Watching as Tadhg moved away, Niall leaned toward Brighit, his voice dropping. "Would ye like to have one last raid as a lad before ye wed, niece?" He winked at her. "I promise ye a night ye'll not soon forget."

"That would be wonderful."

He beamed. "Consider it done."

"What did ye have in mind?"

"Ah, now 'tis a surprise but rest assured, the rest of the lads are up for it as well."

She could barely contain her excitement. The faces of those gathered around him held the same eagerness. The twinge of guilt at betraying Darragh's trust was quickly set aside. This was different. This was an adventure with her uncle! Besides, Darragh need never know.

Beaming, she said, "'Twould be the best of

wedding gifts. Thank ye, Uncle Niall."

"My pleasure."

"Darragh frowns on such things." Her face heated at how whiny she sounded.

He nodded, the corners of his eyes creasing with his smile. "I'm not convinced yer young lad lacks any desire for excitement."

"He's far too responsible to do anything that his father would disapprove of."

Niall raised both brows. "Then certainly my bonny niece will have to change his ways and turn him toward a life less predictable and staid."

"I will do my best." Brighit kissed her uncle's cheek. "But I do thank ye for taking us out one last time. When shall we meet?"

"Well, *ye'll* be meeting me as soon as they've tucked ye off safely to bed." Niall winked again before turning his gaze to the eager faces of the lads surrounding him. "Ye all can join me as soon as ye can sneak away unobserved. With all these clans gathered for the celebration, ye should not soon be missed."

"Unobserved?" Lachlann snorted. "What a way with words ye have."

Her brother Calum shook his head, giving his uncle a sideways glance. "And what a way with the ladies."

"Well, I can't seem to fight them off…"

Brighit didn't miss the dark cloud that passed over her uncle's handsome face. It was no secret that he'd been making his way through the willing lasses, entertaining a different one each night since his arrival. She feared it was more to avoid being alone than from any carnal need.

Niall had just lost his wife to the fever. His arrival in Drogheda had come as a shock—he was still in mourning and hadn't been expected. That first day, Brighit had been taken aback by how pale the normally boisterous man looked. Clearly distraught.

"Are ye certain ye're up for this, Uncle Niall?" Brighit wiped the concern from her face at Lachlann's wide-eyed expression of warning. They'd been told by their mother to behave as if nothing was untoward and, above all else, not to mention Lily, his deceased wife.

"What are ye on about?" Niall scoffed. "I'm seeing to my favorite niece's last night of freedom. I do not take that lightly."

Freedom. An unexpected chill traipsed across her skin.

"A great adventure!" Lachlann beamed. "And my gift to ye, sweet sister, is that I promise to not tell a soul."

"And mine," Calum chimed in, his smile radiant.

Brighit snorted. "Well, aren't my dear brothers the generous ones."

Lachlann stood and stretched. "Ye'll be thanking me for covering for ye come tomorrow if ye're late for the blessing."

"Ye canna be late, lass." Niall's serious expression surprised her. "Yer mother will have my head if she learns what I've got planned. She'll never forgive me."

Pressing her lips together to keep from smiling, Brighit said, "Ye need not worry about me. I'll not be getting caught."

"Caught?" Darragh's voice startled her, but her uncle quickly turned back toward the group as if they'd not just been talking. "Are ye getting into mischief again?"

It was suddenly very hot. Brighit dropped again, collecting the dandelions from the ground. "No good wife gets into mischief."

She smiled at her choice of words.

"So ye wish to not be a good wife?"

Her gaze flew to Darragh to find him grinning at her. She sensed no anger, so he must not have heard any more than what he'd repeated.

She stood.

"Did ye not promise ye could make me a good wife?" he said, his tone teasing.

"Did I say that? Hmm. I do not recall."

His hair hung loose, not pulled back as usual, and she had the sudden urge to push it away from his face. She shook herself. "Something about teaching me?"

That look of desire was back, but he held her gaze, mimicking her words. "Something about it." His quiet voice seemed like a caress. "Within hours ye'll be mine."

"We'll be wed."

He tipped his head. "Is there a distinction?"

"I will not only be yers." She paused. "*Ye* will be mine."

She sensed his intake of breath rather than heard it. Darragh took her hand, gently leading her away from the others before turning to her again.

"And how d'ye treat what is yers?"

Brighit hesitated, not sure what the right answer should be. "I will protect it. As ye would."

His expression relaxed into a broad smile. "And so much more."

"And so much more." She mimicked him back.

Although she had no idea what he referred to, she was certain she would find out soon enough. The excitement was back in her belly, more intense even than the thought of slipping away tonight for a late-night venture. That thought stirred the guilt she'd been trying to ignore.

As if reading her mind, he said, "Ye enjoy yer uncle's tales more than the other lasses."

Her defenses went up and she straightened her back. "I am more capable than the other lasses."

"Ah, so ye have said."

"I could... I could easily be one of those riding along with him." She watched him closely. "If I were a man."

"If ye were a man."

Darragh's expression was intense, as if he were looking right into her soul.

She swallowed against the uncomfortable feeling. "I need to get back to my duties."

Brighit flattened the few dandelions she'd collected into the basket hanging from her arm and headed off toward the cooking fire behind the longhouse.

Without glancing back, she knew his gaze followed her. The way his face had lit up at her mention of duties had sent a shiver down her back. Her palms were damp when she finally handed the basket to his mother.

"Thank ye, Brighit." No doubt Tisa's smile was intended to reassure. "Are ye excited for the morrow?"

Tisa dropped the plants into a waiting bowl of water, swishing the dirt from the leaves.

"Certainly." The quick glance Tisa gave her had Brighit averting her gaze, the heat spreading up her neck to cover her face. "I may be a little... apprehensive."

"'Tis expected." Tisa wiped her hands on a cloth,

a very lady-like action, before directing Brighit away from the fire and the rest of the women. "Every bride feels this way."

"Even ye?" Brighit found it hard to believe this self-assured woman had ever felt nervous about anything.

The older woman smiled. A gentle smile that matched the touch of her hand on Brighit's cheek. "Sweetling, ye are no different than me in many ways."

Brighit forced herself to not roll her eyes at the absurd comment. "I know Darragh is a good man…"

"But he is a man." Tisa finished the sentence that Brighit had not dared complete. "And men have needs. D'ye fear the marriage bed? As I did?"

Brighit shrugged, not feeling overly comfortable discussing intimate matters with her husband's mother. Her future mother-in-law was so controlled and soft-spoken. Could she really have feared Tadhg? She glanced toward the benches where the older men had settled to drink and discuss area politics. Their stern voices carried, although the words were lost.

Tadhg was forbidding, to be certain, and seemed relentless in his demands of those around him. Mayhap Tisa had feared him. Feared his assessment of her. Feared her own ability to fulfill her wifely duties. Feared, above all, that she would be found lacking. Those were fears Brighit could well understand, but there was an important difference—for Tisa, those fears had been unfounded.

"Had ye not been married before Tadhg?"

Tisa nodded, a faraway look in her eyes. "Married, aye, but I remained untouched. My husband preferred others to me."

Brighit gasped. How could any man find her less than perfect? And why had Tisa named her first son

54

after such a man?

Tisa must have sensed her thoughts; her eyes rounded with concern and she said, "Oh, no. Not other women. He preferred men."

That was not unheard of, but who would marry such a man to a young girl? If they had been expected to consummate their vows, Tisa would have experienced his rejection firsthand. Brighit's heart filled with new compassion for this woman.

"I am sorry for ye."

Tisa smiled. That quiet smile she usually saved for her husband when he was reproaching someone, and she was sitting demurely by his side as wife to the powerful *ri túaithe*. "Darragh did his best by me. I found no complaints after we came to an understanding. He offered me his protection. And his care. He was a kind man."

Brighit's confusion must have been apparent because Tisa's next words came out in a rush.

"It was a bad time for my father and our clan. He'd had no choice—and no idea about Darragh's preference. No one did, but many suspected." Again that far-off look. "But I had always held a fondness for Tadhg."

And there it was. The difference between Tisa marrying Tadhg and Brighit marrying Darragh. Brighit felt no such attraction toward Darragh. Well, mayhap the Darragh who'd kissed her... he was different and could set her heart to fluttering, but she'd seen *that* Darragh rarely enough. She set the thought aside. "Then the marriage bed was not so dreaded after all?"

"Mayhap not, but I can tell ye, my son will be considerate of ye."

"And ye're his mother." Brighit knew there was no sense in saying what they both knew. Tisa only saw the best in her son.

"And a mother knows her son. He is a gentle soul."

Darragh had joined the group of men, standing beside his father, his arms crossed over his chest. He was not smiling, and from this distance, he did not look gentle. He looked like a man desperate for his father's approval—and if that meant keeping his bride under his thumb, so be it.

"Well, I am sure it will be fine." Brighit stood as did Tisa. "I will survive as most wives do."

"I am sorry I didn't alleviate yer fears."

"My life is about to change—most drastically. I will get through it. Produce the children that are expected of me. No doubt we will be the model of wedded bliss."

"I understand yer fear—"

"How can ye?" Brighit regretted the words as soon as she let them loose, her impulsiveness getting the best of her. "Forgive me, please, but ye were in love with yer husband. I am not."

"Ye will learn to love him."

Not the staid, dominating warrior at his father's side. Never him.

Brighit ground her teeth together to stop the telling statement from coming out. The words lingered unspoken between them until Tisa finally nodded and walked away.

No doubt a mother had a hard time seeing the faults of her own children. Wasn't it the same for Brighit's own parents? Well, mayhap her mother saw her true colors, but her father believed she had no faults. A twinge of guilt shifted in her gut. Niall had promised them a raid tonight. If she wished to honor her father, she would decline. She would stay behind with the women, embroidering or gossiping or whatever women did.

Safe.

Out of harm's way.

Sitting quietly. Listening politely when the men later recounted their adventures. Pretending she didn't wish she'd joined them.

NO!

Tightening her jaw and tipping her nose in the air, Brighit passed the men, who continued their discussion of clan warring and how best to settle disputes in the area. She smiled. A tight smile. A smile that she hoped conveyed her acquiescence to all that the men did, as if she had a choice.

Brighit may have no say in the clan's business, but tonight she would get her last taste of freedom, brandishing her sword and riding like the wind through the dark of night. She would have her last bit of excitement as a man and then? Then she would set aside her trews and tunic, exchanging them for the acceptable garb of a married woman who waited patiently at home for her husband to return to her. She would think no more of raids or adventures. She would accept her bondage to a man who was like every other man—bent on breaking her will to his own. But not tonight.

Tonight? They would not touch her free spirit.

Chapter Five

Niall led the way through the forest, intent on his destination, although he hadn't shared it with the others. Brighit recognized the place as soon as they entered the boulder-strewn path. This was the very same land she'd crossed with Darragh, Tisa and Tadhg. They had been heavily guarded with no explanation for it. So the MacCochlain would feel the sting of their raiding this night. Her excitement increased three-fold.

When the guards accompanying them had quickly turned their group away from this very path, Brighit's interest had been piqued. The serious expressions on Tadhg and Darragh's faces had left her feeling, yet again, that a woman's life was the antithesis of exciting.

For the smallest instant, she wondered if she should

tell her uncle that their group had avoided riding through this area. But, she had no definite information. They'd kept her *shielded* from any such knowledge. Men were always too protective of women, but her uncle was an exception. Even so…

"Uncle Niall?"

Though she'd whispered the words, Niall turned around, his shoulders up by his ears as if she'd shouted in her loudest voice. She immediately regretted the decision to say anything, but he was already moving closer to her.

"We do not want to be discovered before we've even found the cattle, lass." The smell of ale was strong on his breath. "Are ye certain we need to be talking at this precise moment?"

Brighit nibbled at her thumb and shrugged. Niall tousled her hair as if she were still five, then bopped her nose, ready to turn about.

"I am certain." Brighit spat out the words. "When we traveled these lands yesterday, we were heavily guarded. 'Twas as if there was much to be protected from here."

Niall's eyes creased with his smile. "Wonderful. All the more fun for us."

And then he was back in his place, leading their little group. Well, she'd told him all she knew and it hadn't worried him. No sense in allowing it to worry her.

Walls of cold, hard rock towered over them on both sides. They rode single file between the massive formations. With the moon well hidden by thick clouds, they could barely see the rider in front of them.

"Damn dark in here, Niall." Lachlann's statement was met with a quiet hush.

Brighit shivered, trying to ignore the nagging sense that someone was walking over her grave. This was a wonderful adventure—her last—and she was determined to enjoy it. An owl sounded in the distance as if in warning. Swallowing became difficult despite her constant reassurances to herself.

A horse whinnied in the distance. Too far ahead to be one of their own. Shivers tingled down her back and she took a shuddering breath.

A single war cry pierced the darkness.

"We've been discovered, lads." Niall's call held that distinct pitch of surprise mixed with panic. "Toward the river."

They galloped the rest of the way through the trail, immediately breaking left when they finally cleared the narrow pass.

The sound of many thundering hooves carried through the darkness. The mounted men came out of nowhere. The sight of those dark figures waving their war swords and shields was accompanied by that same eerie cry. Brighit would admit, at least to herself, this was less an adventure and more a scary experience.

They'd barely escaped the ambush. A second slower and they'd have been cut off. Trapped. Likely killed. That fact was not lost on Brighit. These men had been waiting for them, prepared to attack them as soon as they crossed onto the land of Clan MacCochlain.

"Hasten, lads. To the water!" Niall's voice rang out above the din of startled horses and the chaotic calls of the men in hot pursuit.

Why were they being chased? They hadn't done anything wrong yet. And they *were* being chased by eight, big, mean-looking men. Brighit only ventured one glance at the pursuers before dropping low to her horse, urging it to top speeds.

"Quick now, lads." So accustomed was she to Niall's low, deliberate way of speaking, the sudden alarm in his voice was causing havoc in her innards. She was certain his repeated call of "lads" was intentional. A reminder they needed to protect her. Regret washed over her. They shouldn't have to worry about her presence when there was immediate danger.

Niall, her brothers, and the other lads quickly surrounded her, but in so doing, they essentially blocked her in on all sides. Their attempt at protection ensnared her, giving her no opportunity to break into a gallop. Mayhap on her own, she could get away.

The raid had fallen apart before it had even begun. And now she was being led away like a defenseless female—protected! This wasn't what she'd wanted. Not at all.

Valiant was the fastest horse she'd ever seen, and agile too—Brighit easily wove between the spindly trees, pitching sharply from one side to the other to avoid the jagged branches as they ventured into the darkened forest. Despite her unfamiliarity with this place, she'd practiced her riding skills in so many different forests over the years she was able to keep to a fast pace. She'd always won friendly riding competitions, something that gave her confidence now.

They were heading due west and away from MacNaughton lands. Good plan, keeping their pursuers from knowing to whom they were pledged. Best if they remained an unknown group of men unless they were engaged, which didn't seem to be her uncle's plan.

They cleared the trees, crossing an open meadow,

and Lachlann was suddenly beside her.

"To Dead Man's Pass." His whispered words were followed by a hard slap to her horse's rump at the same time the men parted. Valiant jerked forward, directly to the opening, and Brighit was nearly dislodged.

Niall's quiet command from behind was unmistakable. "Make haste."

And so she did. The others were turning back and spreading out, preparing for a confrontation. A shift in tactics? They were readying for attack, and here she was riding off by herself. The sound of the other horses quickly faded, but the unmistakable sound of steel on steel carried to her. A twinge of disappointment settled in her chest. She would have liked to test her skills in such a battle.

The realization that there had been no attempt to even include her was hard to swallow. She'd bested each of these lads one on one, so why wouldn't they want her to stay with them? To help with defense even?

Darragh's comment about her lack of real fighting experience had stuck with her, diminishing her pride in her own accomplishments. It was true her fighting had only been against the lads of her clan. She didn't want him to be right and this would be the perfect chance to prove herself. So she reached beneath her heavy, wool *brait* and fisted her trusty dagger, blade side out. She wasn't fool enough to ride back. If they were bent on protecting her and sending her off, her return could be a deadly distraction, but at least she would be ready if anyone came upon her.

The clouds parted to reveal a steep hill directly in front of her. Brighit smiled.

"Come now, fair Valiant, show them what ye can

do." With a slight squeeze of her mount's sides, the horse sprinted ahead, covering the space to the top of the hill with little effort.

She glanced behind to gauge if the fighting continued behind her, only to discover there was one warrior still after her. Dogging her. Intent on her capture. His dark figure, tall in his saddle, turned toward her as he cut across the hill at a lower level. Given the path he'd chosen, he would easily intercept her at the base. A sudden thrill brought a smile to her lips. She may indeed have a chance at engagement yet.

Holding the reins in a one-handed death grip, Brighit focused on the forest ahead. She would do her best to escape as her uncle had intended. If she could make the trees, she would have a chance. If not, she would turn and engage this devil's spawn who thought to chase her. But despite her increased speed, the sound of his laboring horse was growing louder. When she heard the rider's heavy breathing, she experienced a sudden pang of fear.

Brighit hunched closer to the horse's neck to urge the courser to greater speed, shifting her weight forward. "Do yer best to run like the wind, Valiant."

And if 'tis not enough, may God show me favor in my first honest battle.

"Ye've picked the wrong clan this time." The man's low, menacing tone quickened her heart.

Word play is an attempt to break the opponent's concentration.

She shut out all around her, aside from her horse's gallop and the trees ahead blurring with the intensity of her gaze.

"Ye're mine." He sounded closer, but that couldn't be.

She spared a glance behind her and frowned. There was no one. How could he—

Oomph.

A solid wall smacked into her chest, knocking her right off her horse and onto the ground. As she lay flat on her back, the unbearable sensation of not being able to breathe gripped her. Her chest burned. Desperate, she was struck by the fact that she might die right here for lack of air.

The sight of him coming at her, a nasty looking sword in his grasp, forced her into action. Rolling away from him, she jumped up on her feet and crouched low in a flash, her own weapon in hand.

He stopped an arm's length from her, tipped his head and asked, "D'ye seriously want to do this?"

His words, delivered in a low voice, sent a sharp pang of fear straight into her gut. Admittedly, he was huge. His arms alone could crush her, and his fierce expression confirmed he had no qualms about doing that very thing. If he got close, he could easily overpower her, and she had no doubt that was his ultimate goal. He was giving her an out as if she had no chance against him. She'd have even less of a chance if he knew she was a female.

She gritted her teeth but raised her own blade, shortened to accommodate her smaller size, to ready position. Her terse nod was met with a *you-asked-for-it* look, and his blade was pressed against hers so quickly she barely had time to step forward and brace her arm against it.

The man smiled, and she could have kicked herself. He saw the fear in her eyes.

"A lad yer size should know better than to engage a seasoned warrior." He pressed his arm more firmly against hers with little effort, and she struggled to hold her ground. "Ye need to be put in yer place."

With barely any effort, he shoved her away from him and lowered the point of his blade directly at her. "Show me what ye're made of, pup."

The distance was a gift and she knew it. He was giving her more of a chance than she deserved. Light on her feet, her speed was her most powerful weapon. She'd experienced it over and over again. The lads she'd trained with had grown stronger over the years, but they'd also become slower. Surely this man's momentum did not match his strength.

Shifting from foot to foot, she didn't dare to say anything in her defense. The big man merely watched her maneuvers, his eyes narrowing. When she jabbed at him, he turned his body aside to easily miss the blade. The only problem with this *miodóg* intended for her shorter height was its shorter reach.

"Ye'll have to try harder than that."

She bent her arm, raising the hilt of her blade as high as her shoulder, and slashed at him, catching his *brait*. It was her unexpected step forward that caught him off guard. He jumped back, obviously surprised by the tactic. Confidence welled in her chest.

He had thought so little of her abilities that he hadn't even shoved the heavy material from his shoulders to give himself full maneuverability. He did so now, and she used the opportunity to repeat the same tactic going the other way, once again catching him unprepared. The thin line of blood where her blade had sliced through the sleeve at his forearm was a minor wound, but it emboldened her.

With a fast shifting of her slight weight from side to side, she pressed her advantage. The dagger tight in her grasp, she pulled her elbow back to ready herself for the shove into his belly when he was within reach. He appeared too dumbfounded to withdraw. She'd drawn first blood, but this would be the first time she'd actually impaled anyone. When the moment was upon her, she hesitated, giving him the time required to shift away from her lunge. He dropped the heavy material back into place before she could pull back. Instead of making contact with his body, her arm became tangled in his mantle. She was unable to clear her weapon.

With a growl and a shove, he easily toppled her backward. The pursuer dropped on top of her, straddling her with his heavy weight. His massive legs easily pinned her arms to her sides, the weapon still clasped in her fist. She moved her shoulders back and forth in an attempt to work herself free.

She was helpless, and that fact sparked a hot rage deep within her.

"Ye little shite." He growled through tight lips barely discernible against the heavy growth of beard. Dark, wide eyes filled with anger peered down at her. When he backhanded her, she gasped.

The sting at her cheek spread into a burning sensation across the side of her face, and her mouth flooded with blood. Struggling to move her arms and free her hand, she was lurched forward when he grabbed her by the front of her tunic.

Nose to nose, he said, "Give me the name of yer leader. He'll not get away this time."

Just as suddenly, he released her and was squeezing his knees into her again, backhanding her for the second time. The wave of pain exploded across the other side of her head.

"Ye'll talk, or I'll kill ye straight away."

With the taste of her own blood mixing with the rotten stench of his breath, her stomach threatened to heave. Her fingers wiggled on the hilt of her dagger.

"What swine enlists the aid of a smooth-faced lad? Who sent ye?"

Blood trickled down her throat and she was forced to swallow it. Clamping her jaw tight, her attempt at a fierce scowl merely caused him to laugh.

"Ye think ye can withstand my fists?"

He shoved her shoulders flat, his legs clamped to her sides, and set about proving her wrong. The first punch was to her side and the pain was more intense than anything she'd experienced. She squeezed the hilt so tight, it pierced her flesh.

"A name is what I want and a name I'll get."

When he punched her in the stomach, her gut gripped tight and she bit her tongue to keep from crying out.

"How much d'ye think ye can bear?"

Despite the pain, she kept alert. Escape was imperative. He flattened himself against her with his massive hands gripping her sides, pressing into her ribs, his stinky breath again in her face. She was suffocating beneath his weight and panic set in.

"A name is all I want." Spittle accompanied his word and dripped down her chin.

She shuddered in a tight breath that barely reached her lungs, but he immediately stopped his assault, tipping his head and studying her with intently. Her bindings! He could feel her bound chest. When she tried to hold her breath, the pain was too intense. A painful high-pitched moan escaped.

He scowled in displeasure and scooted low enough

that he could yank at the V of her tunic.

"This better not be true." He worked at the leather belt, tugging the material, and shifted his knee lower. His hold of her slackened. Brighit slipped her small weapon up between his knee and her body. As she bent her elbow out, moving it as far as his relaxing hold would allow, he freed the material of her tunic to reveal the tight binding at her breast.

"And what have we here?" His tone changed, as did his expression, and a flash of excitement lightened his eyes. "Allow me the pleasure of releasing yer bondage, little one."

Her blade cleared her hip. When he reached for the knife at his waist, his exposed side offered her the perfect target.

She buried her dagger into his tight flesh with all the strength she could gather. It made a sickening sound.

He stilled as if frozen in ice before he turned his face toward her, a look of incredulity in his eyes. Filled with wrath and an unquenchable desire to survive, she pressed the blade deeper still, stopping only when the hilt snagged at his rib. Hot, sticky blood covered her fist, but she held fast, clamping her jaw, his eyes locked onto hers.

It took an eternity for the man to die. Brighit dared not move. She dared not breathe.

At long last, his eyes rolled back in his head and he collapsed on her, forcing her hand to release its death grip on the weapon or snap at the wrist.

Relief swept over her, but it was short lived when realized she was trapped beneath his dead weight. Whimpers of frustration filled the air as she bent her knees up in a desperate attempt to dislodge him. Brighit heaved her body up, her hips pushing against him. He was as heavy as a horse. Shoving against his lower body, she finally managed to roll him off.

Her mouth gaping open and her eyes focused heavenward at the stars twinkling overhead, she took one, two, three deep breaths of fresh air. Sighing loudly, she closed her eyes at the pleasant sensation of freely filling her lungs. She blew out a breath before standing. Pulling her tunic back into place, she adjusted the belt, refusing to think about the tremors in her bloody hand.

Her attacker lay flat on his face, his body not moving. Bending closer, she thought to check if he was truly dead, but a movement in the distance caught her eye. A lone rider sat mounted on a huge beast at the top of the hill. Stray puffs of breath from the horse's muzzle were the only sign that the rider was indeed real and not summoned by her imagination. She didn't recognize him.

She straightened her clothing. Her breath ragged, she glanced back at her victim. He could easily have killed her. Or worse.

The horse snorted as the mounted rider began to move closer, covering the distance between them with plodding steps. She began shaking uncontrollably. For the smallest moment she considered calling out to him, reasoning with him, mayhap even asking for his help, but she tossed the idea away just as quickly. There would no help from him even though she had no doubt that he'd witnessed the entire event.

With a low whistle, Brighit called to her horse. Valiant came from wherever she'd been grazing, oblivious to the plight of her rider. The man stopped a few feet away, his face masked in shadows. He was dressed in the traditional *léine*, the long *brait* wrapped around him to ward off the cold and held at his shoulder by a large, shiny brooch. She waited for him to speak, to try and stop her, to ask if she was going to bury the man she'd killed. He said nothing.

So she mounted, put her heels to the horse and sped off. Though she expected the sounds of pursuit, there were none. No horse's whinny. No leather creaking. No foot falls. Today she'd killed a man and she would have to live with that fact for the rest of her life. She followed the path back to the MacNaughton land, away from the violent scene. Back toward her boring life. Refusing to glance over her shoulder the entire ride, she wondered if she'd ever feel at peace again.

Chapter Six

As planned, the masses gathered to witness the vows given and received by Darragh and Brighit at the door to the small chapel. The crowd was silent, whether from tension over the proceedings or overindulgence from the night before, Darragh wasn't sure. He had spent the whole night tossing and turning, and yet Brighit seemed even less awake. Though he had long recognized she had no great love for him, he hadn't expected her to break into cavernous yawns barely hidden by her veil. It did not help that her domineering father looked ready to snatch her away at any moment.

The ceremony was only being performed to appease the strict religious beliefs of Brighit's parents. It was far from simple and already a source of resentment for him. What little patience he possessed for the proceedings was quickly stripped away by his bride's seeming lack of interest.

"Blessings on ye both." The elderly priest did not call for the kiss of unity but instead kissed each of their cheeks. First Brighit's, right over the veil, and then his.

"Thank ye, Father." Darragh answered, always polite.

"Ye've made a fine match." With that, the priest started to turn him away from his bride while Thomasina led Brighit away, several women falling in around them.

Darragh dug in his heels. "A moment, please, Father?"

The room hushed, all movements stilled. His mother's eyes widened in warning, but Darragh ignored her. "Have ye forgotten? This is a wedding."

The priest puckered up his face in concentration before shaking his head at Darragh. "No. I do not believe so."

"The kiss?"

When the priest smiled and shifted closer to him for another kiss on the cheek, Darragh pulled back in exasperation. "Not me. Between husband and wife?"

Clearly perplexed, the man looked to Thomasina for an answer.

"Not her." Darragh refused to try and hide his irritation any longer. Speaking to the priest as if he were an idiot, he said, "May I bestow a kiss on my wife? A sign of unity? Sealing the agreement with a kiss?"

"Oh, well, I suppose." The priest huffed as if he'd never heard of such a thing. But marriages were about the contract signed between two families, not the church. If Thomasina had wanted some elaborate blessing on them, Darragh would not gainsay her, but he would have this symbolic act as well.

Brighit had not returned to his side, much to his chagrin, so he had to take the few steps toward her. He'd chosen his words to the priest carefully, hoping to remind her of their earlier kisses. He knew he had certainly not forgotten them.

"Brighit?"

When he lifted the material over her head, the first thing he noticed about his bride was the fine powder she'd applied to her face. It made her skin unusually pale, even sickly. And with her eyes as wide as a doe caught in the forest, he was suddenly afeared of his own strong need for her. He would go slowly, giving her his total focus so as not to frighten her. With that thought, all around him disappeared. He no longer saw the onlookers, her meddling parents who sought to dictate everything according to their own wishes, or even this man of the cloth. He saw only his beautiful wife, her lips sharply pink against her powdered skin.

"Aye?"

"A kiss to seal our agreement?"

There it was. Her eyes lit with recognition and some of the fear drifted away. With gentle hands at her small waist, he pulled her toward him, allowing her to meet him halfway. Her lips were as he remembered, soft and pliant. A boon for certain and he wished to offer her the same. Reassurance. Pulling back, he whispered to her, "Ye will come willingly, I promise."

That flash of a smile disappeared just as quickly, replaced by dread when Thomasina took her by the shoulders to again turn her away. This time the ladies surrounded her in an impenetrable shield and moved ahead of the crowd toward the castle. The look of irritation Darragh gave the priest had the older man raising his hands and backing away in a show of surrender.

Darragh proceeded with the crowd of well-wishers, keeping his eye on the women ahead. When they reached the great hall decorated for the festivities with leaves and wild flowers, he watched helplessly as the women continued up the stairs at the far wall that led to the chambers above.

The ridiculousness of the situation grated on him, as did the ever-growing number of people Darragh did not recognize, all offering best wishes and slaps on the back for a job well done. Job well done? He'd not even been able to speak to Brighit, let alone see any job done.

Trained to be suspicious of everyone, his mind and body had been on high alert for days now. He was exhausted from seeing plots and schemes everywhere he looked. Sleeping had been difficult despite his father's reassurance there was no cause for concern, and he'd risen near day break, roused by some noisy late-comers to the hall. Niall's voice may have been among those who'd awakened him, but he couldn't be certain. And here was Brighit's uncle again, staring at him.

"Relax, Darragh." Tadhg's tight smile seemed more intended for the onlookers than for Darragh. "Sean told me this is how Thomasina preferred it. They're preparing yer bride for ye."

Darragh cringed at the mere thought of them "preparing" her for the marriage bed. This wedding seemed more of a farce than ever. Worse yet, he knew they would have to face the bedding ceremony.

"Can they not allow us a few moments to sit together? Mayhap enjoy some of the wine *dear* Uncle Niall procured for us?"

Niall's eyes had been on him since they'd crossed the yard to the castle. Darragh finally nodded at him, but he'd swear the older man scowled back.

"'Tis not their way, son. Trust me that yer mother is hoping to convince them to desist in following through with the practice. She had a bad experience herself and would not wish the same for Brighit."

"Do they really plan to witness my deflowering of the lass?"

Tadhg frowned. "Do not be so crude."

Pressing to a halt, Darragh frowned at his father. "Certainly ye do not believe I would be unkind?"

Others continued past them, headed toward the refreshments lavishly displayed for their consumption. Tadhg moved closer to him. "*I* do not."

The crowd passing to either side of them seemed to never end, and the longer Darragh had to wait to have his say, the angrier he became. Finally alone, he pierced his father with his glare.

"I did not wish to take a woman to wife who was so opposed to the idea, as I said. Over and over again. 'Twas not I that insisted."

He refused to share his own hopes that he was winning her over or his disappointment at how uninterested she'd seemed at the chapel doors. She was a beautiful, alluring lass, but there were many beautiful lasses. He would as soon marry one who wished to be his wife—or be given the opportunity to entice Brighit into his arms before bedding her. What a wretched arrangement he was walking into.

"They cannot hand ye over to her without some show of... of... protection," Tadhg said, his last word nearly growled. "I do not claim to understand their reasoning, but I choose to respect their wishes. Can ye not see yer way clear to do their bidding?"

"With a lass a bit more willing..." If given half a chance, he believed he could spur her interest, which was the reason behind his whispered words to her. She was certainly passionate. He could ignite her fire again as she had his. If she chose to remain stubborn, it could be awkward.

"Ye believe she'll resist ye?"

"D'ye see the way she is with her brothers? She may now dress like her mother, but she sees herself the same as a man. More importantly, she sees nothing of value in what a man can offer her. Just the opposite."

"I see." Tadhg rubbed his chin in a thoughtful manner. "So they fear she will continue to resist. And with the onlookers—" Tadhg raised a hand at Darragh's gasped protest. "—not exactly onlookers."

Darragh relaxed his shoulders.

"They want to be certain she cooperates with the bedding."

Darragh glanced toward the heavens. Then he shook his head in disbelief. "And not a spot of wine or mead to dull her reactions to me, to her first experience of intimacy with a man? This is going to be hell."

The two men stared at each other, neither one daring to speak their morbid thoughts.

"And how will this play out?" Darragh asked, admittedly afraid to hear the answer.

"The ladies will come to the hall and escort ye to her once they've prepared her."

That word again... Darragh smacked his hand to

his forehead. "Prepared. It sounds like a chicken rather than a wife."

Tadhg smirked. "Mayhap we can resist a wee bit ourselves."

Searching his father's face for any show that he hadn't understood his meaning was met by a beaming expression. "What d'ye have in mind?"

"A celebration. That's what this should be."

"And?"

"We shall celebrate."

Darragh's heartfelt sigh of relief was met with a smile. "Come, my son. Let us liberally partake of the bounty that has been prepared. We shall make this a memorable night even if we have to dull yer senses enough for ye to ignore any crowds gathered around ye."

At that moment, it sounded like a fine solution. Sometime later, not so much. After indulging in far more wine than he would usually allow himself, Darragh's thoughts wavered between morose misgivings and Brighit tumbling down the back stairs in her attempt at a harrowing escape. No one had yet approached him to say his bride was "prepared."

His father, Sean, and many of the kings from the other clans had settled close to the exit and far from Darragh. He felt a bit like an outcast. The occasional glances the guests darted at him assured him they were discussing him. Terrence finally took mercy on him and came to keep him company.

"Ye being here makes no sense as she is up there." The scruffy blond pointed upward. "Is there something they're forgetting about?"

Darragh couldn't agree with his friend more and said, "Well, apparently, there is more to be done with

77

a bride than with a groom."

"How so?"

A shrug was all Darragh could offer.

"I believed," Terrence said, his tone held a definite air of being right, "that it was something they did together." He scrunched his face in confusion. "Or are ye not to touch the sainted daughter of the great *ri túath*?"

Laughing behind his hand as he made to rub his face, Darragh looked away from the room. They both turned to face the wall and Darragh lowered his voice. "Sainted? God save us."

"D'ye think she'll glow like a bright candle after?"

"How about before?" Their idiocy was being spurred on by the mead, the lack of food since no one would eat until both bride and groom were present, and the ridiculousness of the festivities in general.

"I wouldn't doubt it." The tapestry that hung behind the head table gave an intimate feel to their conversation with none of their words bouncing back into the room. "And if I have to ask permission to touch her golden breasts? I'm thinking I'll set her aside before I subject myself to that."

"Ye'll set Brighit aside?"

They both jumped at the booming voice of Brighit's father.

Sean stood opposite the table, his arms about his chest and a scowl on his face fierce enough to make any enemy shake in his boots.

Terrence giggled awkwardly; his face paling as if he were about to vomit, but no words came out as he stood beside Darragh, who remained seated.

"Well, Sean." Darragh was irritated just enough to not be intimidated by the huge man. "'Tis words between friends ye've interrupted and none of yer concern."

"If my daughter is to be set aside, I would find it very much my concern."

Before Darragh could respond, all thoughts escaped him at the vision beyond the man. Brighit herself was entering the hall. His mouth fell loose, and he stood to watch her as the large entourage of females around her clucked their displeasure. Her dark hair was brushed out now, soft and flowing around her shoulders. A multi-colored ribbon adorned her hair and the baby's breath had been removed. A sign of her innocence, which he would experience soon enough.

That she still wore her dark blue gown from earlier was at first a relief. Her stern expression was also very telling. Darragh would guess she had resisted the bedding ceremony as much as he had, which may explain why he'd not received his summons to do his husbandly duty.

So entranced by his bride, he didn't notice Brighit's mother beside her until Thomasina was headed straight for him. "Darragh."

Spoken in a pleasant tone, but Darragh prepared for the worst. "Thomasina."

"Oh, Mother. Please. Call me Mother. After all we are now mother and son, are we not?"

Fighting the grimace that seemed stuck on his face, Darragh coughed into his hand before answering. "Beg pardon... *Mother.*"

Thomasina smiled brightly before tipping her head. "Verra nice. I was wondering how ye would feel about a bit to eat before the bedding ceremony?"

"Well, I had actually—"

"No bedding ceremony." Brighit came to stand

between the two of them, her back to Darragh as if he was of little importance. Instead, she faced down her mother, a hand to her hip. It was the only way to describe this encounter. Though not much taller than her mother, Brighit did appear quite imposing. "I have said as much to ye, Mother. Repeatedly."

"Brighit," Thomasina's scolding tone grated on Darragh's nerves. "Yer father and I—"

"And that is all well and fair," Brighit's interruption left Darragh wondering what exactly his mother-in-law had intended to say. "…for yer children—whatever it is ye and father want should certainly be seen to—but I am a married woman now."

"In name only."

Bridget's loud gasp seemed to echo around the room. As still as a doe caught unawares by a hunter, she stood there, mouth hanging loose. Thomasina was demonstrating a stubborn side Darragh had not yet witnessed, but she was going too far, and his own ire was rising. The scathing glance Thomasina sent to him halted the words he was about to say.

Sean, forgotten until this moment, moved casually closer to the women, who had the attention of everyone in the room. He made eye contact with Darragh, the smug smile on his face declaring that his new son-in-law certainly did not appear to be a man about to set his bride aside. No. He no doubt appeared as befuddled as he felt. Befuddled. Bewildered. And beyond words. When the older man placed a hand on him, squeezing his shoulder in a reassuring way, Darragh realized his reaction to what was happening was easily read. And that irked him.

"Ladies?" Sean gave him a reprieve by engaging the two. "Why this scene?"

"Sean." Thomasina now used the same tone Darragh had heard her use with her youngest son, Lorcánn. A tone meant to elicit her husband's support. "We've been preparing our dau—"

"My wife." All eyes turned toward Darragh, showing an assortment of reactions. Though surprised at his own words, he suddenly realized their importance. He would not be forgetting that any time soon. "She is my wife now."

Thomasina's face turned a bright shade of red, and though her lips parted, no words came out. Turning to Sean, Darragh waited politely, brows raised, for any denial of the fact. There was none. Instead, Sean inclined his head, took his wife gently by the upper arm, and led her away from Brighit. The rest of the group followed and the two of them were left alone. As alone as two people could be with a throng of people focused on them.

"Sit with me." Darragh indicated the large chair beside his own. Places of honor for the bride and groom. "Please."

Brighit kept silent but came around the trestle to join him. Not a moment too soon, as Darragh plopped down again, feeling the full effect of the excess libations. She didn't seem to notice.

Picking up the goblet beside his own, he pulled it toward Brighit and filled it to the rim with wine from a clay pitcher. "I hope ye find this pleasing. A friend brought this to me when he was visiting from Castile."

"Not from my uncle then?"

"His has long since been dispatched."

She took the goblet to her mouth. The room swayed gently around him, but his eyes remained fixed on her sweet, full lips parting for the liquid. That

81

lighter powder was still visible on her jaw and cheeks, giving her skin a strange discoloration.

Brighit closed her eyes as if in appreciation and he allowed his gaze to wander over her. Admittedly, he studied her. Or more accurately, *appreciated her*. Her generous curves, the slope of her elegant neck, and the gentleness of her hands, again clasped in her lap. And her expressive eyes, flashing with anger or outrage. Quite a change from a year earlier dressed like a lad. A dirty one at that. He would like to see those eyes filled with passion.

Darragh pressed back against his own chair and gazed out at the guests still milling about despite the food about to be served. The others appeared to be giving them little attention. He was certain, however, that they had their ears wide open.

"I prefer not to have a bedding ceremony." Despite the quietness of Brighit's words, a few heads turned toward her. Her voice had lost the edginess she'd used with her mother.

Darragh glared back at those who had turned toward him, anticipating his reply. Some took the hint and went to their table, but others lingered. Finishing his wine, he refilled it before answering. "Then we are in accord."

She beamed at him, a lovely smile. "Ye agree?"

"Of course."

Her expression shifted back to concern. "But they'll try to insist. They could—"

"They will not succeed." His lips curved at her look of disbelief. She had much to learn about the difference between being a daughter and a wife. "I assure ye."

Brighit's chest expanded with her deep breath and

her eyes brightened considerably. She was pleased with him, which would make things much easier later.

Later.

He remembered how she'd looked that day by the water. Dripping wet. Enticing. Exceedingly desirable. And all that sheer, uncontainable outrage just for him. His smile widened at the memory and she returned the gesture. The urge to move in for a kiss was strong, but after considering the possible outcomes, Darragh cleared his throat and turned away. Best he didn't get ahead of himself. One step at a time. He placed the gold vessel down and moved his hand to cover hers. It took but a moment for her to turn her palm up, holding his hand in return.

One step at a time.

Chapter Seven

"That relieves my mind, Darragh." Brighit took in his softened features, finishing her own wine and hoping it might give her that same relaxed demeanor.

"*We* are the ones who have taken vows. Not them." He turned to her with a mischievous glint in his eyes. "Ye do remember the ceremony? 'Twas quite long."

Heat worked its way up her face.

"Certainly I do." She hoped he hadn't noticed her exhaustion and bleary-eyed state. "I am sorry for my lack of enthusiasm. I got very little sleep last night."

Brighit clamped her mouth shut. She hadn't meant to share that detail. If he questioned her, what excuse could she make? There was no way she could tell him about her encounter with that man. She hadn't even spoken with Niall about it.

Returning home with no one the wiser, Brighit had stopped at the stream that bordered their village to wash her bloody hands and clothes. While she'd tried to get some sleep, the stickiness on her hands didn't seem to go away no matter how much she wiped them. No sign of the blood remained, but she could still feel the sensation of the man's blood dripping down her wrist and arm. Even now.

She'd seen Niall this morn, in view of all, but he'd merely taken her into a close hug and whispered, "Well, ye've had a greater adventure than I'd planned. Glad I am that ye're safe. All the lads made it home without injury as well and the attackers were all sent off in one piece."

Not all...

She'd have dropped to the ground but for the hold her uncle had on her. How could she tell him of her ordeal? He would only feel guilty. Better for him to believe there had been no loss of life.

Truth be told, there was no way she could tell anyone about it. Darragh, in particular, could never know. What was she to say to him, after all?

Well, I murdered a man last night, and unfortunately, I found it more upsetting than I thought I would.

Using her empty goblet as a shield, she raised it to her mouth and glanced down at their joined hands. His covered hers completely, its strength undeniable.

A pitcher passed in front of her face, making her jump. Darragh nodded to her empty vessel. She lowered her cup for him. Her idiotic attempt to hide from his piercing gaze had fallen far short. They exchanged glances and his kind smile lingered.

85

He winked at her and said, "Ye didn't say how ye like the wine."

She exhaled slowly in an attempt to calm her racing heart. "'Tis quite good."

Taking too big a swallow in her feigned enthusiasm, she nearly choked. His concern was obvious, and he took the cup, patting her lightly on her back.

"Bones in the wine again? I will speak to the man."

Brighit's confusion quickly changed into delight at the joke and she laughed aloud, relief washing over her. She took back her drink, sipping more slowly, and glanced at the guests gathered in front of them. Their observers were finally turning away again. "I wouldn't expect humor from ye."

"And why would that be?" Darragh asked.

Tracing the rim of the goblet with her finger, Brighit struggled to respond. Certainly he must know how he appeared to everyone. His expectant expression didn't lessen. She had to say something.

"Ye seem much more… reserved."

"Reserved? As in stoic?"

She averted her gaze, turning away slightly. With the lightest touch to her chin, he turned her face to him.

"I have heard it said that is what ye think of me." His tone said she'd been caught in a lie.

"Who would tell ye such a thing?" She was mortified. How could anyone betray her confidence?

Darragh touched her lips with the pad of his finger, a touch that sent a shiver deep into her gut. "From yer own lips."

He kept his eyes on her lips, his voice low and pleasant to her ears.

"I must beg yer forgiveness then, since 'tis clearly an untruth."

When he lifted his gaze to meet her eyes, she was surprised at their sudden darkness. A heated expression.

"Ye are forgiven," he answered in the same low tone.

She had difficulty swallowing. She had difficulty breathing. She had difficulty. Snatching the goblet back to her lips, she choked down the remaining liquid.

"Is it the heat that makes ye so parched?" He shifted closer. "For me as well."

No one watched this time. The guests were too deep in their own conversations, having been drinking for hours now. It was a celebration after all. His hand dropped to her thigh, the material so thin it seemed more like skin-too-skin contact, nearly burning her.

"I look forward to our joining, Brighit. We may leave at yer pleasure."

She glanced at him, taking a shaky breath, but said nothing. His hand gripped her thigh, a gentle pressure.

"We can sneak away even now. Unnoticed."

She realized that was true enough. No one would notice them sneaking down the hall to his left. Climbing the stairs to his bedchamber.

"We can see this done now, Brighit."

"But—but we've not eaten yet."

He quirked a brow and grinned. "I will start with my dessert."

"Ye have sweets in yer chamber? How indulgent. This castle reminds me of the great kings before us and how pampered they must have been."

Darragh looked out across the expanse of the great hall, the crumbling stone and drafty arrow slits along each wall. An expression she could not read passed over his face. Moving close enough that his expanding chest nudged her elbow, he took a deep breath and closed his eyes. "Ye will be my sweet, wife."

Her body shifted toward him, unbidden, before she could check the movement, but he merely smiled, staying near to her. A glance around confirmed they were no longer the focus of anyone's attention.

"If we could do it unobserved." She matched her tone to his.

He beamed.

Darragh leaned away and she shivered as cold air filled in the gap where he'd been. His gaze went to the three men standing off to the side of the hall. She recognized only his friend Terrence. They all appeared quite drunk, but at the lift of Darragh's chin, they moved with purpose, filling in the space in front of them, effectively blocking the new couple from the rest of the hall. They hunkered down behind the men and Darragh took her hand in a tight grip to lead her to the stairs. She giggled at their escape and he held a finger to his lips. That made her giggle even harder.

His wide-eyed, exasperated look of warning made it even worst. Before she could break into a full guffaw, he scooped her into his arms as if she weighed nothing at all and bounded up the steps, two at a time. They were both laughing by the time he opened the door and he set her on her feet. She gawked, suddenly quiet, struck by the overwhelming manliness of the room. Dark wood lined two walls. A huge four-post bed set upon a raised dais in the middle of the room. Heavy brown linens hung at every corner, tied back to reveal a matching coverlet on the bed, embroidered with a slightly lighter brown and blue field flowers.

Darragh closed the door behind them. Glad for the

amount of wine she'd been able to consume, Brighit gulped at the suddenly intimate scene, keeping her back to him. He dragged her hair aside and pressed his lips to the nape of her now-exposed neck, sending shivers down her back. She closed her eyes when he kissed her sensitive skin again, his arm wrapping around her waist to pull her against his solid length. He was quite a bit taller than her, but somehow she fit against him perfectly.

With his hot hand, he stroked over her belly and she tensed, so afraid she would wince in pain at the tender area there. But he quickly moved up to cup her breast at the same time that his teeth grazed her shoulder. All thought of possible pain faded. Despite the material covering her, his mouth was hot on her skin.

"Ye smell of roses." He rubbed his nose at her nape, his voice husky.

"They bathed me with rose petals, then rubbed my skin in an oil of the same." Her response sounded like it came from outside her body.

"Mmm. They prepared ye for me."

So *that* was the reason for the endless ablutions? She had been so afraid they would notice the bruises from her assault, but no one had said anything. The bruises on her face were hidden beneath the powder she'd applied that morning.

Darragh nipped her ear and she was again focused on his touch.

"I wish to unwrap my rose-drenched bride." His breath against her skin sent another shiver much lower. Somewhere in her mind, she knew he was unlacing the ties of her wedding gown, sliding it down her arms, leaving her top bare since she wore nothing beneath it. Now, he stood before her and she was deliciously attuned to the sensations rushing through her. His mouth and hands touching her. His palm, surprisingly smooth as he gripped her naked breast, bringing the hardened nipple into his moist mouth. That was when she opened her eyes to see him there, suckling her, his hands dragging her gown along as they slipped up her bare legs.

Darragh pulled back and shoved the last of the material over her hips to a puddle at her feet. She watched him, mesmerized when he smiled in pleasure, his gaze roaming over her.

He took a deep breath before he finally spoke. "Ye are exquisite, wife."

Brighit held her breath while he continued his perusal, his eyes finally stopping on her face. She thought he might say something, but his gaze was dark when he pulled her against him, his hand sliding down her belly to slip between her thighs, touching her where she'd never been touched. Without thinking, she tightened her legs.

"Let me touch ye." He spoke against her cheek, a soft, persuasive tone, and her body obeyed.

His sigh sounded needy. Her eyes closed at the pleasant sensation of him touching her.

He groaned, his fingers working magic on her fear. All she wanted was more from him and her hips canted even as she tried to still her body's response to him.

"Mmm." His breathing was heavy in her ear. "Let us see to this bedding."

The word sparked an alarm that was quickly forgotten when he pressed into her, taking her mouth at the same time. This was the kiss she remembered.

The kiss she'd thought about so often. The kiss that told her that—at least in this—she would be pleased with him as her husband.

Darragh slid his hands up her sides, urging her back toward the bed, lifting her at the step to deposit her into the middle of its great expanse. It was a feather bed, softer than anything she'd ever lain upon, but then he was there again, taking over her senses with his mouth and his hands. When his hips slipped between her legs, she realized he was naked as well. He hovered above her, kissing her. Long, languorous kisses that swept away her nervousness. She was surprised by how much she wanted him. She wanted this. She wanted to be joined to this man.

Cupping her face, he broke the kiss to gaze down at her. His eyes closing slightly before focusing on her again. She knew there would be pain, but his look of longing set that fear from her. He pressed into her with one swift movement. A sharp pain quickly forgotten when she heard his guttural sound of pleasure.

Darragh rocked his hips into her, entering her slowly, sending sweet sensations through her body. A nip at her shoulder, followed by a sigh of pleasure at her ear, elicited her own groan. This was not at all what she had expected. This total abandon to the pleasurable experience, the rightness of having him here. Overwhelmed by emotion, tears stung her eyes.

He gathered her close and settled on top of her, thrusting more firmly and setting off an intense need inside her. She reached for it, lifting her hips to meet each stroke until it exploded inside her. Overwhelmed with wave upon wave of deep fulfillment, she could only groan while he continued filling her, prolonging her pleasure. His own sounds of satisfaction reached her when he stilled, pressing deep inside her. He covered her. His entire body blocked out everything else. The weight of him seemed to get heavier and heavier. She turned away from his chest but couldn't catch a breath. The soreness of her belly was manageable, but the sudden sense of suffocation came back with a force strong enough to jolt her out of her pleasure.

All she knew was that she had no breath in her lungs. Full-blown panic swept over her and her breath came in short gasps, fanning her fear of suffocation rather than offering relief. With the flat of her palms she shoved at his shoulders with all her strength. He was killing her.

Darragh's confused expression was a blur, his features unrecognizable to her in that moment. She continued to buck against the intruder, frustrating whimpers filling the air.

"No. No!" Her quiet pleas showed her weakness and she despised them. She reached for her dagger, only then realizing she was naked and powerless. She had no weapon.

"What is wr—" Darragh said. He was rising off her and she didn't hesitate to knee him in the groin. When he dropped on her again and grabbed himself, moaning in pain, she pushed as hard as she could and got out from under him. Feeling like a trapped animal, Brighit scrambled off the bed and backed away toward the far wall. The air safely filling her lungs slowly brought her out of her panic enough for to see her husband writhing in pain on the bed where her virgin's blood was visible beneath him.

The reality of what she'd done hit her as hard as any fist. Darragh could kill her for such behavior. It was his right as her husband. She dove for her gown, holding it against her like a shield, and made for the door, desperate to escape his wrath. Just as her hand touched the cold metal of the latch, Darragh bellowed behind her.

"Ye will not leave this room!"

Chapter Eight

By his third glass of mead, the throbbing in Darragh's groin was finally subsiding. Wiping at the powdered hand mark he'd left on the gold vessel, he looked at his bride, huddled in the heavy wool blanket he'd procured for her when she had begun shivering. He'd refused to allow her to don her gown again. She had explanations to give before he would allow her to dress... *if* he allowed her to dress. He'd been too outraged to say anything to her as of yet.

Brighit had actually kneed him. He couldn't say which had surprised him more, the satisfaction of breaking through her maidenhead and then her moan of pleasure or the sudden she-cat she'd turned into trying to get away from him. Was the pain that bad?

But it couldn't have been the pain. He would have known it. Despite his own pleasure, he had remained acutely aware of everything about her. Her quiet gasp when he broke through her barrier. The soft exhale as he moved in a steady rhythm. And the slightest moan when he'd begun to move more urgently. He'd never been so enraptured with a woman. His wife. And then she'd attacked him.

"So why exactly did ye feel it necessary to try and unman me? D'ye not wish to have any children?"

"Oh!" Brighit's wavering cry finally roused his pity for her. If he didn't know better, he'd swear she was mortified at her behavior.

"So ye would like children?"

Brighit's eyes rounded and flooded anew. "Aye."

The banging on the door startled them both.

"Hey! They're coming." a laughing voice whispered.

"Best get the sheets ready," another voice snickered.

Loud laughter followed.

Damn them. Did they need to get drunk when he had assigned them such an important job? He did not want to have his wife embarrassed at their joining but then again he hadn't expected her to assault him.

He didn't miss her gasp at those first words or her covering her mouth or that expression of horror on her beautiful face. A second look revealed where the white powder had been removed. The skin appeared to be discolored beneath, no doubt an illusion from the flickering candlelight.

"Let me help ye with the gown."

He slipped it over her head and she offered her back so that he could see to the ties, which he did. He took his time though, tugging up along her spine, thoroughly appreciating the smoothness of the skin presented him. The shadow beneath the material lent an unexpected darkness to her fair skin.

"I didn't mean to hurt ye." She said it in a quiet voice, her face lowered. "I really did not."

Darragh quickly donned his trews and tunic before responding.

"Was it so repulsive to ye? Our love making?" Darragh tried for a light tone, but he wasn't sure it was successful. When she didn't respond, he knew her answer must be yes. Despite her initial reaction, it *had* been that repulsive to her. Which meant they were in a very unfortunate position.

Bang! Bang! Bang!

"They're here." His friend called out over the muffled voices of the approaching intruders.

The door was flung open so hard, it slammed against the wall. Thomasina stood there with her hand on her hip and a scowl on her face. If looks could kill, Brighit need never worry about him touching her again.

"Thomasina." Darragh used his chiding tone. "I would expect better from ye."

Sean's head bobbed above the others as he pushed his way past the people crowding around the door. Darragh only hoped it was an attempt to curtail his wife.

"Ye know I wanted a proper bedding ceremony for my daughter," she said.

"My sweet, Tommy." Sean wrapped an arm around his petite wife and tucked her close to his side. "Forgiveness, please, Darragh. We didn't mean to interrupt ye."

The look of outrage Thomasina turned on her husband was almost comical, but he stared her down.

"Did we, Thomasina?"

She hesitated before turning to Darragh. "Of. Course. Not," she ground out the words between tight lips.

Sean kissed his wife's cheek, but the stiffness of her expression didn't bode well for him.

"I am fine, *Mamaídh*." Brighit stood beside Darragh, even taking his hand, though she didn't look at him. "I have been well bedded. The sheets are yonder."

She pointed toward the bed, and like a swarm of bees to a flower, the women rushed to retrieve the stained sheet with its telltale proof of her virginity.

"I had no thought of such trivial concerns, Sean. I am pleased with Brighit as my wife." Darragh turned to the woman at his side, with her upturned nose and fierce appearance. The woman who still refused to even glance his way. "As I hope my wife is with me."

The silence in the hall seemed to go on and on until Brighit finally spoke. "Of course. I am well pleased."

Thomasina beamed, then took her daughter into her arms, whispering things Darragh couldn't hear. Sean clasped hands with Darragh. "Then we shall return below unless ye wish to remain here?"

"Below," Brighit said with far too much enthusiasm.

She pushed to join the crowd, making her escape from him. Darragh's sense of having fallen short was far from eased. And with his groin still sore, he knew what a stiff upper lip felt like as he forced a smile and followed them to rejoin the celebration.

The talk in the great hall quieted as soon as the musicians took over and the dancing began. Brighit enjoyed watching the unmarried ladies flirt shamelessly with every one of her brothers, save Lorcánn. He managed to find some pretty lasses his own age, sitting amidst them and dazzling them with his wit and charm. Since his trip north, he seemed to have grown a foot and acquired an attitude to match.

Brighit sighed as she watched the carefree merrymaking all around the head table where she sat silently with her new husband. He'd assured her mother he was pleased to take her to wife, but surely that was not the case. Shading her face with her hand, she relived the shame at what she'd done. He would certainly never forgive her, and she didn't blame him.

So wrapped up in her own worries, Brighit didn't notice the rowdy crowd coming toward them until they started to drag her and Darragh from their seats to join in the festivities. At first hesitant, she gave in as gracefully as she could. Darragh did the same, even taking her hand as they joined the revelry. The lads on one side and the ladies on the other, the dancing did not allow for one-on-one discussion with anyone, which was fine with her. Embarrassing though her parents' intrusion had been, at least it had put an end to his questions. Brighit understood her parents' wedding had included very little in the way of tradition and ceremony, and it was important to Thomasina that Brighit should have what she had not.

Lachlann picked up a fiddle to join in with the musicians, loudly stomping along to keep the beat from slowing down. The ladies in their best attire created a colorful border while the lads—some in the *léine* that came down to their knees, and some in trews and tunics—faced them. Turning, the single-file line of dancers moved up to cast off in opposite directions, only to meet in the middle again. With hands raised, they moved toward each other, stopping short of their palms actually touching.

This dance was followed by a slower version in which the men made their way down the line of ladies, pairing up. Each couple circled around, palms nearly flush. When Darragh came to Brighit, their eyes held as they circled about, the rest of the guests forgotten. Though his face was peaceful enough, she wondered about his thoughts. Was he thinking of a way to set her aside? Did he wish he'd never agreed to take her to wife? Or did he wish they were alone so that he could hold her in his arms and kiss her again?

Brighit stumbled, but Darragh was quick to catch her.

"Is ought amiss?"

She straightened her gown to avoid looking at him. "I am… exhausted. Nothing more."

"Then, 'tis time to rest." Darragh raised his forearm for her to place her hand on it, and she allowed him to lead her back to the head table.

As soon as they sat, he took a sip from his golden chalice. Brighit feared he would ignore her, but he turned to her and said, "They are enjoying the dancing. I did not realize ye were so agile on yer feet."

She snorted. "Are ye referring to my near fall?"

Darragh's eyes creased at the corner with his smile. "I would never call attention to something ye had not intended to do. I would prefer to overlook unintended offenses."

When his smile faded, Brighit realized he was seeking an explanation, an excuse at the very least, for her treatment of him. He held her gaze, but she didn't know what to say. It was suddenly difficult to swallow, but then he broke the contact, looking away.

"I referred to yer dancing. Ye seem very comfortable with the music."

Before she could answer, the large door to the great hall was shoved open with so much force that all in the room gasped. The dancers froze mid step, their eyes locked on the entryway, and even the musicians halted their playing to turn toward the sound.

Five large hooded men, covered with mantles of wolves' fur, well-armed with axes, shields, and swords entered the hall. Warriors. An intimidating sight. They stood in the doorway, glancing about at the revelers as if not quite understanding what was going on. The man in the lead took a few more steps into the hall before removing his hood, revealing long, black hair and a beard to match. His eyes darted about the room as if searching someone out. His gaze landed on Darragh and Brighit, where it hesitated for the slightest moment before continuing around the room.

Tadhg stepped toward the men, his hand outstretched to their leader. "Seigine. Ye're late to the festivities."

They'd been invited. The tension in the room lightened a bit. All the neighboring tribes were called to a celebration unless they were enemies. The more important the person being wed, the more neighbors invited.

And yet… the newcomer's dark eyes assessed Tadhg with what appeared to be disdain. Darragh tensed beside Brighit, but she dared not say anything. No one spoke. Seigine finally dipped his head, a show of acquiescence. "Forgiveness please, Tadhg.

They clasped hands and the entire assembly seemed to heave a sigh of relief. Brighit was fairly certain she had never met this man and his warriors. Over the past few days, many of the clans from the surrounding area had come to the castle to pay their respects, but it was impossible to keep track of them all.

Seigine continued. "I do not come to celebrate."

"Where is yer king?" Tadhg searched the faces of the men behind him. "I do not see yer brother with ye. Has he intended an offense against me?"

"Cathair is dead."

The collective gasp from the crowd sent a sensation like cold fingers sliding up Brighit's back.

"In battle?"

The large man's eyes seemed to bore into Tadhg's. "No *battle* ensued. We *found* his body."

"An accident?"

Brighit started to shiver. Uncontrollably. She sought out her uncle in the crowd, but his expression revealed only mild curiosity.

"Yer hands are cold." She started at Darragh's words, at the sensation of his hand gripping her own. Without looking, she knew he watched her.

"I am fine."

"Let me get ye a—"

She shook her head, the movement causing shooting pain behind her eyes, and suddenly the room grew blurry all around her.

"No accident. He was murdered." The tall man's words were met with stunned silence.

Chapter Nine

"Who would wish him dead?" Tadhg asked.

Brighit could barely hear him through the pain in her head.

"That is the reason we've come to ye for help. We've signed yer treaty."

The room erupted in speculative chatter until Tadhg raised his hand for silence. Motioning Sean closer, he responded, "Of course. D'ye speak as the *rí túaithe*?"

Seigine glanced at the men with him. When all nodded their agreement, he turned to face Tadhg again and said, "There was little choice. We must seek revenge. A leader is required."

"Ye signed the treaty and we will give assistance as agreed."

"I need only the blood of the man who killed my brother."

Darragh stood beside Brighit. She had difficulty swallowing. She had a notion that Seigine's bloodlust would not fade should he discover it was a woman who'd killed his brother.

"And the treaty states that a man shall not be found guilty and killed in cold blood. He will be brought before a combined council of the *derb fine*," Sean said. "There is no question that ye have our assistance, but we must not act in haste."

His words, though meant to be calming, led to an eruption of shouted words from the men before him.

"What of justice?" Seigine's outrage was uncontainable.

"There will be justice when our laws are followed. Justice for *all* the clans," Tadhg said, his voice loud so that his words were heard above the din.

"Our laws must be obeyed," Sean insisted.

"I want the blood of this murderer." Seigine's bellow was filled with such rage, the others in the hall backed away from the five men. Darragh stood firm, his attention on his father.

"I signed yer treaty. I demand yer assistance."

With each word, the man pressed closer to Tadhg until they were almost nose to nose.

"And ye shall have it." Tadhg stood his ground, his voice remaining calm. "We will call a meeting of the council with a member from each clan that signed the treaty. That will take time."

The tall man backed away, but he was not appeased. With a scowl, he looked around at each of them. When his gaze came to rest on Brighit, her body tensed. She clenched her jaw against the bile flooding her mouth.

Seigine came toward her with plodding steps. "Is this the new bride?"

"This is my wife. Brighit." Darragh moved a step closer to the man, intercepting his course to her.

Her breath quivered so badly she had to part her lips to let in air.

"A lovely lass." When Seigine reached toward her, Brighit jumped. She looked at the man's hand hanging in the air before her, convinced her knees would give way at any moment. It took all the strength she could rally to force her hand toward him. Seigine immediately bowed over it, kissing her knuckles lightly.

"May ye bear many strong children."

Brighit struggled to steady her breath. Guilt was making her overreact. The man was being as polite as all the other neighbors had been. There was nothing to worry about. No one would find out.

"My thanks." Darragh spoke the words she was unable to say, lest offense be taken.

She dropped her shoulders and was about to bow her head when Seigine raised his eyes to meet hers. The dark orbs seemed to pierce right through her, and she had the overwhelming sense that he knew she was the killer. She would have yanked her hand away to break contact, but there was no need. Darragh stepped closer then, lowering a hand on the man's shoulder and turning him back toward Tadhg.

"Please stay and partake of refreshments before ye return home. We are sorry for yer loss, but ye and yer men must still eat."

The rest of the words were lost on Brighit. Those around her were beginning to disperse and she backed her way to the table, unsure of how she could make her escape.

"They are fearsome looking warriors." Terrence was beside her, extending a hand to assist her to her seat. "But ye do not need to look quite so frightened. We could best them in a battle and they know it."

The man's boasting brought a curl to her lips. It was so like Darragh's closest friend to make such statements. "And ye know this from experience?"

The man shrugged, his lips puckering slightly. "Some things a warrior simply knows. That we could best Clan MacCochlain is one of those things."

Terrence took his leave and Brighit was left to observe the festivities. The dancers prepared to resume while the musicians saw to their instruments. Brighit would not be joining them. Her legs were shaking too violently. Darragh had fallen in with the circle of men escorting Seigine and his clan to the table laid out with food and drink. Her eyes remained on him, watching as Terrence joined them.

The treaty the clans had signed was intended to avoid unnecessary bloodshed, to help them find other ways to work out differences, but there were many clans with long-held grudges that went back generations. Her father and Tadhg had worked so very hard to form this treaty. If even one tribe had not agreed, it would have all been for naught.

When the music started, the group of men left the hall through the main door and slipped out of Brighit's sight.

"Ye're quite pale. Drink this before yer husband becomes concerned." She turned to accept the wine, but her heart leapt to her throat at the sight of the bearer.

Seigine settled himself in Darragh's seat, leaning back as if he belonged there. A strange smell drifted to her. He looked out over the dancers with a thoughtful gaze. Brighit gulped down the wine, frantically thinking of a way to take her leave. She could not sit with this man. The colors swirled at the corners of her eyes as the dancers moved past. When they retreated, he finally turned to look at her.

"Ye do not recognize me?"

"I do not."

Seigine pushed his mantle back over his shoulder, revealing the blood-soaked tunic beneath. The source of the tangy smell, she realized.

"Mayhap ye would like to see my horse?" he asked.

The sparkle of the large brooch holding his *brait* at his throat seemed to wink at her.

"I do—" She forced herself to swallow. "I do not care to see yer horse."

Shifting forward, he pushed the wolf skin back and put a hand to his waist. "Then mayhap ye'd like to see this?"

In his grip was the serpent head of her dagger, the two sapphires eyes sparkling at her, tucked into his belt. She gasped, but he merely smiled, turning back toward the room and allowing the material to cover it again.

"So d'ye recognize me now?"

When she started to stand, he gripped her arm so she could not move.

"It appears ye do. Sit. Let us talk."

The music changed into a faster paced song, the colors a grotesque mix swirling before her. She said nothing.

"Ah, Brighit? Is it? We only have a few moments

before yer husband returns and so much to discuss. Are ye certain ye wish to remain silent?"

Movement from the entryway caught her eye and she sat up straighter.

"When he returns, I will reveal the murderer's weapon. Such a unique blade." He turned toward her, a tight expression on his face. "I am certain they will realize who has killed my brother in cold blood."

A small shake of her head became violent, but he gripped her chin to hold it still, searching her face. "And where are the marks from that attack? Is it a powder ye've used to cover them? Another piece of truth that a good washing will reveal."

"Do not."

"Good. Ye speak."

"And *ye* watched! Ye saw what he did to me. I was defending myself when I killed him."

His pink lips widened, peeking through his dark beard when he smiled. "And what a defense ye gave, little one, for a lad... and for a lass?"

His eyes darted down her length, and he wetted his lips. "As a lass, ye intrigue me even more."

She sucked in her breath, but he turned now toward the men re-entering the hall and dropped his hand. "But ye have wasted much time. Mayhap 'twould be best for me to show them what I found buried in my brother's chest."

There would be no mistaking the serpent-headed hilt of the dagger. Her father had given her that weapon.

"Please do not." Her voice squeaked, but his gaze remained on the entryway. He stood and removed himself a respectable distance from her before finally giving her his attention. Seigine shrugged as if it mattered very little to him then took his leave.

Darragh intercepted the man, leaving his father and Sean with the others in the group.

"Darragh!" Brighit stood as she called out his name, desperate to have her say before the man revealed her.

Both he and Seigine turned toward her. Darragh's expression one of concern. Seigine's one of amusement.

"Darragh, I have been speaking with yer new bride." His voice was loud, calling the attention of the entire gathering since the music had stopped for the moment. "From Clan Cruadhlaoch. A clan as powerful as yer own."

Crossing his arms about his chest, Darragh nodded at the man.

"Please, Darragh." She couldn't help the fact that she sounded desperate. "Come here."

When he began to move, Seigine checked the movement with a hand on his arm. "Are ye not spending yer honeyed moon apart from the others?"

The tradition was still kept by many. Her heart leapt with hope. If she could get him away from the others, certainly she would have time to explain what had taken place, how there had been no choice but to kill the man who was assaulting her.

"Aye, we will, Darragh."

"If that is what ye wish." Darragh's face clearly showed his confusion, but then he turned to his father and said, "Although I would prefer to be present for discussions."

"As well ye should be," Tadhg said, his hands on his hips. "Ye and Brighit may need to remain near for yer time of seclusion."

Seclusion was all she wanted. Here or somewhere else, it mattered not. She required time to get the courage up to tell her husband what she had done. Her gut tightened at the thought.

Seigine eyes were on her again. "My men and I will continue to hunt down this killer. I feel certain he has not gone far. Mayhap we will find him with the blood still on his hands."

"Even with proof that strong—" Tadhg's warning tone drew Seigine's, "—ye must wait to have yer justice seen to. It must be agreed upon by the council."

"A punishment befitting the crime." Sean's eyes narrowed. "And it must be carried out in the presence of the council once they have decreed the judgment."

"A murderer is put to death."

Sean nodded at the dark man's declaration. Brighit's skin crawled. Was there truly no consideration for a killing that had been done in defense? She searched her mind and realized she'd paid such little attention to her father's work, she had no idea.

"My men and I have searched the area and examined Cathair's body."

"D'ye have the weapon?" Tadhg's words sent a chill down her back. "It must have be—"

"It *was* with the body."

"Can we see it?" Sean asked.

Brighit squeezed her fingers so tightly together they ached. Her mind searched frantically for what she would say when the man revealed her dagger to all.

Seigine shifted, reaching beneath his *brait*. She didn't miss the glance he shot at her, or the flash of his white teeth. He was enjoying this!

"Forgiveness, please," he said, lifting his empty hands for all to see. "My wife is not well, and I did not wish to leave her. In my haste to get here, I must have left it at her side."

Sean and Tadhg exchanged glances. Her lungs refused to work.

"Was there anything distinctive about the weapon? Something ye may have noticed?"

"Ye have seen the body? The mutilation my brother suffered?"

Her heart sped up. The man she'd murdered was beyond those doors? Was his body cloaked in a burial cloth even now? Or had he been thrown onto a cart just as he was, his side bloodied from her blade?

"We have." Sean tipped his head in a show of respect. "A most vicious attack."

No! It was done in defense.

"I do not remember anything about the weapon, only the destruction it caused."

"The sharpest of blades, to slice so clean—"

"An angry strike. I will bring it with me for yer examination when next I return." Seigine paused before continuing. "Unless we can find the murderer and can bring him to ye, we will wait until ye send us word that the council has assembled."

The need to confess what she had done—to put an end to this terrible mess—shifted in Brighit's chest. She set her feet to the floor, preparing to stand and yet… it was a real possibility that she would be killed if she could not convince them of her innocence.

She remained seated.

Seigine turned to the others listening, their eyes intent on him.

"I do not wish to take away from this celebration," he said. He extended a hand and Darragh clasped his wrist. "May yer time in seclusion be fertile and produce a son as great as the father."

A child. Brighit searched her memory. Was there

any mention in the treaty of a woman being given leniency because she was with child?

"My thanks."

Seigine's threats did not demonstrate any willingness to cast her as an innocent. He had her weapon in his possession. If he wanted her punished, he needed only to reveal it to them now, or even describe the distinctive hilt to them. He did not.

"We have taken enough of their time. Come." Seigine motioned to his men, who gathered around him, and they headed toward the door as one.

Stopping at the entryway, Seigine turned back to Tadhg and Sean with a twinkle in his eyes. "There is one more thing I must ask ye before I leave."

Brighit's relief was short lived and she slumped in her seat, no longer able to even consider standing.

"I wish to know that both of yer clans will support me as king if there is an outcry from Clan Dubhshláine."

"Why would there be an outcry?" Sean asked.

"My grandmother was of their clan and they would prefer that our clan, small as it is, should join with theirs."

Tadhg nodded. "I know of the dispute, Seigine." His tone indicated both his understanding of the matter and a lack of patience for it. "Yer land is the better land. It is located along the river. Did yer brother not recently consider joining with them?"

"My brother is dead." The words spoken with such finality raised a few eyebrows, but no one said anything. "I will speak with my council. I will follow their advice."

"As ye should." Sean's reassurances were not repeated by Tadhg. "We will gather the other *rig túaithe*. Capturing the murderer before that time—"

"I will bring the murderer before ye." Seigine bowed his head then led the men through the outer doors.

To Brighit's ear, it was both promise and threat.

Chapter Ten

Tadhg signaled for the celebrations to continue and all seemed happy to comply. He had feigned interest in the festivities for all of ten minutes before huddling with Sean and Darragh at the table opposite Brighit to discuss their visitors. Though she felt compelled to remain in the great hall, her seeming abandonment suited her fine. She preferred not to be part of any conversation about Seigine. Instead, her mind kept reviewing everything he'd said to her.

He had her weapon, the proof she had murdered his brother, and an eyewitness—himself. That was all that was needed for justice to be seen to. The punishment would fit the crime. So why had the man approached her with the information instead of revealing it to all and pointing the finger at her?

He'd said he wanted the council to support him as his brother's replacement. Could that be why he was waiting?

The men continued to discuss how they should proceed. This was the first true test of the treaty so many had been opposed to signing. The tradition was for important agreements to be memorized, often recited by the bards and *fili*. The idea of putting the terms down in a document had set many against the agreement.

"And this is acceptable to ye, Darragh?" Sean asked.

Something about her father's tone—and mayhap the mention of her husband's name—caught Brighit's attention. Several of Darragh's closest friends stood beside them now, intently listening.

"There is no choice in the matter," Terrence said. "Their leader was murdered. They demand satisfaction."

"And they watch and wait to see what we will do about it. How quickly we will move on it," Tadhg added before emptying his horn of mead.

Brighit felt the hair on her neck rise.

"Was it some random act? Did he travel alone like a fool?" Darragh asked.

"Seigine told me they were set upon by a group of men they did not recognize," Tadhg said.

Brighit averted her eyes, the sound of her heart beat loud in her ears.

"On their own land?" Sean asked.

Tadhg nodded. "They took chase and somehow the leader was murdered. There was no sign of the attackers."

Sean glanced at Brighit, but he did not seem to

notice the petrified look on her face.

"The closest neighbors, and even many from far away, have been here. Among us." Terrence stated the obvious. "How could a group that large go unnoticed?"

"And more confusing is why Cathair and his men were out in the dark of night. I am wary of their truthfulness."

Tadhg merely shrugged. "But if the men who attacked them are the same ones who have been killing our deer and leaving them to rot in our woods, I would like to receive just compensation as well."

"I worried that this clan might become a problem. They were so reluctant to sign the treaty and tried to get others to reject it as well," Sean said.

"I feared the same, which is why this union between Darragh and Brighit is so important. Their land stands between our two *túath*, and they could make life difficult for us."

"Was it not Seigine's brother who approached us about their joining Clan Dubhshláine?" Darragh asked.

Tadhg nodded. His face a grim mask. "He was looking into the joining of the clans to ensure continued peace, but he assured me it could wait until after the wedding."

Cold horror filled Brighit. After prolonging their betrothal for her own selfish purposes, had she managed to kill the one man who might have sought a truce in the area?

Tadhg turned to Darragh. "Are ye prepared for any trouble ye might encounter?"

His ominous words had her searching Darragh's face for any clue, but he merely smiled. A quiet smile intended to calm any concerns. "I will be traveling with my new bride. Why would I be a threat to anyone? Besides, I believe I will find more trouble bedding my wife."

Darragh winked at her and she gasped, her eyes widening at the unexpected jest.

As one, the younger men turned to her with a mix of expressions from avid curiosity to complete shock. Tadhg and Sean pretended not to be listening.

"Is this so?" Terrence asked, looking ready to explode with laughter. "This wee bit of a lass gave ye trouble? Did ye leave her disappointed?"

Brighit's face tightened when he looked at her as if to discern the truth.

Darragh said, "I would never leave her disappointed, as well ye know."

"Oh, ho ho!" Terrence stood as if he'd learned something of great importance. "How ye speak of yer own prowess—and in her presence, ready to set ye aright."

The three turned to her as if ready for some reaction; she had none. Her face heated considerably, but she wanted to scream at them.

Stop! Ye have no idea what I am capable of.

"Is something amiss?" Darragh had moved closer without her noticing. He took her hand. "Yer skin is like ice."

The others were once again paying them no attention. "I'm... I'm fine. Thank ye. Mayhap a little tired."

"It has been a long few days."

He didn't know the half of it.

Sean inched forward on the bench and Brighit recognized her father's speculative gaze. She wasn't certain he could hear them, but she became overwhelmed with the idea of going to him, crying in his arms and confessing all that she had done. Surely he could protect her.

Her father finished off his mead and came to stand beside her.

"How fare ye, daughter?" His fingers smoothed down her hair. Tears pricked her eyes.

"I am fine," she forced herself to say. "Thank ye for yer concern."

When he dropped to his knees in front of her, taking her hands in his, his intent gaze startled her. "I will always be here for ye if ye need me, ye know that?"

Brighit nodded, afraid to speak.

"But ye must go with yer husband. He will care for ye now." Sean glanced at Darragh. "He is a good man and he will be a good provider and protector."

"I do not…"

Her father's eyes widened when she did not finish her familiar complaint. She couldn't say the words. They were no longer true. She *did* need his protection.

"Ye are correct," she said instead.

Pressing his lips against her forehead, she swiped at the tear slipping down her cheek before he would see it.

"I am most proud of ye, Brighit. Ye are the light in my life and I will miss ye more than I can say."

When tears filled his eyes, she wrapped her arms tightly around him. "I am sorry I have been such a disappointment to ye."

"Never! Never were ye a disappointment to me."

Brighit couldn't voice the feelings ripping out her heart. When he found out what she had done, he would be glad to be rid of her.

"I will love ye always," Sean's words were

muffled against her hair.

"And ye are the best of fathers."

He kissed her cheek and rose to include Darragh. "Ye will see to her needs?"

Darragh moved closer, accepting Sean's hand. "She will be well taken care of."

When her father's gaze shifted to the crowds of merry makers around them, Brighit knew without asking that he was seeking out her mother. They never slept apart. The moment Thomasina sensed his gaze, her eyes went directly to him. When she turned her nose up in the air and turned away, Brighit's couldn't help but mumble, "Oh dear."

She immediately regretted saying it and hoped no one had heard.

Sean patted her on the head before dropping a kiss in the same spot. "Rest easy, *ghráidh*. I'll win her back. She can only stay mad at me for a short time."

Tadhg, Darragh, and the other men kept their eye on Sean's swaggering retreat, their heads close together, as if they were watching a play being performed before their very eyes.

"D'ye suppose he'll be looking for another place to sleep?" Tadhg spoke without turning away from the scene unfolding before him, as if afraid to miss any part of this—Sean's overtures to his irritated wife.

Darragh was also intent on the scene. "I doubt it. The two seem inseparable."

Brighit offered no information but would admit to being concerned about the outcome. Sean was saying something. It only received a curt nod. Not a good first move. But then he stroked her in the pretense of moving Thomasina's long hair off her shoulder, he said something into her ear—a whisper. When her mother's smiling face turned up for Sean's amorous kiss, Brighit sighed in relief. They would be fine.

"Ah! Not this time." Tadhg chuckled. "The man's got the touch. Always has." He turned back to the others and reddened when he realized Brighit was also listening. He cleared his throat before standing. "I'm for bed."

Darragh nodded. "I thought we'd set out in the morning."

"And how does Brighit feel about traveling south? I'm sure it will be an adventure."

"An adventure to start off our married life? Would that please ye?" he asked her with a smile.

Excitement, unbidden, simmered inside her. They would be leaving for their honeyed moon in the morning. It would be an adventure *and* an escape from her troubles. Mayhap she need never return. Struggling to keep all emotion from her face, Brighit nodded. "I have never been south."

Tadhg smiled and said, "Do take care. We don't know who may have set about to murder this *ri túaithe.* I admit I would prefer ye be away from here with Brighit at least until the new moon."

"I will take care of what is mine, Father." Darragh glanced at her as if measuring her response when he answered.

"Go with God. Both of ye." Tadhg offered, kissing Brighit on the cheek before leaving them. The others drifting away as well.

Brighit met Darragh's eyes. He studied her before he spoke.

"This will not be the kind of honeyed moon I'd wish for us. I've agreed to bring the news of the treaty violation to the other *rig túaithe.*"

119

Guilt flooded her. It was her fault—all of it.

"We will travel with warriors for protection, but the trip will not be easy. The rains are nearly upon us, which can make the routes impassable. Without many places of protection along the trail, we must prepare for the worst."

She simply nodded. A single short, quick movement.

"Still, we will have time to ourselves, as we should," he said. "We should get ye to bed. Sunrise is not so very far off."

Standing, he offered her his arm, his face again that stoic visage. Overcome with sadness, she placed her hand on his arm and they turned toward the stairs. The music stopped, and all eyes were on them as they ascended the steps. Applause broke out, but rather than pause to acknowledge the cheers of encouragement, Darragh seemed to quicken his step.

At the door to his chamber, he turned to her, the torch on the wall casting dark shadows on his face making it impossible to read his expression. "And here we are again."

He leaned into her, easing her against the wall with a hand on either side of her, before capturing her lips. The gentleness of the kiss wiped away all other thoughts and when he grasped her chin to tip her head, his tongue slipped between her parted lips to spar with her own. The heat was there again. If he touched her *there*, he would find how easily he roused her.

He pulled away, sliding a single finger down her face. "My lovely wife. Have ye nothing to say to yer husband?"

A jumble of words flitted through her mind. Apologies. Explanations. A plea for forgiveness. She remained silent.

He turned away from her and opened the door, giving her room to precede him. The bed had been remade and a sheer chemise lay across the foot of it, the silky material no doubt meant to entice.

Darragh cleared his throat before speaking in a brusque tone. "We best get to sleep. I plan to leave before the sun is up."

He gave her his back, removing his tunic, calfskin shoes, and trews with little ceremony. She struggled with the ties but managed to disrobe, quickly donning the chemise. Darragh neither watched her nor offered his assistance. He seemed to be fulfilling her first impression of him just fine. When he crawled beneath the covers and turned away from her, she did the same, shivering despite the heavy fur covering. The wedding night was truly not everything a young lass might hope for.

Chapter Eleven

Brighit had been dreaming of her own bed, but it was her husband who roused her from sleep. She groaned, and her eyes flew open. He was leaning over her, a hand on either side of her head, and a knowing smile on his face.

"Were ye dreaming of me?" His voice barely a whisper.

When he leaned closer to kiss her, covering her with his body, Brighit couldn't take a breath. She panicked, shoving at his chest. "No!"

He yanked back, quite a far distance, and she realized he'd moved more than a knee's length away. His expression of confusion quickly shifted to irritation. "Get yerself ready. We need to be off."

Darragh left the room, stopping barely short of

slamming the heavy wooden door closed. The tears came fast and hard. Her dream had been so sweet—she'd been lying across his chest and kissing him back. Sweet, tender kisses that sent all kinds of delicious sensations throughout her body. She remembered wanting him to take her again. But just now, he had been too close to her. She'd felt trapped. Jumping up from the bed, she quickly bathed in the cold water from the pitcher then dressed. The last thing she wanted to do was to anger him more by making him wait for her.

When Brighit entered the inner bailey cloaked in her heavy mantle, she was surprised by the number of mounted men gathered there. Darragh approached, the reins of his horse held loosely in his hands.

"Ye'll ride in the carriage, hidden and well-guarded by my men."

It was then that she noticed the small wood-sided conveyance. Attached to a single horse, it could probably hold two people in close proximity. For once, she eagerly embraced the notion of traveling in a carriage. She required time to herself, time to think. Her earlier reaction to Darragh had come from some irrational fear and that did not sit well with her. She hoped he wouldn't share what she'd done, for the men would certainly see it as cowardice as well. No doubt another woman would care very little if the men saw her as a coward, but to Brighit, there was no worst label.

"Let me help ye in." Darragh joined his hands, fingers locked, for her to use as a step up into the carriage. It swayed like a ship on a sea and she couldn't sit quickly enough.

His hands on either side of the door frame, he leaned in to look around the inside. "Seems a comfortable enough way to pass the day, would ye agree?"

She tightened her jaw, disgusted with the fact that she wanted to agree wholeheartedly with him. To be in here? Away from prying eyes? Alone to ponder how best to handle the situation? A godsend! "'Twill be most pleasant, I'm certain."

He tipped his head, his eyes narrowing the slightest bit. "D'ye still wear the powder on yer face?"

Brighit's bruises seemed even more prominent today, so she'd had no choice. "I do."

She didn't dare offer any more information but prayed he would let it go rather than question her. Her own father always insisted her mother was beautiful enough without adding foreign concoctions to her skin. Surely Darragh did not feel that way about her looks.

Ye are exquisite, wife.

The unexpected memory of his words sent a ripple of longing through her. If only the horrible thing she'd done didn't stand between them…

"I do not remember ye wearing it before our wedding."

Brighit shook her head, her lips pressed tightly together.

"Is there a reason a married lass would choose to wear it? I remember ye having lovely, soft skin."

Her breath caught at the kind sentiment and she lowered her eyes. She hadn't thought he'd noticed her at all. He'd always stood there at his father's side with a stoic, untouchable look, ever the obedient warrior.

He must have read her reaction as uneasiness because his face hardened, and he drew back. "No matter."

He closed the door to the carriage and soon they were on their way.

The group stopped mid-day for a fortifying meal, resting for a time before resuming their journey. There was some talk about the order in which they'd relay the message to the various kings. If she hadn't been beset by her own concerns, she would have looked forward to seeing these new sights.

Watching the men on their horses from inside the carriage, she realized it was her conveyance that was dragging out the undertaking. On horseback, they could have easily made their first destination within a few days' ride. The men's decision to continue through the night made her feel even guiltier. They were accommodating her presence. But when the time came to finally stop and rest, she was more than ready to quit the confining space.

Darragh's men saw to the setting up of their camp while he came to assist her.

"Are ye stiff from yer ride?"

Brighit forced herself to straighten as they walked away from the carriage. The pain across her body was near unbearable today. "A bit, I'm afraid. I am usually much more active."

"Traipsing around dressed as a lad, if I remember correctly."

Her sharp gaze took in his teasing smile and she relaxed. He referred to when he'd caught her with the lads a year earlier, not her misadventure with her uncle the night before her wedding.

"Yer threats certainly saw an end to that." She was too tired and sore to hide her irritation with him.

"So yer brother saw the error of his ways?" He was undaunted. "Shame on him for putting the daughter of the overking at such risk at all."

Brighit glared at him.

"Not to mention my betrothed." Darragh's expression softened and he stroked a fingertip along her jawbone, his voice quieter. "Even with the ash on this face, yer loveliness could not be denied."

She swallowed, not sure how to respond. The other lasses were often complimented by lads currying favor with them, begging for time in their presence, but she'd had none of that.

"I like the powder even less than the ash. I would prefer ye not use it." He watched her eyes, glancing from one to the other. "Will ye fight me on that as well?"

Fight him? Brighit couldn't hold his gaze. He spoke of the bedding, of course, but for the life of her she couldn't figure out how to explain what she didn't understand herself. Not without telling him what she was still not ready to tell.

"I prefer it on occasion." When the bruises faded, she would have no further use for the disgusting stuff.

His eyes were on her. She could feel his gaze boring into her, as though judging her defiant.

"I'm sorry," she said. "Ye have been most kind to me."

"And why would I not." He stepped closer, raising her face so she could no longer avoid him. He studied her intently before he spoke again. "I have taken ye to wife… and ye have taken me to husband."

More teasing. She smiled at the reminder of her earlier words.

"Ah, a genuine smile. I would like to see more of that."

When his gaze dropped to her lips, she knew he

wanted to kiss her. She wanted the same. The heat pouring from him was intense, but then she recognized the look of resignation crossing his face. Instead of kissing her, he reached for the sack beside him and said, "I need to see to my duties. I will return for ye."

Her heart sank, even more so because Darragh didn't look at her again before slipping off. She wiped away the tears dripping down her cheeks, her palms came away white from the powder. Glancing around, she realized he had taken her belongings with him, including the powder. The lads who'd stayed behind were going about their business, none of them paying her any attention.

"Darragh?"

"He's gone off to catch our supper," Terrence emerged from the woods, his arms loaded with twigs and dried leaves. "Is there something ye need?"

He bent down to the ground to start the fire, giving her only a cursory glance.

What could she do? Darragh had just said he'd prefer she not to wear the powder. It seemed rebellious to now ask for it.

Terrence finally faced her, the fire catching nicely before him. He looked like he was about to speak, but he frowned instead.

"What—?" He crossed the distance between them and wiped along her cheekbone. She winced in pain. "How did ye get these bruises?"

Brighit turned away, draping her hair alongside her cheek to hide herself from him.

"Not Darragh." Terrence appeared to be making a statement, but then he moved up close, turning her face to the light. "Tell me it was not Darragh who did this to ye."

She could tell he believed it to be true—but was desperate for her to prove him wrong. He searched her eyes.

"Of course not," she said immediately, her tone sharp. Her mind frantically searched for an excuse. "I am... susceptible to hives, and when they clear, they leave my skin... marred. I usually cover it with powder until it fades."

His brows slashed down and he nodded, but she could read his disbelief. Terrence, whom she had only ever seen smiling and teasing, looked ready to do someone harm.

She grabbed at his arm, imploring him with her eyes. "Please. That is all it is. Let it go."

The sound of the hunting party returning put Brighit in a panic. If Terrence could see the bruises, others, including Darragh, would see them, too, and then... and then she'd have to explain here and now in front of everyone. Her lips quivered. She would prefer to explain the situation to her husband before sharing the truth with anyone else. With a start, she realized she wanted Darragh to tell her what to do. When had she decided his council was worth seeking?

"Terrence," Darragh called to the man.

"Oh dear," Brighit said, turning from the fire.

"Go back to the carriage, I will find the powder and bring it to ye." Terrence's whisper was followed by a gentle shove in the right direction.

"Where is Brighit off to?" Darragh held up the

sack. "I have her things here."

Darragh ruffled through the bag of items and pulled out a skin of mead, blowing out a wooden mug before pouring himself a liberal amount. Terrence gave him his back, tending to the fire while the others saw to the preparing of their meal.

"Isn't that meant for ye *and* yer wife?" Terrence dropped a log onto the fire, the sparks flying high into the air, but he still didn't look at Darragh.

"When she returns, I do hope to share it with her," Darragh answered.

Settling on the ground, Darragh rolled up his heavy *brat* and positioned it behind him. The mead would be much better enjoyed the way it was intended, shared between a husband and wife who found pleasure in each other's company… and enjoyment in each other's bodies.

He sighed. Her declaration that he had been kind to her had caught him off guard. If she believed he was kind, why did she keep pushing him away? Mayhap keeping his distance from her was not the best approach. And hiding away in the carriage instead of riding beside him? That did not seem like the Brighit he knew. If it was him that she feared—and he would swear she had found pleasure in his arms—spending time with him should put those fears to rest.

All he knew was that being near her flooded him with an overwhelming desire to have her again. Like a moth to a flame. That wasn't anything he'd experienced before, so he couldn't be certain if the urge was so strong because she was his now or because of the woman herself.

Terrence grabbed the sack of Brighit's belongings,

jarring him from his thoughts.

"What are ye about?" Darragh asked.

The man headed off in the direction Brighit had gone. "Seeing if yer wife needs anything from this."

"She *is* taking a long while to join us." Darragh glanced down the path she had taken, then narrowed his gaze at his friend. "And why are ye the one to bring it to her?"

Heaving another sigh, Terrence stopped and turned toward him. "Because ye do not seem to be held in high regard by her." He shook his head. "And here ye are, seeing to yer own relaxation, oblivious to her plight."

"Plight? What plight?"

Darragh started to rise, but Terrence lifted a hand to stop him. His usually jolly friend gave him the most insincere smile he had ever seen. "Relax. I will charm her with my wit and set her mind at ease."

"I did not realize her mind was not at ease." Darragh realized it was a lie as soon as the words came out. She was extremely ill at ease, only he didn't understand why. He'd assumed the marriage itself was the cause for her disquiet, but now his suspicions were ignited. Terrence was not a deep thinker. If he had an idea that Brighit was upset with him, he must know something. "What did she tell ye?"

"Darragh, sometimes ye are an arse." With that, Terrence followed the dimly lit path back toward the horses and carriage.

Finally standing, Darragh roughed his hand through his hair and stared down the pathway.

"*A thighearna.*" Iain came toward him, a look of concern on his young face.

"What is amiss?"

"I believe we are being followed."

Relief flooded him. He'd been feeling out of sorts all day, but he attributed it to his problems with Brighit. This new information seemed to confirm his concerns. "Show me."

The man led the way across the open meadow before coming to a sudden stop.

"Can ye make out the firelight in the distance?" Iain asked, pointing off in the distance.

After watching several moments, the slight flicker showed through the darkness, the hills a backdrop that nearly hid the telltale sign of another camp. "Ye believe they have something to do with us?"

"I found the tracks of several mounted horses along with a few men on foot." Iain put his hand to his hip. "They backtracked to where they are now, as if they had followed us, saw that we were staying the night, and left to see to their own camp."

Iain was very good at assessing the enemy's plans and Darragh didn't need to question that. "D'ye have any thought of who they could be?"

He shrugged, shaking his head. "I do not. The only clan in the area that did not remain at the festivities was Seigine's."

"And he was beside himself with grief." Darragh searched his memory and realized Iain was right. There was no reason for anyone to hurry home from the festivities. The harvest was in, and it was expected that visitors would remain until the rains had passed.

"Mayhap 'twould be best for us to do some tracking of our own? Learn who it is that follows us?"

Iain nodded, his expression thoughtful. "We could set out after they believe we have bedded down for the night."

Darragh nodded, trying to ignore the way his tarse twitched at the word "bedded"—irritated with himself for having the idea of bedding his wife again foremost in his mind.

"Or we could approach now," Darragh said. "Take another man with ye. When ye return, we can make our plans."

The lad left and he was alone with his aching desire for Brighit. How quickly she'd become a need to him, like eating or sleeping. And like any other need, bedding her again would be the only way he'd be satiated.

Chapter Twelve

Brighit had tried her best to spread what powder remained on her face over the worst of her bruises. It didn't help that there was no flat surface of water nearby—nothing she could look in to help assess where it was most needed. Her face was sore, but her stomach was even worse. Misleadingly so, since she could sit for a long time and not even think about it, but when she went to stand, the pain was excruciating enough to double her over.

Near enough to see the others going about their duties, she could just make out Darragh sitting alone by the fire. The rest of the area around her was dark, the leaves in the trees rustling their warning that the rains would soon be coming. When they finally did come, she would be grateful to be ensconced in the carriage. However constricting, it kept her safe.

"Brighit?"

She hadn't heard anyone coming over the wind in the trees.

Terrence came toward her, the sack of her belongings in his outstretched hand. "I think ye'll find what ye need in here."

She rummaged through it and pulled out the jar of powder. Other men from their group mumbled greetings as they passed them, but the lack of light made it impossible for anyone to see what the firelight had revealed to Terence. Still, she turned away to apply the stuff, then wiped her hands against each other before facing him again. She said, "Hopefully that works."

He shook his head, staring at her with somber eyes.

"No?" As soon as she said the word, Brighit realized he wasn't commenting on how well she'd covered the damage done her face.

"I need to hear how the bruises came about."

The compassion in his voice unleashed her tears. She gave him her back again and replaced the clay jar, disgusted with herself for such an open show of femininity.

She cleared her throat, trying for a forceful tone. "I cannot tell ye."

"And that concerns me even more." He shifted behind her. "I am unable to figure out why something hasn't been said to the rest of us about yer attack." His hand on her shoulder made her jump. "Unless the person who hurt ye is the same one that should be protecting ye."

She squeezed her quivering lips before responding. "Darragh knows nothing about this."

"How can that be? The bedding…"

"I kept it from him and so will ye."

"Never! How can ye ask that of me? If someone has abused ye, he will see ye avenged."

"He cannot." She slammed her teeth together to keep from saying what was right there on her lips. *That man is dead.* Instead, she huffed and said, "It does not matter because it will not happen again."

"How can ye be so sure?"

Her mouth opened to shoot off a thoughtless response, but she slammed it closed again. Nodding her head, she said the only thing she could think to say, "Ye must trust what I tell ye."

And that was the crux of the dilemma as she saw it. Trust. She had betrayed him by going behind his back and doing as she pleased. The result was that she would be marked as a murderer.

Ye are a foolish lass.

He had been, without a doubt, correct. Now she bore the result of her foolishness—and so, too, would he. Overcome with emotion, Brighit dropped to the ground with her head in her hands.

Terrence was beside her in an instant, his hand on her arm. "Do not fret so. Please." He paused before continuing. "Is this the reason ye keep Darragh away from ye?"

She gasped at him. "No… I do not… Oh God!"

Quick to placate her, he mumbled, "No. He never said as much. I assumed. I did not know. Please. He needs to know."

"He needs to know what?" Darragh asked, suddenly behind them. His menacing tone was undeniable.

Both Brighit and Terrence jumped up, startled.

"I asked a simple question. I do expect an answer. Simple or not." He was visibly seething with anger. "And I would like ye to remove yer hand from my wife," he added.

Terrence whipped his head around, looking at Darragh with an astonished expression, but he withdrew his hand. "Darragh—"

"I think I would prefer to hear from Brighit," he snapped.

"I… I do not know what he is speaking of. There is nothing." Brighit was proud of her even tone. Inside she was a quivering mess, and her knees trembled and threatened to collapse.

"There is nothing I need to know?" Darragh turned to the man, one hand circling the air in front of him impatiently. "So? Have yer say, Terrence. Tell me what ye believe I need to be told."

His closest friend dropped his gaze. Brighit could feel the tension coursing through his body, his warring loyalties. And she prayed he would hold his tongue. Darragh was already angry—this was not the right way for him to learn the truth.

"Forgiveness, please." Terrence faced his friend without balking. "There is nothing."

"*A thighearna.*"

Iain's return could have been better timed, but before Darragh could voice his irritation, Iain continued.

"They are Seigine's men."

His winded delivery of the information caught

Darragh by surprise. Terrence moved closer while Brighit stayed in the shadows. He would have liked to pull her closer, demand that she tell him all, but this news was unsettling. With great effort, he set aside his concern for his wife and looked at the man.

"Is he with them?"

"*A thighearna.* He is here at our camp."

Darragh shoved past the man to trot down the path toward the fire, searching in the darkness. The men were not hard to find. Eight of them, standing around the flame and warming their hands.

"Seigine?" Darragh attempted a cordial tone. Much better to approach them as friends. He saw no reason to reveal he knew they had been following them, as such suspicion would be met with a less than amicable response. That the man had reinforcements was disconcerting at the very least.

"Darragh." The large man bowed his head in a show of respect. His lips turning up at the corners in a closed smile, he said, "My men have been discovered."

An odd response, but Darragh checked his reaction, instead widening his own lips into a pleased expression. "And were ye hiding?"

Seigine laughed. A deep sound that rivaled the loudness of the wind high in the trees.

"Forgiveness, please." The man paused and glanced at Terrence and Brighit, who were right behind Darragh. "I am merely hunting down a murderer."

Darragh glanced around in a joking manner. "And ye believe he has come this way?"

"I am following the very trail taken."

Darragh allowed his surprise to show on his face.

"I do not think we passed a single person on our travels here," he said, casually looking at the others for confirmation. His men had taken up positions around the MacCochlain warriors. A protective outer circle.

They nodded, also appearing relaxed. He knew they would be ready to spring into action at a moment's notice should a threat present itself.

"But please, join us." He motioned for Iain to see to sharing their ale and food. "We have more than enough ale and food for yer men. We will continue our celebrating."

Seigine motioned for his men to partake of what was being offered before grabbing a horn of ale and settling on the ground. Darragh caught Terrence's gaze and tipped his head the slightest bit. The signal was received. The men would be welcoming, but they would remain watchful.

"I am surprised ye did not approach earlier rather than setting up so far from us. We are a greater force joined together." Darragh took a mug of ale, no longer of a mind to drink the honeyed wine, and returned to where he'd spread his *brait* to settle himself. "If the murderer and the men that attacked ye show themselves, we will easily defeat them and bring him to justice."

Seigine stopped, his horn halfway to his mouth and his face darkening. "D'ye believe I wish to see to my own justice still, Darragh? Ha!" He drank from the horn, emptying it one gulp. "Ye do not realize how persuasive yer father is. We signed the treaty. We will see this done according to what has been written down."

Darragh shook his head and smiled, an easy smile meant to reassure. "I know ye understand the importance of the agreement. To disregard it would cause nothing less than chaos."

"Agreed!" Seigine smiled, accepting more ale from Iain. "We had hoped only to give ye and yer bride some distance."

The man's eyes were on Brighit. She averted her gaze from where she sat slightly behind Darragh, away from the others.

"That is very thoughtful of ye, my friend." Darragh took a long draw on his mug, glancing back at Brighit, who looked uncomfortable with the attention. "As ye can see, we travel with many men already. Not exactly alone, but we will have time alone."

The men chuckled around them.

"The son of the *ri túath* goes nowhere unprotected." Terrence remained standing a few feet from Brighit, his arms about his chest. He did not glance at Darragh, which was unusual. "Just as *ye* go nowhere unprotected."

Terrence gazed over the well-armed men, who made a show of relaxing around the fire even though none of them had yet touched their drinks.

"Our group is *intended* to be seen as a show of force." Seigine's eyes, twinkled but there was no smile. "Intimidating… but only to our enemies… never to our friends." He raised his full horn to the men around them. "Let us relax and drink with our friends. Tomorrow will be soon enough to worry again."

Darragh raised his drink higher, and the warriors from both sides did the same before emptying their horns. The ale and mead flowed, and the different clansmen relaxed around each other, allowing the repast to end without incident.

Brighit kept to herself—Terrence annoyingly at her side. Darragh had little choice but to entertain his guests rather than fight for the opportunity to engage his own wife. Besides, he was no longer in a fighting mood.

"Have ye thought of any reason for the attack?" he asked Seigine.

"On us? Or on my brother?"

"Are they not the same men?"

Seigine belched and put his food aside. "I believe they intentionally sought him out to kill him."

A gasp drew Darragh's attention, but he couldn't be certain who it had come from. A glance around the fire revealed little. "How so?"

"A particularly vile death. Would ye not agree?"

Darragh nodded. The man's body had been attacked with a fierce blade, intending to do harm. Blood had covered the man's clothing.

"The murderer should be scorched before hanging," Seigine continued. A particularly vile death as well. "I considered who would seek to kill him and I was reminded of the men who came recently to our clan."

"Men?"

"Warriors from Clan Dubhshláine. Their *ri túaithe* is an old man. Good for nothing. He was not among them."

"Yer grandmother's clan? It sounded to me as if Cathair was on good terms with them. Did the men come uninvited?"

Seigine shook his head. "My brother welcomed them, but not everyone in our clan was pleased with the idea of joining. The notion had come about because of an unprovoked attack on our women fall last."

"An attack?"

"When the men were away. The women had no defense against them." He glanced at Brighit. "Not every woman can defend herself against an enemy."

"I did not know of any attack." Darragh's concern was genuine. They were near enough that word should have reached them. He searched his slightly befuddled mind but found no memory of an attack on the women of Clan MacCochlain.

Seigine shrugged, throwing his heavy cloak over his shoulders. He stretched back in a comfortable position and finished his drink before he began his story.

"It took place when many clans were called to a great gathering." Seigine snorted a laugh. "*We* were not invited, so instead our clan traveled west where the hunting was better.

"We traveled with our women and set up a camp to see us through the hunt. Our warriors were gone two days, mayhap three. We had found a great herd that we tracked until we felled our catch. Excited with our blessing, we returned to our camp with much celebration in our hearts.

"In our absence, the camp had been attacked, and our women had been ravaged." He emptied his horn again and held it for Iain to refill it. "A few vicious warriors. Above the law."

"No one is above the law."

Seigine sipped his ale, peering at Darragh over the rim, before speaking again. "Some believe Clan Dubhshláine's offer, first made less than a month after that attack, came at an overly opportune time."

"Ye believe they had something to do with the attack?"

The man shrugged. "My brother did not believe so

and that is all that matters."

"Such treachery is unheard of."

The barking laugh that followed seemed full of condescension.

"My friend," Seigine said, "treachery is everywhere. Let us set aside this serious talk. We need to celebrate," Seigine announced, then raised his horn toward Brighit.

Darragh would swear she had touched not a drop. She appeared to be sulking in the shadows, her guard at her side. So be it. "Certainly, and ye should join our camp tonight."

Seigine nodded his agreement.

With the decision to combine the two camps, Darragh saw no reason not to send Terrence and the rest to help move the other warriors' camp. He wanted the opportunity to see to Brighit himself. Mayhap alone, she would tell him what she had refused to share earlier.

"My hope is that ye will sleep with me this night." Darragh spoke quietly without looking directly at her. Though they stood at arm's length from each other, the gap between them felt far wider than ever.

"Of course. I am yer wife." The lack of hesitation was promising.

"And ye can tell me what ye may not choose to say in front of others." He held his breath, wishing for some sign from her.

When he turned to her, he again saw the innocent lass who'd so enjoyed his kisses. How she must hate her youthful appearance. Darragh moved closer to take her into his arms, her scent arousing him more than he cared to admit. Roses. He cursed himself for his lustful thoughts, but it didn't prevent him from reaching for her.

Her lips were more demanding than he'd expected—they parted with little urging and he accepted the invitation. Or was his besotted mind, now laced with strong ale, playing tricks on him? Struggling to keep his need for her in check, he focused on the signs of her enjoyment—her quickening breath and the way her small hand gripped the tunic where it covered his chest.

Gliding his hands along her curves, he stopped to cup a breast she pressed into his palm. Her nipple tightened. With a start, he remembered her just like this. No fear. No pushing him away. And he was reassured that her disinterest was the lie. She *had* wanted him on their wedding night, just as she wanted him now. His spirits soared and he pulled her close, needing to feel her against him just like this.

He glanced around and realized this was not the best place for such a private moment. The men would return soon.

Reluctantly releasing her, he searched her face. Her dark eyes revealed her own arousal. "I will find a quiet place for us."

She nodded, as if so overwhelmed with her own need she was unable to speak and his pulse quickened.

The heavy air around them crackled with anticipation, the thunder in the distance like a promise of what was to come.

"Darragh!" Terrence called from atop his mount, two other men close behind him. "They've found something that looks like blood."

Darragh shook his head to clear it, then answered brusquely, "Here?"

"They've asked if ye could come to take a look."

Brighit tensed beside him, her face a mask of

terror, and he was reminded that she was still hiding something from him. Despite her brave front, mayhap she was shaken by all this talk of the murdered man.

"I will be back anon." He halted his instinct to kiss her on the lips, instead opting for her cheek. "Will ye be fine alone?"

He smiled at the way she pulled back, looking very near to outraged. Before she could start in on him, he withdrew his own dagger from his side and placed its hilt in her hand. "In case there's any trouble."

Brighit's fierce appearance softened into open adoration and his throat tightened. That was the look he would prefer to see on his wife.

"I will be back. Keep the fire burning." He followed behind the other men, already looking forward to returning to his lover's arms. If given the right persuasion, she would trust him—he felt certain of it.

Chapter Thirteen

Brighit hugged her knees close and stared into the fire. Why was Seigine here? What game was he playing? The air was thick, saturated from the impending rains and clogged with suspicion. The clouds overhead lumbered across the sky to block out the stars. She tightened her grip on the mantle, hoping it would warm a chill that had little to do with the cold.

"Mmm. That was quite a show." Seigine came toward her from the darkness. "My guess is that ye have said nothing about yer dagger being buried in my brother. I am glad ye have waited until we could talk again."

She jumped up, struggling to appear calm. "I did not murder him. I was defending myself."

"Tsk. Tsk. Is that what ye will claim?"

"'Tis the truth and well ye know it."

He shook his head, his lips compressing as if considering a great dilemma. "A wild lad taking on a seasoned warrior twice his size? Who would believe such a tale? Certainly ye snuck up on him." He quirked a brow, and her body tightened with outrage. She would have liked to slap that smug look right off his face.

"Ye will lie outright and say it was a sneak attack?" She guffawed. "No one would believe that of me."

Seigine did not answer. He simply watched her—his stare so long and intense, fear tingled down her spine. "Well?"

"Ye are most desirable when ye are defiant."

That was not the answer she had expected. When he moved closer to her, she instinctively backed away.

"Is this the game ye will play, little one?"

"Ye are a horse's arse." She threw the words at him without thinking through what he might do, but he moved swiftly for such a large man, twisting her arm up behind her, the pain excruciating.

Through tight lips, he asked, "Did ye learn nothing from yer encounter with my brother?"

Brighit tried to maintain the space between their bodies, but he roughly yanked her closer, painfully flattening her breasts against him.

"I am not a man to be taunted." His gaze roamed over her face before landing on her lips. "Kiss me."

"I will not."

With the slightest movement, he bent her arm further up. White-hot pain shot through her upper body while his lips moved ever closer. Demanding. She closed her eyes to block him out. He jerked her forward, crushing her lips to his. Then he released her just as quickly, and the pain was gone. She caught herself before she fell, gingerly testing her shoulder and arm for damage. When he turned away, she wiped the feel of him from her lips.

"Am I not as pleasing to ye as yer new husband?"

"Ye don't please me at all."

"And ye did not seem so very pleasing to yer husband since he did not see to yer... obvious needs." He glanced at her, then laughed as if he saw something in her expression.

Her face heated. She hated to think Seigine had seen her and Darragh together. She'd been so lost in her husband's kisses, and then he'd warmed her heart by giving her his own blade. Her hand reached for it now, but Seigine stopped her. He gripped her hand so tightly her fingers felt as if they were about to be crushed.

"Making the same mistake twice would not be wise." He released her hand and waited until she dropped her hand again.

The huge man threw his brait over his shoulder at the same time that he squatted down in the spot where Darragh had been. "Let us discuss this husband ye want so badly. How will he react when he learns he has married a murderer?"

Her gasp was unbidden, and she clamped her jaw tight, angry with herself for revealing so much weakness to her enemy. She flexed her fingers, the thought of Darragh's dagger giving her confidence. Taking a calming breath, she spoke in a low voice. A quiet voice. "I am not a murderer."

"D'ye not know our laws? Women and children are protected by our laws. The belief is that *they* would never harm another."

She stilled.

His smile widened. "Ah, ye did not realize another would be forced to pay for yer crime."

Not sure if she should trust what he was saying, she held her breath and waited for him to finish this latest taunt.

He glanced out into the darkness, his eyes narrowing as if he were searching for words at the very edge of his memory. "Hmm, 'tis the father of an unmarried woman who pays the price and…" His wide eyes turned to her, impaling her with a smug gaze. Her body went rigid with fear. "…the husband of a married woman."

"Pays the price?"

"Either with money or his life."

Reeling as if she'd been slapped, she shook her head, denying what he was suggesting. Her own guilt or innocence was not even her own to face?

"'Twould be better if no one ever found out."

She struggled not to reveal the hope his comment had sparked in her. Until Seigine had come to the feast, she had been prepared to live her life without anyone ever knowing. She could do no more than nod in agreement.

"If ye give me what I want no one ever need know."

Did he seek to bed her? She shuddered at the idea even as her imagination worked at how terrible it would be for this man to touch her the way Darragh had.

The decision hadn't even fully formed in her mind before she hurled it at him. "No!"

His cruel scowl sent her into a panic.

"No?" His voice was tight with incredulity. "Did

ye tell me... no? Ye will not give me what I want?"

The sound around her was being muffled by the blood rushing through her veins at top speed, her mind struggling for another way to get out of this, but she couldn't back down now. Not if *that* was the price she would have to pay. "I will not."

"So ye wish everyone to know that ye are a murderer?"

"I am not. I defended myself against his assault."

"An assault ye baited him into making. How reprehensible yer behavior was to a warrior. Any lad who thinks he can best a warrior must be taught. My brother gave ye more than a fair chance. Ye killed him because ye could not best him. Ye killed him to save yer own pride, and then ye left his body to be eaten by ravens. Who would not call ye a murderer?"

He was right. Guilt washed over her. She had been a coward. A rumble of thunder sounded in her ears. And if she was found guilty, *she* would not be paying the price.

"What is it ye want?"

Seigine smiled, tipping his head down to look at her like an affectionate puppy at his feet. When he moved to pat her head, she reacted without thinking and swiped his hand away.

"Oh no." He yanked her closer by the front of her gown, her feet only skimming the ground now. "That is not how ye will react, little one."

Petrified of what he might do, Brighit dropped her eyes. "Forgiveness."

Not a twitch of a muscle, not an audible breath. Seigine remained still as a stone. She knew without asking what he wanted. By her words she conceded. By her apology she showed her weakness. And now he wanted her eyes on him again for total submission.

Closing her eyes for an instant to gather her courage, she slowly raised her gaze to meet his dark expression. So fierce, it felt like a blow. His lips turned up at the corners.

"Mayhap I will keep ye close. I enjoy this battle of wills with ye."

Brighit seethed inside, but she kept herself from tightening her jaw, instead keeping her eyes rounded in supplication. Was it truly only an act?

"Ye will do as I say, and I will keep Cathair's murderer a secret."

She glanced at the bulge in his trews. She would die before she allowed him to touch her, but he noticed her glance and laughed again. "I am referring to something else ye can do for me."

Her relief did not last long. He would demand a high price.

"Ye need only convince yer husband and yer father to side with my clan over the Dubhshláine."

With her mind frantically searching through what he'd told Darragh, she forgot to be afraid. Instead, she blurted out the words, "*Ye* were the one who didn't want to join with them."

"Very good. I will always have ye this attentive to my desires."

She cringed at the word, but he was clearly pleased. So much so that he lowered her so her feet touched the ground then smoothed out the material he'd gripped near her breast as if testing her willingness to have him touch her. Her mind reeled, and she struggled not to react even while her gut churned in revulsion.

"But I have given it much thought." He dropped

his gaze to her bosom, his breath quickened. "If they wish to join with our clan, so be it, but I have as much right to become overking as their ri túath."

Seigine had described the Dubhshláine's *ri* as an old man, which meant he was no longer able to lead his warriors into battle.

"With the support ye provide for me, little one, I will become overking, an equal to both yer father and yer husband's father."

A show of prowess in battle was the normal way to become overking. The entire clan relied on the *ri* for protection, so they were usually asked for their blessing. This man was hoping to obtain kingship by overstepping the process—and he was looking for her to help him.

"D'ye not have the ability to gain the kingship on yer own?"

Though her tone was merely questioning, his face shifted into a look of rage and his eyes darkened. The fear blasted out of her stomach right up into her chest.

"A pampered princess who believes she can fight as a man cannot be expected to grasp the finer points involved in gaining support from other kings." His tone was surprisingly calm compared to his scowl. "It matters not if ye understand, only that ye obey."

He tipped his head, questioning if she agreed or not. When he raised his brow, his irritation was irrefutable. Her stomach tightened, but she forced the question out.

"How do I make this happen?"

Seigine watched his fingertip as it slid along her jaw. "Cleave unto yer husband for now. Speak to him of how dangerous the divide is among the clans." His eyes piercing her made her jaw tighten. "Mention how impressed ye are with me."

His gaze dropped momentarily to her throat when she swallowed.

"And what a wonderful king I will make as yer neighbor."

"He'll never believe I've put that much thought into ye."

He seized her chin in a death grip. "Convince him."

His hold made it impossible for her to respond but, just as suddenly, he released her.

"Ye have the choice on how things will go for ye."

The sound of the men returning, laughing and talking, put an end to his intimidation. She stepped away, moving into clear view of those now approaching. Her nose in the air and her breath heaving.

"Careful, little one." Seigine's quiet words sliced through her pride, his eyebrows raised in question. He was amused by her discomfiture.

Brighit would be his puppet and well he knew it.

Chapter Fourteen

The next few days passed in a haze, Brighit's mind fixed on Seigine's threats. The sight of Seigine riding side by side with her husband made her sick with nerves, which was no doubt his purpose. He hadn't approached her again, but his presence alone set her on edge. She had begun to give up hope that he would ever leave when he and his men finally parted ways with the group, claiming they may have lost the trail of the murderer.

There'd been no opportunity to broach the subject with Darragh, which was just as well—she was stuck in an endless circle of thoughts with no answers. Each day left her feeling exhausting and hopeless. Despite Darragh's sweet attempts to find some quiet time with her at night away from the others, she could barely find the strength to converse, and each night ended the same; with him turning his back to her and falling asleep.

"Ye're deep in thought."

Brighit jumped at Darragh's voice. She was so wrapped up in thought she'd forgotten he'd decided to join her in the carriage this day, professing she must be lonely. Despite her adamant objections to the contrary, here he was.

"I did not mean to startle ye." His slight smile seemed genuine.

She forced a smile in return. "Ye did not."

Darragh nodded. He didn't believe her. "Very well then. And what were ye so deep in thought about?"

"The strangeness of life." Brighit regretted the words when he frowned. She was learning her husband was a deep thinker. Even with his men. He would ask questions and listen to their answers. If he questioned her further now, what could she say to avoid having to explain herself?

But he glanced away, his thick brows coming together. "It is that."

The answer shouldn't have surprised her, but it did—like when he'd mentioned he may never be king. "Did ye not tell me that kingship may not be yer destiny?"

He shrugged and turned back to her. "I thought ye should realize ye may never be the wife of a king. Would that displease ye?"

"It would not. Though ye men enjoy commenting on my father's closeness to my mother, his kingship has cost them much. They have spent far too much time separated."

"Apparently he has always been quite good at his sweet talk."

"And what of yer father? He believes ye will be *ri*."

He sighed, a loud sound in the small space. "My father has always had high hopes for himself and now he passes that on to me."

"D'ye believe what Seigine said about his grandmother's clan?"

She didn't miss the flash of surprise that crossed his face before he answered. "Cathair was always the calmer of the two brothers."

Brighit cringed at the memory of that man's fists. If *he* had been the calmer one, they were all doomed.

"Though both lean toward violence. I am not convinced my father would care whether the two clans were joined or not."

"It sounds as if the Dubhshláine are trying to coerce them into joining." The words felt insincere coming from her own lips, but she forced them. Their lives might depend on it.

His lips tipped up on one side. "Coerce? Is this how ye understood what he told us?"

She squeezed her jaw shut. He saw through her feigned interest. "It sounded as if they may have had a hand in the attack on the women," she pressed.

"To what purpose?"

Brighit cringed at how quickly he saw through her attempt to make them appear the victim. Something warned her to choose her words carefully. "If the MacCochlain has the better land and the river, is it unheard of for another clan to wish to subdue them?"

"Subdue? Possibly, but I believe Cathair had worked out a peaceful plan." His eyes remained steady on her. "Why the interest?"

Brighit's fumbled lies had roused his suspicions, but she had no recourse other than to continue lying. "My father has always encouraged my interests. He taught me battle strategy, but he also taught me about negotiations. I was only trying to help. Clans getting along well is of the utmost importance."

The air stilled in her lungs. She had spoken the truth about her father and avoided the truth about her line of questioning.

"Tell me how it feels to be able to do whatever ye want to do." His voice sounded almost wistful.

"I… I do not…" With a start, Brighit realized she *had* lived most of her life just as she pleased. Whenever she asked her father about battle, he taught her what she needed to know. Whenever she asked him about clan politics, he shared his experience. Because as a woman there was no need for her to know these things, it wasn't surprising that Darragh believed she always got to do whatever she wanted. "There are things I must do that I would prefer not to."

"*Prefer* not to?" He nodded, an odd expression on his face. "Such as?"

"Working beside the other women, listening to their endless complaints about this or that—"

"Wedding me?"

He had the same stoic expression on his face that he oft wore while standing at his father's side. "I would not say so."

"No?"

He measured her words as if trying to figure her out. She knew what he was thinking. His every attempt to rekindle her passion had only increased her trepidation. "I wish ye to be happy. I do not appear to

156

do that."

"Ye have been very... patient and I appreciate that."

"And yet ye share things with others that ye do not choose to share with me."

When she opened her mouth to defend herself, he raised his hand and said, "I know. There was nothing."

He sighed, a sad sound, but his expression softened. "Would ye prefer to ride?"

An eager light shining in his eyes at the suggestion was not well hidden. Did he truly prefer for her to ride with them? With him? And not be tucked away and out of sight?

Brighit ignored her own desire to gallop through the clean air, free and unencumbered. What she preferred mattered very little in the big scheme of things. Having murdered a man in cold blood and then returned home in time to attend her nuptials in the morning, she was having a hard time figuring out who she *was*—never mind what she wanted. The things she'd once cared greatly about struck her as unimportant now. And now she would do whatever she needed to do to keep her sin a secret. How far she had fallen from the warrior her father taught her to be...

"I'm fine in here."

Mayhap it was the clipped way she spoke, or the way she'd turned from him, but the rest of the morning was spent in silence.

Darragh would admit to being greatly perplexed

by this behavior from Brighit. She was not an overly talkative woman, not like some he had met, and that pleased him. But she was usually willing to have a discourse. A lively one. Not anymore. No matter how many times he tried to engage her, she shut him down. And he couldn't figure out why.

It eased his angst some when he noticed her doing the same with the other men in the party. They were his own men, previously unknown to her, but they attempted to be cordial to her. All of their overtures had been met with single word answers, and they'd learned to keep their distance. Terrence stayed nearer to her than the rest, but Darragh never witnessed her speaking with him either. Could Darragh have misunderstood what he'd witnessed? No, Terrence had told him he was missing something so why did the man keep refusing to tell him what he knew?

She'd always seemed so sure of herself, so eager for an adventure—and certainly traveling south would be considered as such. He'd hoped some time on the road would excite her. Instead, she remained aloof and uncommunicative.

With his days filled with preparations for his upcoming meetings, they passed by quickly. While his nights seemed to grown even longer.

This night, as with every other night, he set them up near the fire. He again tried to share with her the mead intended for them as a newly married couple while the rest of his men made themselves scarce. She remained aloof, her disdain clearly directed at him, and it was killing him.

"There's a skin for every night, Brighit. Ye're leaving me to drink our mead alone and even after ye'd expressed yer desire to keep to the tradition. It does not bode well for us or our children."

Brighit barely nodded, so deep in thought with her eyes on the firelight. It was the first clear night they'd had on the road and the warmth was definitely appreciated. The impending rains had shifted north.

"Can ye not even rouse yerself enough to speak with me?" Anger was nipping at him.

She shrugged, her knees tucked up close to her body. "I have nothing to say."

Darragh watched her as she stared at the sparks flying heavenward. He wanted her the way she used to be, always ready to argue with him. Feisty. The firelight cast her in a soft, seductive glow. He sought to woo her. The more he partook of the mead, the more he wanted her. He held her small hand ever so lightly, testing her boundaries, then wrapped an arm around her shoulders. When she didn't pull away, he caressed the silky locks that fell down her back, holding them close to smell her scent.

"Mmm, lovely." He opened his eyes to find her looking at him.

"What?"

He smiled, tracing a finger along her jaw. Such soft skin. "Ye look lovely sitting there."

"I do not feel lovely." Brighit turned back to the fire.

Sitting close, he kept his voice low. "And that may indeed be our problem."

"Our problem?"

Though her response may have put him off at another time, Darragh did not feel compelled to back off right now. He had done his best to get her to share with him whatever Terrence refused to disclose, but if she continued to say there was nothing then this needed to stop. They needed to move beyond it. Whatever their situation, he believed they could work things out if she but tried. He'd seen her spark of passion, and he'd felt her surrender to it. He wanted that again.

"A husband can usually expect to bed his wife more than once."

"Oh." She faced the fire again, shaking her head as if that was of little importance.

A fist to his gut. He exhaled slowly, his patience at an end. "Or did ye believe ye needed only submit to me once?"

Brighit's eyes flashed at him. "Submit?" Ah, the tone he recognized so well. *This* was the Brighit he'd longed to see these last days.

"That is indeed the word I used. If ye'll not come willingly to my bed, there are other ways to have ye."

"Other ways? To have me? And what is it ye're thinking exactly?"

That gently flaring nose. Excitement raced to his groin and he stuck with the same belligerent tone. "I will wait no longer."

"Wait? For what?"

"I want ye. Yer my wife and I'll have ye. I will no longer be put off."

"Put off? Who has put ye off?"

"*Ye* have. Now take off yer gown. Or I will be happy to take it off for ye."

"Ye'll do no such thing."

"Do not tempt me." Though his words were merely a ploy intended to kindle some spark in her—and it was working beautifully—his body didn't seem to understand the difference. His need was painful.

"Ach, why would ye hold yerself back from me,

lass?" He searched her lovely face, her eyes closing slightly as he stroked her. Leaning into her because he hadn't the strength to watch her obvious desire for him when he was so damn in need of her, he said, "If ye want me, why aren't ye with me? Why d'ye keep me away, *mo mhíle stór*?" His voice was hoarse and low, feverish with desire.

He rubbed against her with his thumb, and she moaned. "I cannot. I... cannot."

"We are wed. We may enjoy each other. Let me have ye?"

He dipped his head down, kissing her alluring neck. His fingers moved with a steady rhythm, while he thought of the pleasure he'd have were it another part of him inside her.

"What are ye—" She sounded torn between decency and desire.

"Hush." He took her mouth, pulling her closer with a hand at the back of her head. "Mmm, just as I remember."

As always, she was lost in his kisses, giving of herself with abandon. When she flattened her chest against him, he knew they must either stop immediately or finish this. More than anything, he wanted her willingness.

"Let me love ye." He nibbled her ear, urging her back onto the *brait* he'd spread out under them. "I'm in desperate need of ye."

Her groans set him on fire and he pushed her shoulders back until she lay before him. One-handed, he loosened the ties at her bosom, using his teeth when necessary, and paused to suckle each gorgeous pink nipple before loosening it further, leaving behind a trail of kisses.

Dropping a kiss to her belly, he sucked on her there as well, while his hands worked at pulling up her skirt. He kissed a bare hip, keeping his eyes on her, and worked his way lower. He knew the exact moment she opened her eyes.

"What are ye about?"

"This is having my sweet." He ran the tip of his tongue along her wetness. "And ye are very sweet."

Her breathing remained stilted, as if trying to reason out the sensation with the act. Clearly she enjoyed his attention, and he certainly enjoyed giving her this attention. Relief filled him when her eyes drifted closed in pleasure.

Thinking nothing of his own need, he responded to every moan, learning the places that pleased her most by the tightening of her hands in his hair. And the lovely sound of the groans from deep inside her throat. He pleasured her until she quaked, receiving her release.

"Nothing but pleasing ye, sweet wife. That is what I would give to ye."

A guttural sound of agreement and she pulled his face up to hers, their lips locked for a tighter exploration. He settled atop her, and she immediately stiffened beneath him. The suddenness of the change surprised him, but when her hands ceased their caressing and the cadence of her breathing shifted, he knew to stop.

Her noises of pleasure were sounding different. She was suddenly afraid of him, though he didn't understand why. Before he could fully pull away, she shoved against his chest with the flat of her hand.

"What is amiss?" His brain was foggy, but he knew her fear. He tried to move to alleviate her panic.

"No!"

Darragh yanked himself to stand before her. "Tell me, Brighit. What is it ye fear?"

Brighit wagged her head from side to side, covering her face.

"How have I hurt ye?" He was torn between compassion for her fear and irritation that she still wouldn't tell him what caused it. "How am I to avoid what I do not know I have done?"

"'Tis not ye." Her words came out between her sobs.

"*I* am the only one with ye." His mind worked frantically, grabbing at every passing thought to reach her. "Ye were untouched, Brighit. How is it that ye are so fearful, ye must push me away?" Beside himself, he squeezed his scalp with his fingertips. "I have pleasured ye in every way I know how. If ye find me lacking still, I can offer ye nothing more."

Darragh stalked off, away from the small encampment, certain he'd spoken so loudly in his frustration that each of his men knew the breadth of their estrangement.

His hopes dashed, he pledged to stop seeking her out. This was indeed a miserable existence for the both of them.

Chapter Fifteen

The heavens unleashed rain in the middle of the night. Their travels were slowed by the heavy, unrelenting downpour, which washed out the trails the carriage needed to travel. The mood of the group quickly plummeted. Heavy clouds pressed against them and blocked out the sun, and nights were spent huddled under leather *braits* that didn't provide much warmth and never allowed their clothing to dry completely.

"A roundhouse ahead." Terrence came back into the group of riders that halted and encircled him. He'd been sent up ahead in the hopes of finding some place dry they could rest. "'Tis a small house but no doubt hospitable."

The men's eyes lit up, their expressions relaxing

for the first time in days. Darragh looked forward to the respite as well. He'd been avoiding Brighit again, but they needed to come to an understanding. They were bound together and could not continue this way forever.

"Will ye go ahead and see if they'll open their doors to us?" one of the men asked, speaking loud enough to be heard over the rain pouring down around them as they stood huddled under a tree.

"I will go ahead with my bride." Darragh glanced toward the carriage that had stopped half a wheel deep in the mud. "But 'twould probably be easier to travel by horse."

"A cumbersome vehicle to be certain, but no doubt it gives her some comfort," Terrence said.

Darragh bristled at the protective way he spoke of her, as if *he* were the husband, but he also knew she showed him no preference despite the way he spoke of her.

Terrence nodded. "And if they've no room for the likes of us to stay, they will certainly make room for ye and Brighit. Rest assured a warm meal would be welcome enough to us." The others added their agreement.

Darragh appreciated the suggestion that he and his wife could use some distance from the others, but Terrence's attitude toward Brighit still baffled him. There seemed to be nothing untoward between them, and yet...

Did his friend believe Brighit needed an ally? Against *him*?

"I will see to it." Darragh opened the carriage door to find Brighit leaned against the far side, a heavy wool wrapped tightly around her. "Did ye hear the news?"

Brighit's eyes seemed unusually bright, and her teeth were chattering as well. Immediately concerned, he pushed his way inside to kneel before her, warily raising a palm to her forehead. "Ye're burning up with fever."

He was struck by the fact that she was sick and hadn't felt it necessary to tell him. How little did she think of him? He'd been more than attentive and still she held herself at a distance. Even now, she shook her head to deny the truth while her eyes drooped closed again.

"Ye most certainly are." Over his shoulder, Darragh shouted the men into action. "Water! Start a fire as best ye can and see to some warm broth."

Terrence moved in close to look at the two of them within the wood-sided conveyance. "What is amiss?"

"She has a fever."

"Some of the men were not well this morning. Was it something they ate that's sickened them?"

"I'm not sick." The weakness of her protest belied her statement.

"If not, then why are ye soaked through in your own sweat?" He pulled off the blanket and then immediately opened her cloak, blocking the other man's view of the curves nicely displayed through the dampened material. "Terrence, can ye fetch a cloth for cooling her? And ask the men to set up a shelter for her. She'll not be able to travel to the roundhouse like this."

"Cool? When she's taken a fever?"

Darragh realized that wasn't the normal procedure, but it was the only thing that made any sense to him. Why keep her bundled when she was so hot her skin was reddened? "Please do as I ask."

A short time later, an older man came to the door with a mug of a hot brew. "A few herbs to cool her fever." Duncan was the oldest warrior among them and, as such, much respected.

"My thanks." Darragh held the clay vessel to her lips. She had trouble swallowing so he adjusted it until it was easier for her. "Healing herbs?"

"'Tis what my own mother would give her. The others that were sick are fine now." Duncan remained in the entrance, his large gray mustache drooping over his turned down lips, watching them.

Darragh felt the tension working into his shoulders. "Is there something ye wish to say?"

"I wonder how long she's been with fever." The simple question was full of accusations. Darragh may be in command, but without question, it was Duncan whose advice he sought out most often.

Darragh brushed the dampened hair from her face and pulled at the ties to slip the mantle from her shoulders. "As do I."

"A new husband should know these things."

Darragh held his retort, the man was right and he had little defense. "She seeks neither my company nor my bed."

"Nor d'ye seek hers."

The man had an answer for everything. Darragh's ire rose, but wisdom oft came with age. If Duncan had something to say, he'd be a fool not to listen. "I'd hoped to give her some peace."

"Peace?" The older man spat the word out like a fish bone. "She needs coddling, not isolation."

"I do not need protection." Brighit mumbled even as her head lolled back, coming to a rest on Darragh's shoulder.

Duncan and Darragh exchanged glances. "I know ye have yer work cut out for ye but seeing to the men to avoid seeing to yer own bride on yer honeyed moon is not the way to go about being a happily married man."

Darragh wanted to ask how a man never married would know such things but knew better.

"Ye've left her to herself almost every night." And the man was relentless.

"She prefers it that way."

Duncan's thick brow lowered. "And how d'ye know that is so?"

Done with the niceties, Darragh turned to face the man, though he was careful not to jostle Brighit awake. "Because when I did my husbandly duties, she felt it necessary to knee me in the groin for my effort. Message received, thank ye."

Duncan's dark brown eyes widened, and then he nearly fell to the ground laughing.

Darragh only scowled. "Ye can stop acting like an arse."

Duncan appeared unable to stop, laughing so hard he was grabbing his sides and bending over. Terrence appeared with the cloth and cool water.

"What are ye about?" he asked of Duncan, but his eyes remained on Darragh as he lightly rubbed the cloth over Brighit's face.

"She kneed our young man." Duncan spat out between bouts of laughter. "Right in the balls!"

Darragh rolled his eyes. It had been a poor lapse in judgment to tell *this* man what had happened. He'd hoped for some bit of advice, understanding in the very least.

Terrence's frown darkened. "Why would she do

that? What did ye do to her?"

Duncan shrugged, getting himself under control, but Darragh was surprised by the question. There it was again—Terrence's strange protectiveness toward his wife, which neither of them would explain.

"I did nothing a husband is not expected to do." Darragh's explanation left little room for comment. He ignored them both, turning his attention instead to Bright, who appeared to be rousing.

"I'm sorry. I am very hot. I didn't mean to bother ye," she said.

"What ye are is sick. This damn rain is making us all sick."

"'Tis nothing. I'll be fine."

Her head rolled to the side and all three men jumped forward to catch her before she fell.

"We'd best get her some place dry," Terrence said, and Darragh bit back a retort.

Clasping her small body in his arms, Darragh did his best to protect her from the unrelenting rain as he followed the other men, who had finished setting up a small lean-to for her. The fire within cast a gentle glow and the men had made a heap of whatever dry material they could find and covered it with a heavy fur for a makeshift pallet.

Darragh removed her soaked mantle before gently laying her down. Duncan retreated with the others while Terrence handed him a freshly cooled cloth.

"She's pale, Darragh." He spoke loudly to be heard above the rain.

"I can see that." Darragh struggled to keep the irritation out of his voice. Her dark eyelashes against her cheeks made her look even more vulnerable. He felt his own failure miserably. It was his job to look out for her.

"Terrence? Check the accommodations at the roundhouse. I need to get her some place dry come morning."

His friend left without a question, closing the flap to their makeshift alcove, leaving them alone together. Brighit's clothing was damp and he worked at the ties, loosening her outer gown until he could work it off her. She lay there in her chemise, vulnerable and pale.

Supporting her head, Darragh held the cup to her mouth until she had finished the warm drink. When he dipped the cloth into the water and rubbed it along her neck and chest, Brighit still didn't stir.

He refreshed the cloth, "Ye have my sympathy."

"No. No sympathy."

Darragh snorted, working the cloth beneath the neckline to cool her breast. "I did not say ye deserved my sympathy, only that ye have it."

"I do not want it."

His hand stopped midway to the bowl of water. Her words cut him to the quick, but it struck him with sudden clarity why she didn't want him caring for her. Even in her weakened state, she would behave as if she disliked him? How she'd hate him caring for her. With sudden clarity he realized it was a lie. She needed him, but she didn't *want* to need him. It was her damn pride.

He thought back over these past two years, how easy it had always been to bait her. How her eyes would flash with resentment when he selected the best meat for her, offering it to her on his own dagger. How very irritating she was to *him*… and how much he wanted her.

Alone in their cocoon, the driving rain overpowering

all other sounds, Darragh stopped listening for Terrence's return and adjusted himself so that he held her securely in his arms, her head resting on his shoulder, before drifting off himself. His dreams were of their first time. The sound of her sighs. Her fingertips pressing into his back, urging him on in her passion. The overwhelming sense that he was where he belonged.

He awoke with a start, his breathing labored. The sun had gone down and the fire was nearly out, leaving even their small space chilled. Brighit rested peacefully beside him, her skin now cool to his touch. Whatever had made the others ill had left her as well.

As quietly as he could, he eased himself away from her to feed the small fire and then doffed his *brait* to use as a blanket to cover them. She appeared very peaceful. And desirable.

"Brighit?"

"Hmm?"

Her eyes still closed, he lowered his mouth to hers. Her lips pressed against his with a surprising urgency.

"Are ye awake?" he whispered the words against her parted lips, but she moved closer, deepening the kiss when he would have withdrawn.

"How are ye feeling?"

Her responding moan cut right to his own desire. She reached an arm around his shoulders, holding him closer. "Ah, much better now."

He didn't dare move, but she found his hand and placed it against her breast before she started kissing him again. Her breath quickened and Darragh had to resist the overpowering yearning to explore her body more fully, to satisfy the fire she was igniting in him.

"Yer fever may be gone, but ye should probably rest," he forced himself to say.

When he withdrew from her, she yanked him back. "Do not leave me. I am cold alone."

She held his upper body tight and nuzzled against his ear, sending a rush of blood to his cock. Her nipples teased him, pressing into him through the thin material of her chemise.

When he started to pull away, she whimpered in protest.

"Ye need to rest."

She shook her head. "I need ye."

The words hung between them. She was acknowledging she needed him—he could not deny her.

Dragging an open palm along her lush curves, he cupped her firm bottom to shift her closer. The passion rushing through him required release, and he kissed her with abandon. His hands slipped beneath her chemise to cup her bare bottom.

"Ye've a fine arse."

In response, she leaned up and over him, giving him better access to her curves.

Darragh groaned, her weight heavy on him and her thigh rubbing his manhood. This could definitely be his undoing.

"I'm not… I don't know…" Why was he still fighting something he wanted more than his next breath? He groaned right before he pulled her the rest of the way on top of him. Her light weight was a blessing against his heated stiffness.

"I would like to take ye again."

"Aye." Her eyes were open now, a smile on her face as she looked down on him. She stretched to kiss him again, grinding her hips into him at the same time.

Her answer surprised him, but his hand was

already slipping betwixt her thighs and he was beyond talking. He tucked his head into the curve of her neck. That alluring curve he'd been in too much of a hurry to truly appreciate their first time. Was that the problem? Had he moved too quickly? He slipped his finger along her wetness as he nipped at the sensitive flesh beneath her ear. No, she had been just this ready. He had not taken her unprepared.

Brighit's strangled groan, barely heard above the winds overhead in the trees, urged him on, but then her hands were pushing against him, trying to break his hold.

"Someone's coming," she whispered.

As if waking from a deep sleep, Darragh struggled to get his bearings and make sense of the sounds around him. The rustling of disturbed leaves.

"Darragh?" Terrence's quiet call cut through his lust. Darragh cursed, hitting his head in his haste to move away from his wife, and cover her with his mantle.

"Will they accommodate us?" He was happy his voice didn't betray his frustration, but he rolled his eyes at Brighit. She giggled, pulling her chemise down and over her hips before scooting deeper beneath the covering.

Terrence's face appeared in the doorway. "How is she?"

Brighit's eyes widened more. "Better. I am... better."

"Well?" Darragh sounded about as irritated as he felt.

His friend hesitated only a moment. "They are expecting ye. They've pulled the carriage from the mud and laid down some branches to ease it over the

173

worst of the trail."

"Good. We will be out anon."

Terrence flashed a smile and was gone.

Darragh roughed up his hair. "Not the best timing, that one."

"Wait." She pulled on his arm when he would have left her. "Thank ye for caring for me."

He nodded and helped her pull on her nearly dry gown. When he cradled her in his arms to carry her out, he was humbled by the rightness of her being in his arms. A sense of pride filled him—his wife had a fierce passion, and now that they were getting beyond whatever issues had stood between them, he felt certain their relationship would only grow stronger.

Darragh carried her to the carriage and settled her inside. "I'd prefer to ride with ye, but ye'll stay drier in here."

"My thanks."

He gave a dubious look to the men around him, and said, "Are ye certain the carriage will get there?"

After the way things were moving along in the lean to, Darragh was in no hurry to be separated from her. Especially not if they were doomed to get stuck in the mud.

Duncan laughed. "I've checked the trail myself. We've seen to the worst ruts. Ye'll be fine." He moved in closer, glancing around to be sure he was not overheard. "One thing about that tea. It makes 'em very… needy, if ye know what I mean. Best to keep her with ye."

Darragh sent him a withering glance. "I would prefer not to have known that."

The older man nodded in understanding then shrugged. "A tea can only do so much, Darragh. If she

174

didn't desire ye at all, no herbs would make her direct her affection toward ye."

Darragh glanced toward the wooden conveyance, considering a stop along the way. Not the most comfortable spot for him to take her. The men circled around him with expectant expressions, and he knew his needs would have to wait.

"Take yer time, lad." Duncan moved in closer. "If ye handle this right, she'll not know when the herbs wear off and when yer own prowess takes over."

Nodding his head, a smirk on his face, Darragh asked, "Did ye do this apurpose?"

"The lass had a fever. I'd never put her in harm's way." Duncan crossed his arms about his chest and planted his legs into a warrior stance. "I help where I'm able."

Darragh hopped up onto the seat, quirking a brow at him. "Do not feel ye need to hurry."

Chapter Sixteen

The roundhouse had definitely seen better days. The walls had gaps where the weather had worn away at the structure, but it was clean and there was no sign of damage to the two small sleeping areas toward the back. Fitted with straw pallets and draped with material for privacy, the space looked much more inviting than the makeshift lean-to they had fashioned. The elderly couple that lived there seemed genuinely pleased to have guests, claiming they seldom had anyone pass by.

"My wife is excited to be cooking for yer men as well." The gray-haired man stood tall. Mayhap nearing sixty, but the years seemed to have been kind to him.

"Ye're far from anything here."

"We've been seeing to the sheep our whole lives," he wrapped an arm around the woman who came to stand beside him. She was a small woman, with long gray hair and hazel eyes that twinkled with humor. "Gwen and I do fine."

"We appreciate yer welcoming us all in like this," Brighit said, her eyes slightly glazed.

"Ehh?" The man named William scrunched up his face.

Gwen's eyes widened, and a small smile touched her lips. "My husband is in good health except for his hearing." She turned to him. "But he does well if he can see lips."

William nodded, tucking her closer to him.

"Please, sit." The small woman gestured with her hands then went about setting the table with a clay pitcher of ale and mugs.

The three of them settled at the large trestle table, scarred with age—no doubt from playing host to many such meals over the year. Gwen turned from the fire, a heavy cloth wrapped round the handle of the battered iron pot. "Hope ye enjoy soup, 'tis hardy and filling."

Darragh nodded. "The others should be here anon."

"Ach, she's made plenty. Had several nephews on both sides we helped to raise and she still cooks as if they're with us."

"Where are they?" Brighit faced William when she asked the question, then reached over and broke off a piece of the hardy brown bread in the center of the table as she awaited his answer.

"Not far but far enough." William winked at her. "How about ye? Any bairns?"

Darragh cleared his throat, trying to ignore the

telling glance exchanged by the couple. "Not yet. We've only just wed."

Her sigh of relief was audible, at least to him, but Gwen was settling beside her husband. "Soon enough."

She stretched out the word 'soon' and Darragh kept the grin from his face. Was his need for his wife that obvious? He let the smile escape as he accepted the bread, which Brighit had slathered with thick cream.

She prepared a slice for herself and closed her eyes in pleasure as soon as she bit into it. "This bread is wonderfully sweet."

"It has honey in it." Gwen answered, pleased with the compliment.

"What a wonderful idea." Brighit's eyes widened. "I have never heard of that before."

Gwen's cheeks blushed in embarrassment. "I can show ye how I make it if ye like."

Darragh could only describe the expression on Brighit's face when she turned to him as exhilarated. "Could I? May we stay long enough for her to teach me?"

He couldn't be certain it wasn't the herbs from the tea causing this reaction, but her sheer pleasure at the idea of learning something to do with cooking was nothing short of a miracle. "If that would please ye."

"I *would* like that." Her bashful smile of appreciation was accompanied by another small gesture—her hand finding his and then resting them together on her lap. "Thank ye."

"I have many hives that we keep. Helps make for a sweet life, eh, Gwen?"

The older woman smiled but kept her attention on Brighit. "How are ye with oats? They've a fine taste with the honey as well."

Again Brighit responded enthusiastically. Darragh sipped at his ale, watching his wife have an animated conversation for the first time in days—and about cooking no less. He was totally perplexed. Were the copious amounts of ale, mixed with the strange herbal concoction, loosening her tongue? Her fever and any sickness from it were long gone.

Duncan had assured him the herbs only heightened things she would already have a liking for and yet her repeated disdain for women's work seemed to disavow that idea. Gwen's ready smile and quick wit seemed to make Brighit at ease enough to ask many questions.

"Ye are a great one with questions." Gwen ladled out more hot soup for Darragh before he could stop her. "Are ye interested in learning more?"

"Oh I am." She nodded eagerly, turning to Darragh. "Gwen would be a wonderful teacher."

Gwen dropped her gaze, clearly embarrassed by the compliment. "I'd be happy to show ye the things I've learned over the years."

When Brighit covered the woman's hand with her own, Darragh had the odd sensation he was witnessing a side of Brighit she preferred to keep hidden, though he didn't understand why that would be.

"I would be happy to learn from *ye* all ye can teach me," Brighit said, her voice pitched low purposefully, so as to convey how genuine she was in her appreciation.

Darragh squeezed her other hand that sat in her lap where their hands were still joined. "Then if ye're willing to keep us for a few days, that's what we shall do."

Brighit's eyes sparkled when she glanced at all of them. He felt a strong sense of accomplishment that he was able to give her this simple pleasure. Terrence and the others arrived without incident, but it was Iain he told about the change in plans. He had no patience for Terrence's evasions. Darragh and Brighit would meet up with them at week's end at Terrence's former clan. The men were settled in the empty stable for the night and would leave at daybreak to continue their mission.

Brighit wrinkled her nose. "Are there leeks in this?"

"Aye. Ye can put in soup anything ye have stored," Gwen said.

"They are difficult to clean."

"Ah, it does take patience."

Brighit nodded thoughtfully. "Soup does not seem difficult to make."

"Not at all. We can make more on the morrow."

Brighit caressed Darragh's hand where it rested on her thigh while continuing to speak to Gwen. "This is very tasty and ye say there's no meat in it?"

Darragh grasped his wife's leg, noticing she didn't look at him and she didn't miss a word. When he repeated the gesture, she again caressed his hand—but in encouragement or discouragement he couldn't be certain.

When he gripped her thigh more firmly, her eyes widened the slightest bit, but her words remained conversational. William coughed across the table from Darragh. When he looked toward him, the man's attention was on his soup.

Again, he gripped her leg and she shifted it slightly closer. Encouragement? He believed so, imagining the slight parting of her thighs beneath her lovely green gown.

"We are not always able to get out and hunt. Isn't

that right, William?" Gwen spoke louder whenever she included her husband in the conversation. He nodded in agreement, his lips puckering as if the answers required deep thought.

Working his fingers closer to the imagined cleft between Brighit's legs, Darragh squeezed her thigh again. Her hip moved beside him and she sat up straighter.

"And ye have no help here?" Brighit didn't miss a word. "How d'ye keep it all up with just the two of ye?"

Darragh marveled at her composure—*he* could think of nothing but getting between those legs. He noticed William's questioning expression with a start and realized he'd missed something.

"Say again?"

William smiled, his eyes creasing with the gesture. "I think 'tis best we get some sleep, Mama."

He stood and his wife did the same, though she wasn't successful at hiding her surprise. William may be hard of hearing, but Darragh had the impression he knew exactly what was happening beneath the table.

"I'll see to these things in the morning." Gwen offered apologetically before disappearing within the sleeping area to the right.

"Ye two stay up as long as ye like," William said, looking back at them. "Ye'll not bother us. We sleep like the dead."

Darragh would swear the man winked. He turned to hide his smirk, but when he turned back, he was met by Brighit's urgent kiss. With a hand on either side of his face, she pulled his lips to hers, shifting restlessly on the bench beside him. Her raspy breathing told him she shared his need. She was

181

simply better at hiding it.

He pulled her onto his lap without breaking the kiss and slid the material of her gown high.

"Well, aren't ye the sly little fox?" Darragh whispered. "Asking all those questions while ye had only this on yer mind."

He rubbed against her without hindrance since she wore nothing beneath. She moaned into his mouth, rocking her hips in rhythm with the insistent movement of his fingers stroking her.

Breaking the kiss, she seemed to purr in his ear. "I have wanted ye something fierce."

His arousal came on him so fast, it was almost painful. Even though he'd prefer to take her without people a few feet away, his cock had no such qualms. "And I would like to give ye what ye want."

Sliding her gown to her waist, he guided her legs to either side of him so that she was straddling him. He closed his eyes in ecstasy when he pushed his solid bulge along her most intimate area.

"How is this?"

"More."

Her voice was so husky, he had to see her expression. Darragh stilled. Her eyes were closed, a slight frown knit between her brows as if her complete attention was devoted to rocking her hips against him. Like a slap to the face, he realized it *had* to be the tea making her act this way. Disappointment overwhelmed him. He wanted her willingly, not like this.

"Brighit?"

It took her a moment to focus on him when she opened her eyes. "Nice."

Well, that was a yank on his prick, but he needed to protect her from herself. "The tincture ye had in the tea? D'ye remember?"

She nodded, rubbing her breasts against him until he cupped one solid globe in his firm grip, thumbing the nipple into a firm peak even through the course material. "It may be causing ye to feel this way."

"I always feel this way with ye."

Those words knocked the breath right out of him. He searched her expression, feeling an odd sense that she was speaking the truth to him. Mayhap he should stop and wait until the herbs were out of her system, but his need for her was only growing stronger. God knew she was doing nothing to help him quench his desire.

"I want my husband," she whispered huskily. Her need was killing him, and he didn't doubt that she wanted fulfillment, but it seemed he was taking advantage of her. "Now," she urged.

Suddenly desperate, he slid his hands beneath her dress, trailing them up her flat stomach to grip a firm breast, his nose slipping along her neck before nipping it. Shifting closer without the slightest impediment to his pleasant grasping of the underside of her breast, she moved nose to nose so her face was a blur, and said, "And we shouldn't wait."

He hesitated for as much time as it took her insistent hand to find the bulge and run her fingers along his length.

Guilt washed over him. "I am—"

She squeezed his length through the thin material.

"—not certain ye would want this had ye not been giv—"

Her insistent stroking and pulling was doing him in.

"—en the tea."

Her hand worked its way into his trews so that they

183

were skin to skin, and he stilled at the tremendously pleasant sensation nearly sending him over the edge.

"Ye're wanting this, too." She whispered against his lips, rubbing his nose, and looking at him with eyes hooded with desire even as she stroked him mercilessly.

With a groan, he loosened the waist of his trews until his cock was presented, stiff and proud. With not even a pause, she sheathed him to the hilt in her womanly depths and gave a deep-throated groan of satisfaction.

It was heaven and he moaned. Loud. But before he could think to worry about the noise, she was riding him, demanding his undivided attention. Her exquisite tightness threatening to undo him.

He could only moan. For some reason this seemed right. He decided she could have her way with him and prayed he'd be able to see her satisfied.

Making mewling sounds like a cat in heat, she shifted forward and back as she rose and fell on him in a very satisfying way. Helpless to her ministrations, he had to grip her hips at one point to keep her from setting him off too quickly, she felt that delicious.

When he lifted her *léine* to suckle her heavy breast, she stilled and threw back her head in pleasure. He prodded her again and was rewarded with a gasp of pleasure. Holding her hips still, he thrust into her until he met her in the heights of satisfaction.

Exhausted and covered in sweat, she collapsed against him, turning her face away to heave in great lungfuls of air. He did nearly the same, unwilling to remove himself from a place he'd longed to be for more than a week now.

They said nothing as their hearts began to slow

along with their breathing. She was extraordinary and showed no signs of shoving him away.

A deep snoring resounded from the hidden pallet. They stilled like possums. Then burst out laughing.

"Shhhh." Darragh put a finger to his mouth. "Do not awaken our hosts."

Brighit giggled, her body quaking with the movements where his body should have been softening inside her. That didn't seem to be the case. She nodded right before her wide-mouthed yawn took over.

"I have exhausted my lovely bride." Darragh pushed the hair back from her face then traced her sweet pink lips, bruised a bright red from their passionate kisses. "My delightful wife."

Her sleepy expression shifted into a smile, but she said nothing.

"Tell me ye will remember this come morning? That ye found great pleasure in my arms?"

Brighit nodded right before her head lowered to his shoulder and her quiet snoring began. Darragh sighed, content to hold her a bit longer and to wonder at how one woman could fit so perfectly against him. It was indeed as if she belonged there.

Chapter Seventeen

Brighit awoke to the tantalizing smell of sweet cream and honey. The scent reminded her of her favorite childhood treat—oats dripping with both. Her insides rumbled, and she stretched her arms overhead.

Beside her, Darragh slept soundlessly, his arm still wrapped around her waist as if he were afraid to lose her even in sleep. She turned toward him, tracing the beard that grew along his strong jaw. A handsome man indeed, her husband.

Despite his concerns, she remembered everything about the night before. It had been wonderful—everything she'd hoped for.

"Yer belly is loud enough to wake the dead." Darragh spoke with his eyes closed.

Her stomach growled again. "I cannot help it. I

smell food and I'm hungry."

"As am I." Darragh yanked her close, his breath heavy in her ear, and said, "Ye are most satisfying, *a ghráidh.*"

"As are ye."

"Ah, ye remember?"

She blushed, and he nuzzled into her neck. "My hope is that ye enjoyed it enough that we may try it again," he continued.

"D'ye think they'll hear us?"

He put her hand to his hardened length, covering it with his own hand. "They left a while ago. I've been waiting patiently."

The idea excited her as did the feel of his heat beneath her hand. The slamming of the door jerked them apart.

"They're satisfied, Mama. Do not worry so." William's words were followed by something heavy dropping onto the table.

"William," Gwen hissed the word. "Our guests are still sleeping."

"A moment," Darragh kept hold of her hand, though he moved it to his heart, when she would have stood. "Ye cannot know what ye mean to me." Her breath caught, and he glanced at the closed curtain as if he could see through it to the elderly couple probably working over the fire. "How pleased I am with ye."

Her eyes widened, and she glanced away, embarrassed. "Are ye speaking of our love making?"

He turned her to face him before pulling her closer, surrounding her with his arms. "I am. And so much more."

"Sit yerself down." Gwen's loud hissing carried

through the curtain, her annoyance with her husband obvious.

Darragh snorted. "I should have picked a better time to speak my mind, mayhap when we were completely alone, but I wanted ye to hear the truth." He cupped her cheek, stroking her bottom lip with his thumb, "I'd have taken ye to wife even if we'd not been promised to each other at birth."

Almost afraid that she hadn't heard him correctly, she placed a kiss on his palm before pulling back with a very slow movement to search his face. His brown eyes were rounded, his expression soft with emotion. His sincerity tugged at her heart and she didn't immediately know what to say, how to put her feelings into words. He'd always held her interest, from the first moment her mother had said he was to be her husband. Her attitude toward him had only changed when she started to believe he didn't feel the same. When he ignored her after she had sought him out. She only wanted his attention like the other lasses received from the lads.

Darragh shrugged, smiling sheepishly as if he may have shared too much.

"Ye are very pleasurable in my arms, but yer stomach is still growling. Ye sound near to starving." He slapped her bottom.

She hesitated a moment, wanting to give him some indication of her own feelings. Awkwardness threatened to overtake her, so she quickly kissed him before pushing open the curtain to join the couple.

"Good morn to ye," Brighit said, her smile feeling wide enough to light up a room.

"Ah, did ye sleep well?" Gwen was wiping her hands on a cloth, while her husband sat quietly at the table.

Brighit's mind flashed back to the intimate night of loving she'd shared with her husband. She wondered at the woman's knowing smile and her face heated. "Most certainly."

"I've a few vegetables from the garden for soup, if ye'd like to start there?" Gwen indicated the sack on the trestle, her smile broadening when Brighit nodded.

Unlike the women at home, Gwen definitely seemed to take pleasure in teaching Brighit. There'd be no ridicule from her for what Brighit didn't know. That was a great relief. Brighit opened the bag, surprised by her own sudden interest in its contents. "These will be fine. And the herbs?"

"Plenty have not gone to seed. After we break our fast, we'll decide which to use. Ye wanted to make bread as well?"

"The bread. Let us make a filling, dark loaf."

"Ye sound as if ye've a full day planned." Darragh joined them, nodding a greeting to their hosts.

Brighit's eyes followed him as he came to a stop opposite William, and that knowing smile returned to Gwen's face. "A fine man ye have there."

"Fine indeed."

Darragh had not heard them as he settled at the trestle. "But yer insides are calling for something a bit sooner, wife."

Gwen rubbed Brighit's shoulder as she passed her to reach the iron pot beside the fire. "I've taken care of the breakfast. We cannot have yer bride cooking on an empty stomach."

The porridge was hot and filling, its sweetness increased by the always present honey.

"Yer cock is having trouble knowing when to

crow, William. I heard him all night." Darragh helped himself to more hot cereal before settling back down beside Brighit. "How are the eggs? Are they plentiful even through winter?"

William wiped his mouth before answering. "We have more than enough. Our nephews take turns coming by every week or so. 'Tis only the meat that has been scarce of late, but we're fine."

"I would not mind seeing what I can get for ye, in appreciation of ye giving us a dry place to sleep."

Collecting the bowls, Brighit followed Gwen to the small work bench behind the hearth. There, Gwen emptied the bag of a large assortment of root vegetables, scattering the colorful array across the top of the wooden surface.

"Are ye up for a little hunting then?" William's voice sounded pleased, as if he'd come up with the idea himself.

"A fine idea," Darragh said.

Brighit glanced up to find Darragh's eyes on her, just as she'd suspected, and his look of interest made her blush. She smiled at him before she took up a knife and started chopping.

While the men discussed a plan, Gwen shared her concerns about her husband with Brighit, careful not to be overheard. William seemed healthy, but his tracking and hunting was taking longer and longer. Although he'd never said as much, Gwen was worried that he'd had trouble finding his way home again.

"And what about ye, Brighit?" Darragh asked.

Brighit's blade slipped and she bit her lip to keep from making a sound.

"Does yer wife hunt?" William asked, surprise evident in his tone.

She glanced up again, but Darragh was regarding William with an expression of surprise. "Why would she not? She is very accomplished."

"Almost like having a man with ye but for the pleasure of her body at night to keep ye warm."

Despite her heated cheeks, Brighit managed a smile of appreciation for her husband. It would be wonderful to be alone with him, the two of them working alongside each other. She wondered if he would enjoy it as well.

"Would that please ye, wife? Be off in the woods with me hunting down small animals to kill for our meal?"

"I prefer the larger animals. It makes it so much more worthwhile." She straightened her shoulders then shrugged. "But small ones are fine if that's all ye can find."

"Ha, now does that sound like a challenge to ye, William?" Darragh asked, his eyes steady on her.

"A bit like she's saying she could fell a deer while ye'd only catch a rabbit."

Brighit feigned outrage, but her eyes twinkled with mischief. "I said no such thing."

Gwen laughed beside her. "I believe I heard the same thing."

"Ye did not." Brighit laughed. "I did not say I was a better hunter than my husband."

Darragh's smile widened and he crossed his arms about his chest. "Ah, but 'tis a challenge simple enough for me to take up and prove."

Her brows raised, Brighit replied "It is that."

"A fine idea," He nodded to William. "and we'll leave anon."

Brighit's excitement was uncontainable, dimmed

only by the thought of trying to do the job hampered by her long *léine*. If she could learn how to cook soup, she could learn how to move with her long, covering rustling about her, announcing her presence to her prey.

The fresh, crusty bread was baked to perfection according to Gwen. She was quite outgoing in her praise of Brighit's ability, making her feel her abilities were acceptable. Quite different from her experience at home. The loaves were packed up for them to take on their hunt. Among the vegetables Gwen had procured for the soup were the dreaded leeks, which Brighit quickly learned was one of Darragh's favorite vegetables. She'd have to acquire a new appreciation for the filthy things. Shortly after adding them to the pot, she'd realized how thick and fragrant they made the broth.

Packing this as well, Darragh and Brighit were soon ready to head out. She settled on Darragh's horse, their supplies packed in the bags hanging behind his legs.

"Do not worry for us if we are not back anon." Darragh held a rein on either side of her while she sat sideways in front of him. He glanced at her and said, "We do not plan to hurry back."

"There's a path along the ridge where ye can see the herds as they're moving. My favorite place to settle down to watch for the deer."

"Then we will head there first." Darragh nodded to Gwen and they were off.

The ground across the glen was saturated and that made their travel slow, but the rains had brightened their color, making the meadow they crossed seem almost dreamlike while they moved toward the mountains in the distance.

Brighit sat surrounded by Darragh's warmth, and they took their time crossing the open field. The birds in the trees announced their arrival and the smell of the damp earth filled their senses. She sighed, content with the world, and rested her head on his chest for only a moment before drifting off with dreams of a hearth and family of her own.

Chapter Eighteen

It was midday when Darragh awoke her with a gentle kiss to her cheek, her jaw, and finally to her lips. A bit stiff from the ride, she stretched her arms wide then wrapped them around his shoulders to offer her lips more fully to him.

"Mmm, exactly what I wanted."

His firm hand at her back pressed her flush against his chest while his tongue teased hers, setting off sparks of longing low in her belly like a gentle breeze fanning a fire.

"Now that ye've slept most of the way, we'll have to find a way to keep ye out of trouble."

"Ha! I am quite refreshed enough to see to providing a feast for us both."

They dismounted and he set about starting a fire.

She took the supplies off the horse, seeing to its comfort before leaving it to graze nearby. Gwen had packed the leftover bread, some honey sweetened cream, and a hunk of hard cheese.

"Well mayhap not such a feast, but our bellies will be full."

"Are ye certain ye never cared for such work? Ye seemed to enjoy learning from Gwen." Darragh brushed the dirt from his hand and watched the fire continue to grow.

His eyes met hers across the flame. She shrugged, removing the wrappings from the food. "I like her. Mayhap I never saw any use for such knowledge before, and besides, 'tis very boring." Turning to him, she continued. "Unlike defense of the clan, which is always exciting. And defense of the clan assured our survival."

"My own mother does little cooking. As the wife of the king, 'tis not expected of her, though she does enjoy her gardens and embroidery." Darragh crossed to her, slicing off a chunk of the cheese to offer her before getting some for himself. "Being able to feed the members of the clan keeps them alive and the warriors strong enough to defend against an attack."

Brighit savored the nutty taste while pondering the obviousness of his statement. Why had she been so opposed then to working in the kitchen? The other lasses' smiling faces and flirty smiles flashed through her mind, along with their disdainful glances at her.

She looked away, feeling as if she was found lacking. "The other lasses cared not for my abilities, always criticizing me. When I was ordered to stop training with the lads, it seemed like there may have been something to what they'd said."

Darragh finished the cheese and took the bread with him to where he'd rolled up his *brait* and propped it against a tree stump. He settled down, leaning back against it. Patting his thighs, he indicated she should sit on his lap. Her awkwardness returned, but she tried to disregard it. When she would have sat closer to his knees, he gently urged her to lean against his heated body before offering her a piece of the bread. They ate in amicable silence, the sound of the breeze high in the trees soothing them.

"They were jealous." Darragh finally replied, his tone decidedly defensive.

"Of what?"

"Ye spent yer time with the very lads they wished to impress." With a hand on her chin, he pulled her in for a passionate kiss, his hand skimming along her breasts before wrapping around her waist. He broke the kiss and waggled his brows. "Not one of them compares to ye in any way."

"The lads were endless in their praise of the other lasses' beauty and abilities."

"And what did the lads say about ye?"

"Nothing. They patted me on the back for a job well done." She looked away. "When I was no longer allowed to train with them, I had no one. The lasses did not care to become friendly with me. They said I was odd because I preferred battle and wore trews."

Darragh brushed her gown out, smoothing it over her knees. "This would be a difficult way to dress for training."

A deep sadness washed over her suddenly. She'd taken such pride in her accomplishments despite the way the other girls had treated her. Losing that might have made her defiant—willful even—because it was something she *was* good at, not like those other duties. Surely not every lass was meant to sit around sewing or being gawked at or fought over.

She sighed in resignation. "It is a silly thing to be speaking of things that matter so little."

"It upset ye. 'Tis not a small thing." Darragh glanced away, looking far off into the distance before turning to her again. "I remember watching ye with the lads when ye were younger. Ye fought better than a lot of them because ye took yer father's direction seriously and it showed."

Her experience with Cathair had demonstrated her uselessness as a warrior. Her training and abilities could not stand against a man with a greater strength. The bigger man had been able to best her as easily as he would have swatted a fly.

"Ye're saying that to be kind." All she remembered about Darragh's early visits was that he'd wanted nothing to do with her. "I do not remember ye ever noticing me."

"Ah, I hid my interest in my future wife." Darragh's eyes widened. "A lass besting the lads is not a sight easily forgotten."

Heat spread up from her chest. "I didn't think ye ever saw me or cared to know anything about me."

"Yer feats demanded attention and the rumors sparked my interest."

"What rumors?" She tapped down her irritation. Those girls did love to talk. She wondered if he believed all that he'd heard.

He shook his head. "That they spoke of ye, not what they said. I did not trust more than what I saw with my own eyes." His gaze caressed her. "And what I saw intrigued me greatly."

Appreciation for him bloomed and she leaned in to kiss him. When he broke the kiss, she was taken aback by his suddenly devious expression. The same look he'd had when they'd snuck out for the bedding.

"What are ye about?"

"I have something for ye." Reaching between the *brait* and the stump, he pulled out a wad of material.

She shook out the piece of rough, dark material to find it was a pair of trews and disappointment washed over her. "Did ye wish me to show ye my mending abilities next?"

He simply puckered his lips and shrugged, holding his shoulders up longer than was necessary.

Searching the legs and seams, she found nothing, so she stopped and leveled her gaze at him. "I do not understand. I see no wear on these."

A large bird settled somewhere overhead, cawing loudly at the little birds that continued to badger it. "They are for ye."

He was wearing her patience. "And ye've given them to me, so now what am I to do with them?"

"They are for ye to wear."

Confusion was quickly followed by excitement. "For me? My own trews? Instead of the *léine*?"

"On occasion."

She jumped up, holding the pair up to her waist. They were cut smaller than her brother's and looked as if they would fit her quite well. "How did ye do this?"

Darragh shrugged and stood alongside her. "I saw no reason not to have some made for ye to use when ye're with me if it makes movement easier for ye. The thought of ye wearing yer brother's did not sit well with me." He crossed his arms about his chest, looking quite proud of himself. "And I wished to see that appreciative look on yer face."

Brighit moved in close, throwing her arms about his shoulders to pull him against her, and kissing him thoroughly. "Ye have made me very happy."

With a firm arm about her waist, he twirled her around until she couldn't catch her breath from laughing so hard. Setting her on her feet again, he gazed down into her eyes. "I never cared to have a dull woman at my side, predictable and staid. Ye? Ye are exciting to me in every way. Forgiveness, please, for not doing a better job of letting ye know that sooner."

She pulled away to again look at the trews, trying to imagine how they would fit her small frame.

"Will ye try them on?"

A sudden shyness overtook her, but she stamped it down and gave him her back to unlace her gown. His knuckles lightly touching her back sent chills of excitement down her spine. Her eyes closed in pleasure. She assumed he was caressing her by accident until his lips touched her as well.

"Ye have such lovely, soft skin."

Reaching beneath the edges of her dress, he slipped his hands along her skin to push the material down and over her arms. He kissed her again, one bare shoulder blade and then the other, the tip of his tongue just grazing her. "Very lovely indeed."

Her breath caught and she leaned back toward him, giving his hands free access to her exposed bosom, which he took advantage of without hesitation.

"What am I to wear with the trews?" Her voice was husky, and his laugh in response made her smile.

"I see ye only have one thing on yer mind."

"As d'ye," she replied.

Darragh slid his hand down her belly. It constricted under his light touch. He pushed the material off until it gathered at her feet, but he stopped short of touching her more intimate area.

"I have a tunic for ye as well."

He whispered the words close to her ear, his voice low, and she waited for the kiss she expected to follow. The firm slap on her bottom made her jump.

"Ouch!" Brighit turned around, her mouth gaping open. "What was that for?"

"It was either that or take ye as is my wont." He raked his gaze down the length of her, taking in all of her nakedness, then moistened his lips. His breathing was slightly heavy when he looked at her again. "Dress quickly before I change my mind."

Brighit squealed and moved to don the trews. He tossed a tunic to her, still warm from his body. She gave him a questioning glance and was struck by his solid torso, lightly covered in dark hair, in all its naked splendor.

"Best ye cover those delectable breasts sooner rather than later." He abruptly gave her his back, moving toward their supplies.

Surrounded by his musky scent, Brighit couldn't deny the quiver of desire that prickled along her skin to settle between her legs. She pulled the garment close around her, closing her eyes as she took in a deep breath.

"Mmm, now that was a pleasure I hadn't anticipated." Darragh had silently returned and was right there in front of her, fully clothed now. Tenderly stroking her cheek, he said, "The sight of yer longing for me."

She exhaled slowly, unable to deny what he could

clearly see with his own eyes. "This can wait. Mayhap we should wait to go out until the morrow?"

Darragh searched her face with narrowed eyes, then shook his head and took another step back. "Tonight will be soon enough for us. Anticipation will only heighten yer pleasure."

Feeling swamped by her sudden desire for him, Brighit swallowed, hoping to clear the lust from her voice. "Ye are certain we should wait?"

She was certain they should not. Never had she wanted something more.

His beaming smile irritated her. "I should set about getting a place for us to sleep tonight."

He had decided to make her wait and he certainly seemed to enjoy seeing her in such need. Disappointment shifted in her gut, and she squeezed her legs together, only to have the strange material between her thighs scratch against her sensitive skin. She had made a small pair of *braies* to protect her when she wore her brother's clothes but had nothing such as that with her.

Her disappointment shifted to ire when he turned around to get to work.

"And I'll see to… something else." The words sounded clipped and she felt sure she heard him chuckle. Well, much better to ignore him. Ignore him and everything about him while she turned her attention to straightening out her *léine* and putting it in a safe place.

Her own bow in hand, Brighit stood beside Darragh

on the ridge William had told them about. The much-used trail a short drop below them seemed promising and as the gloaming moved in, they were rewarded for their patience with a large herd of healthy deer lumbering like shadows across the glen.

"Be my guest." Darragh whispered into her ear and her chest expanded.

She stilled, lined up her arrow and released the string of her bow. Her aim was true.

"Very well done."

Brighit turned a bright smile on him.

"And will ye see to the rest of the work as well?"

Insulted at the mere suggestion that she would leave the lugging, cleaning, and caring for the carcass to another, she ground her teeth together, ready to spout out at him. His sincere expression while he waited for her answer tugged at her heart. He had no way of knowing what she was capable of. She needed to remember that.

"I am able to see to it myself but am happy for any assistance ye may wish to give me."

Darragh kissed her gently. "Let us see to this together."

Their duties were carried about in companionable silence and the remaining soup filled their bellies quite nicely once they were done. When he took out the mead, he smiled at her.

"And shall we enjoy this together now?"

She nodded, slightly anxious about where this was leading even though her earlier excitement had stayed with her most of the day, accentuated by the unusual rubbing between her legs.

"For my lovely wife." Darragh raised his mug to her and they drank at the same time. "Mmm, very good."

He leaned his head back against the stump, his arm behind her where she sat leaning against his chest.

"A lovely night." Following the direction of his gaze, she couldn't hold back her gasp at the sight of a million pricks of light filling the sky as if giving a performance for them alone.

She tipped her head back and said, "So many stars. Very lovely."

Darragh bit her sensitive neck, and she gasped again.

"And ye've a lovely neck."

His tongue stroked her skin like a cat cleaning its fur, with long, slow strokes. He nibbled her again and her arousal bloomed into full-blown need. Somehow he knew and shifted her to straddle his lap, continuing his nipping and licking, stopping only to whip the tunic off over her head and cup a breast in each palm.

"Such lovely breasts my wife has."

She moaned when he sucked her deep into the warm, damp recess of his mouth. He answered her with his own groan.

Putting a hand between her legs, he rubbed against the material that had been rubbing her all day. She immediately jerked away, and he drew back to search her face.

"I have hurt ye?" His surprise matched her own.

"No. 'Tis very… sensitive."

Watching her, he tentatively touched her, again getting the same reaction. "'Tis arousing ye?"

Brighit shook her shoulders, shifting slightly where she sat, unsure of what she was feeling.

He took her mouth then and she opened herself to him, pressing her breasts against his solid chest, needing him to touch her. Darragh pulled her slightly forward to work the trews down, stopping only to apply his hand to her sensitive skin. Immediately, she gave in to the serious quaking that rocked through her body.

He yanked her close to impale her with his fingers, each thrust setting her on fire. Groaning, she threw her head back. When her flesh quivered against him, his shoulders tightened beneath her fingers. His breathing sounding labored.

"Is something amiss with ye?"

Darragh shook his head dismissively, as if unable to respond.

"Am I hurting ye?"

His eyes were wide when they met hers. "Only from my need to be inside ye."

Brighit pulled back to gawk at him. "Then why are ye not inside me?"

With a firm hand around her waist, Darragh yanked the trews the rest of the way off before covering lowering himself over her. Something terrifying sparked in her mind, sitting just outside of her focus like a wild cat ready to pounce. But then he filled her, and his breathy moan and her body's pleasant response called her attention back to him.

"Ah, does that pleasure ye?" His words were spoken on a throaty exhale.

The fear crouched low in the shadows of her mind.

"Mmm," she answered.

With firm hands grasping her small shoulders, he sheathed himself completely into her depths. When he lowered his lips to her ear, blocking out everything else with his massive chest, the nagging sensation nipped at her thoughts.

"D'ye feel me inside ye?" Darragh's low voice

called her back to him.

"Aye." And she could, a most pleasant sensation. But she panted slightly, no longer certain she could get enough air. He shifted, still covering her.

"And this?" His hot breath against her neck, along with his solid thrusts, claimed her total awareness. Most pleasant.

She could do no more than nod.

"Ye are safe with me, Brighit."

Those words echoed in her head until all she knew was the delicious feeling of fullness.

His words from earlier returned to her mind. "Ye're extremely enjoyable. Mayhap I should always make ye wait."

Waiting had been awful. She couldn't hold back the groan of pleasure as his movements increased her need, that tension and pressure building inside her again. Her body instinctively reached for it.

"Ah, I would know yer pleasure." His scolding tone told her he knew exactly what he was doing to her and that realization released the flood gates. Taking her mouth, he accepted her groan into his own body as wave after wave overtook her, the fear fading out until it disappeared. When the waves settled down to gentle ripples, he murmured soothing words of endearment. Without warning, he flipped her on top of him so that he lay on his back, a wicked grin on his face.

"Ride me again."

And she did so with abandon. Her deep moans couldn't be silenced when he shifted her back and forth, sliding her against him. Their lovemaking was certainly not quiet, but there was no one near to hear them. He urged her on, using his hips to ensure each thrust touched that special place deep inside her. Her release was overpowering, taking her like an inescapable summer storm that leaves everything soaked and shivering. She collapsed against him. Exhausted. His hand to the back of her head, he kissed her deeply while he plunged into her depths until his seed filled her.

Darragh turned them both to the side with him still inside her. They lay facing each other, waiting for their hearts to calm, both of them wet with sweat and breathing as if they'd run a great distance.

"Ye give me great pleasure, wife."

"As d'ye, husband."

"I believe we can save the rest of the mead for another night."

Brighit laughed. "I believe 'twould be best."

She snuggled up to him, leaning on his chest. He settled his *brait* over them and they slept right where they were without waking until the cock crowed at dawn.

Chapter Nineteen

The time together went by quickly. Darragh was amazed by how well Brighit could handle herself in different situations. Tracking, hunting, fishing, and even mock battles, which he couldn't resist engaging her in. She was very fast on her feet. Her father had indeed trained her well and she took great pride in her abilities... most of the time. Other times a shadow would fall across her features. In those moments, it was as if she thought very little of what she could do. And when Darragh encouraged her, she insisted he was only being kind.

Darragh hoped to gain her confidence and make her understand she was safe with him, but she had not yet shared her secret, the thing that continued to bring her sadness. The next night Brighit offered herself to him boldly, with no sign of the old panic returning. Afterward, they lay side by side and talked of life.

Three of the kings he had been sent to deliver the message to were not well known to his clan, but the last king was a good friend of Darragh's. He wanted to see how he fared, introduce Brighit to him.

They had to leave soon after bringing the deer back to Gwen and William. The couple was very appreciative and he wasn't surprised to see tears welling in Gwen's eyes when it was time for them to go.

"Oh please, do not cry." Brighit hugged her tight. "Yer nephews are sure to visit in no time."

"One of them came while ye were gone."

"I am sorry I didn't get to meet him."

William put a hand to Darragh's shoulder to direct him toward the door. "Let us see to yer horse. How far is it ye must travel?"

Darragh went with him toward the small *ráth* where his horse rested. "Two days if we go quickly. Our next stop will be at the Meachair."

"Ah, Francis. A good man."

"A good *rí túath.*"

William tipped his head before answering. "I stay away from the clan rivalries. 'Tis what ripped my Gwen's family apart."

"I am sorry to hear that. The true purpose for a clan is to live peaceably with support from others, joining together what ye have to live a better life."

"That may be the purpose, but I've rarely come upon that myself. No offense intended."

"None taken."

"The two sons who were part of the *derb fine* became rivals, so overtaken by the lure of power that

208

they nearly killed each other. Gwen's grandfather banished the fiercer one, Gwen's father. He had a meanness about him that not even a tender wife could soften. She died in childbirth bringing Gwen and her sister into the world."

Darragh nodded thoughtfully. He'd witnessed similar situations, which was why he was convinced of the importance of the treaty helmed by his father and Brighit's father. It made each *ri* accountable for himself and his own. "And is that why ye stay apart from the others?"

"I wish for peace. Besides, we get enough news from her sister's sons. Too much. The two believe they can set things right but instead stir up trouble. Usually upsetting to her, but she continues to ask."

"Is there a message ye'd like me to convey to the Meachair?"

William smiled. "Tell him we fare very well here thanks to ye and Brighit."

Gwen rubbed at her nose, sniffling quietly. "But ye had a fine time hunting with yer husband?"

"I did."

"And who felled the deer? Did he allow ye to do the honor?"

Brighit was impressed by the women's astuteness. "He did."

"And that way his pride remains intact and ye can have a great feeling of accomplishment."

"Hmm." Mayhap she was little too astute. Brighit had taken it down on the first shot. It was not possible to prove he could have done the same.

"A husband and wife can either have a hard time, keeping to themselves, or share with the other who they are. Ye two seem to be sharing just fine."

Brighit couldn't agree more, which only made the knowledge that she was keeping something awful from Darragh that much harder to bear. But she must keep it to herself for his own safety. "Did yer nephew bring some food as well?" she asked, changing the subject.

"Oh." Gwen got up and went to the small work bench, picking up the top of a heavy jar to reach inside. "I have something for ye."

"For me? Ye've given us so much, Gwen. Please nothing else."

The older woman came closer, something glittery flashing in her hand. "Ach, 'tis not from me and we've given ye nothing. Glad to have ye with us even if for only a short while."

The women's patience with Brighit was something she could never repay.

Opening her hand to Brighit, Gwen continued, oblivious to the heightened awareness coursing through Brighit's body. "My nephew—a strange man—thought this would be a fine gift for ye."

The rare sapphire sat in the palm of the older woman's hand like a viper ready to attack. Brighit swallowed down her fear. Gwen shoved it closer. "Take it. He wants ye to have it. He insisted."

I bet he did.

"Ye never told me. What is yer nephew's name?"

"Seigine. He and his brother, Cathair, are my sister's boys. They look after us as if they were our own sons."

Brighit could do no more than shake her head. The woman's imploring eyes filled Brighit with guilt. Gwen had no idea her nephew, who had feigned kindness and appreciation for the visitors, was a cruel tormentor. Brighit didn't doubt that Seigine had been following her and Darragh, not looking after his aunt and uncle at all. Forcing air back into her lungs, she reached to take the thing. "Did he say why he wanted us to have this?"

Gwen smiled broadly. "He said he will soon have enough to buy many more, even fancier, gems, and wanted to thank ye for…" She frowned as if searching her thoughts. "Oh, thank ye for helping him with that."

"I do not understand." The pounding in her ear increased and it was difficult to swallow.

"Strange to me as well, but he said knowing ye were here helped him with what he needed to do."

The words filled Brighit with dread. What had he done? "I cannot really accept this."

"Oh, ye must." Gwen's eyes rounded and unless Brighit wanted to upset the woman further, she had to be gracious.

"I thank ye. And be sure to thank yer nephew. When will ye see him again?"

"Hmm, he said he would not be back until after the snows. He promised to return with great news. But we are more than prepared here for winter's deadly cold, thanks to ye and Darragh."

Chapter Twenty

The ruins of the stone castle overlooking the bay stood as a stark reminder of battles lost and won on these very shores between those who lived here and those who had invaded their lands so long ago. A shiver traipsed across Brighit's skin at the sight of the long boat, barely peeking above the rocks leading down to the sea. The stories of the Norsemen and the terror they brought was not often spoken of. Many of those who now ruled as Eire's kings had the blood of the invaders mixed within their royal blood. A past best left undisturbed.

"Are ye cold? Ye've hardly said a word." Darragh's concern, evident in both his tone and his expression, sparked her defenses.

"I am merely tired of the travel. It's exhausting.

Ye said so yerself just last night."

Last night there had been much talk of this and that, and what would happen when they finally returned home. Feeling the pressure of Seigine's nearness, Brighit had subtly turned the conversation to him. But her husband was a wise man and he seemed to know almost instinctively that the man had no leadership qualities.

"Then we will get ye some rest before ye meet the *ri túath*. He is a good friend of mine."

"I look forward to meeting him. Will ye relay yer father's message as well?"

"That is the reason we are here." Darragh sighed. "And I will listen closely for his response since I have my own concerns."

Brighit parted her lips to allow her shaky breath to remain unnoticed. If she did not succeed in convincing her husband and father-in-law to support Seigine against the Dubhshláine, her part in the murder of Cathair would be revealed and her father and Darragh would bear the brunt of her punishment. All would be lost.

He must have noticed the change in her expression because he took her hand, kissing it before leaning in to kiss her cheek. "*A ghráidh,* I pray ye are refreshed after ye rest. I miss my feisty wife."

"I will do my best."

They were met at the entrance by two well-armed warriors who recognized Darragh immediately. Setting aside their imposing demeanor, they each embraced him in turn, one even lifting him off the ground.

"Ye have been missed." The blond man ruffled Darragh's hair like he was a boy, and Brighit could only look on in astonishment.

"They have known me since I was a boy," Darragh explained, his face reddening.

Still dumbfounded, she nodded open-mouthed while the second man did the same.

"Please, no more. Ye'll have my wife wondering about her husband's ferocity when he can allow himself to be pawed by other warriors."

"Yer wife?" The blond's eyes widened in amazement, then he slapped his friend's back with quite a bit of enthusiasm. "'Tis her. The she-warrior from Clan Cruadhlaoch?"

Brighit's jaw dropped at the title.

"Devin." Darragh's irritated tone did little to discourage the man. "Please. My wife is named Brighit."

"She is indeed." The man got his exuberance under control and, with great solemnity, swept into a low bow before taking Brighit's hands to his lips. "I am honored to meet ye, fair lady."

Flabbergasted, she had no words, and when the second man offered the same greeting, she was beside herself. "Darragh?"

"Is Francis about?"

"'Tis still daylight. Ye know he is practicing with his men." Devin glanced at his friend as if astonished. "What say ye, Liam? Is the young Darragh losing his mind so soon?"

Her husband rolled his eyes. "Gentlemen, if ye could but show us to a quiet place, I wish to sort out the problems ye've started for me."

They both laughed. Devin called over a stable boy to see to their horse while Liam led the way within the new part of the castle, leading them up the stairs that followed along the length of the great hall to, he informed them, the recently added second floor. The new building was attached to the only part of the castle that remained intact.

Liam was at least a foot taller than Darragh and his body was huge. His *léine* was made up of wolf skins, the head still attached on one as if the massive beast were sitting on his shoulder.

"This is where Francis's dearest guests reside and where I presume he would also like ye to stay with yer lovely wife."

Winking, the man closed the door behind him.

"What is amiss here?" Brighit felt totally confused by this attention. "What are they calling me... that name for? Who are these people to ye?"

Darragh put a hand to his mouth in a useless attempt at covering his laugh. Brighit swung her arms around, beside herself, and said, "I need an explanation, Darragh."

"Come. Sit with me." He settled on the edge of a bed very much like his own at home. Brighit sat beside him, an arm's length away. He seemed surprised at her irritation, but she was in no mood to explain what should be very plain in her opinion.

Darragh heaved a great sigh. "I visited often when I was young. My father would leave me with Francis so I could study my letters. When I came here as a lad, I would talk about ye. I admit it. Especially when we traveled here right from yer *túath*."

"And ye called me a 'she-warrior'?"

"No." Once again, he could barely contain his laugh, but at least he had the decency to desist when he caught her cold stare. "*They* were the ones who came up with the name. No harm or insult was intended."

Inside, Brighit fumed. Her eyebrows felt like they were touching her hairline in her irritation. "I can see the harm. 'Tis an insulting term."

"Never. They had great respect for ye and Aednat. Sean is a man who demands respect, make no doubt about that. Those men would never insult anyone he cares for and everyone knows how much he cares for both of ye."

The memories of training with the older Aednat caused a tug in her heart. She had been so proud of their accomplishments. When Aednat shifted her focus from warfare to healing, she had nonetheless continued to encourage Brighit. She wished she could talk to her cousin now, find out how she should handle this terrible predicament.

"Forgiveness?" Darragh's hand covered her own.

"I suppose." Brighit could not remain angry when it was more a childish prank than an intended insult. "They seem to care greatly for ye."

He smiled. "They are as close as brothers to me. Terrence is their younger brother."

It was easy to imagine Terrence here, and those men certainly did put her in mind of him, but the mere thought of Darragh's friend filled her with guilt. What a situation she'd put him in. Terrence always kept a discreet distance from Darragh now. There had been no time to convince him of her husband's innocence regarding her bruises.

"I think I will lie down if ye have no need of me immediately."

Darragh pulled back the dark green blanket covering over the bed. "I would prefer ye rest now. I will see if Francis is about and return shortly to see ye to the feast they will no doubt host for our arrival."

After she lay down, he covered her with the blanket and then kissed her tenderly on the mouth. "Sleep well, *a ghráidh.*"

The large, cold hand on her cheek startled her awake. Darkness surrounded her, though the heavy coverings managed to keep her toasty warm.

"Brighit?" A light came up behind Darragh, casting a strange glow over his face. "Are ye not well?"

An older man had followed Darragh into the room with a candle, which he set in the iron holder along the wall before exiting the room and closing the door behind him.

Her body ached, but she forced herself to deny it. "I am over tired. Please help me to wash and dress. Has someone brought up our belongings?"

"Here is everything." Darragh put down their sack and began pouring water from the pitcher into the bowl. "I came in twice to check on ye, but ye slept so heavy I did not wish to wake ye. Are ye certain ye are up to joining the others?"

"The others?" She splashed the water on her face, dipping the cloth along her throat and neck. When he lifted her heavy hair to aid her, she was caught by the passion in his gaze and her breath quickened.

"They are below and wish to meet ye."

Standing now, she gave him her back so that he could help her unlace her gown. His tantalizingly gentle touch soothed her, and when his lips touched the sensitive area of her neck, she leaned against him ready for more.

"D'ye mind if they wait a bit longer?" Brighit slipped the gown down her arms and pushed it to the floor.

Darragh's quiet gasp was followed by his hands tenderly exploring her breasts. "If ye do not mind."

Excitement ignited low in her belly. "Then ye shall see to me properly? A feather bed once again beneath us?"

Pressing her back onto the mattress, he covered her, his kisses dropping along her warmed flesh like dew on a rose's petal. "Mmm, I am entranced by the sight of ye in candlelight. Yer body calls to me."

Brighit was overwhelmed by this sensual attack and submitted to his touch for her own pleasure. A short while later, she lay alongside his body, both of them still damp from their exertions.

"I do not believe I am ready to share ye with others."

Brighit laughed. "I fear 'twill be *ye* who becomes lost to *me*. I know no one here."

"My men have arrived. Ye know them."

She gave him a withering look.

"These warriors are friends to ye, like family, but I do not know them. They may not be as cordial as ye and my father are."

Darragh beamed. "Ye place me in the same standing as yer father?"

Her eyes widened. "Certainly. Why would I not? Ye are as brave and honorable."

With a start, Brighit realized he'd believed—still—that she thought less of him. "I am well pleased with ye as my husband, Darragh."

Moving over her, he scooped her into his arms to

hold her close and kissed her passionately, sparking little flames that had just begun to cool. She groaned while he continued his assault of her mouth, his hands moving along her curves in a worshipful manner. When he broke the kiss, he was breathing heavy.

"Ye have made me most happy with yer declaration." He rubbed her nose along hers.

"I should have said so sooner."

"Ye have said so now." Darragh looked down into her face. "Are ye ready to join the others?"

"But…" Brighit hated to claim he hadn't finished what he'd started when he had so thoroughly loved her not fifteen minutes earlier. It seemed such a wanton thing to do. "Will ye finish this later?"

Her whining voice was met with a loud laugh. "Try to stop me."

"Then I will do as ye ask."

He helped her to wash and dress, seeing to her hair himself, which nearly forestalled their joining the others for a second time. A knock at the door reminded them others awaited them.

"We will be down anon." Darragh called to the faceless voice at the door. "*Reidh?*"

"I am."

When they ascended the stairs, the group that had been waiting in the great hall crowded into the entrance to witness their arrival. Spontaneous applaud broke out. When Brighit moved to nibble at her finger, Darragh took her hand away and kissed it. "No need to be nervous. I am with ye."

Pausing a few steps from the bottom, he lifted their joined hands for all to see. "May I introduce to ye my bride, Brighit, formerly of Clan Cruadhlaoch, now of Clan MacNaughton."

A lovely woman with black hair and wise brown eyes stepped ahead of the rest to embrace her warmly. "My sweet girl, ye are more lovely than I had imagined even with all yer husband's going on about ye."

Darragh glanced away when she looked at him. "My thanks," she said.

"I am Moira of Clan Meachair, my husband is Francis." She turned about, a concerned expression knitting her brow. "Francis?"

A formidable-looking man with a full head of thick black and white curls stepped up. "Here, dear lady."

"Oh, Francis. Come see our Darragh's bride. Isn't she lovely?"

Francis bowed low over her hand. "An honor to finally meet ye. Ye have quite stolen our Darragh's heart."

Again Darragh would not meet her gaze. Instead, he looked to their hosts and said, "Well, we have made ye wait long enough. Let us enjoy the feast ye have so thoughtfully prepared for us."

"A time for celebration, dear Darragh." Moira led the way, her shoulders back and her head held high.

Darragh was given the seat of honor beside Francis and Brighit between him and Moira. The older woman clasped her hand. "I am so happy ye've come. This is indeed a day for celebration."

"Ye're very kind."

Moira motioned for the servants waiting to the side of the hall, their arms laden with heavy trays of foods of every sort, to begin serving. A young lass came forward with a silver pitcher, bowing slightly to those seated at the table, and offered the wine first to

Francis and Moira, and then to Darragh and Brighit. She filled their bejeweled goblets with a bright red liquid. Darragh sipped at it.

"Ah, my friend from Calais has come by here."

"He was here spring last." Francis took an appreciative sip. "We had expected ye as well."

There was censure in his tone, but Darragh replied, "I was seeing to my father."

Brighit wondered if Francis was referring to the first time their wedding had been postponed.

"Yer first duty. Of course we understand." Moira said, but her glance toward her husband showed her own disapproval, either for mentioning the matter at all or for not voicing his understanding, Brighit couldn't be certain which.

"So tell me of yer mother, Brighit. How fares she?"

"Ye know my mother?"

"Of course, she is from Alba, as am I."

There had never been any mention of Clan Meachair in her hearing, but Brighit realized there may have been much that she didn't give the proper amount of attention to growing up. She answered as best she could. Darragh spoke with Terrence's brothers when they joined them at the table. There was no sign of Terrence himself, though she saw a few of the other men from their group. She would need to remember to ask Darragh about him later.

The fire was stoked up as the food was removed and the entertainment began. A large gathering. Brighit wondered if this were normal or if outlying clans had received word of Darragh's presence.

"Now that we have dispensed with the pleasantries, tell me why ye've come." Francis leaned forward to speak to Darragh.

"If ye will excuse me, I need to see where my daughters have gotten to," Moira said. "Would ye care to join me, Brighit?"

The polite answer would be yes, but she needed to hear for herself the message being conveyed regarding the murder of Cathair. Darragh, mayhap sensing her reluctance, took her hand. "I wish my wife to remain at my side, Moira. Certainly ye understand?"

Moira dipped her head and retreated through the hall where the jugglers and musicians were keeping the crowds entertained.

"We need to call a meeting of nobles. There's been a murder."

"Who has been killed?"

"Cathair of Clan MacCochlain."

Francis looked as if he'd been struck. "Cathair? The lad fostered with me. I heard of no battle."

"He did not die in battle. He was murdered and his brother hunts down the killer even as we speak."

Brighit felt her whole body start to tremble. Darragh turned his gaze to her, planted a kiss on her cheek and whispered, "Would ye prefer to go with Moira? I should have asked."

She shook her head, unable to form words.

"Are ye certain 'tis not too much for ye to hear such talk? It would not be untoward."

Francis glanced at her as if he knew what they discussed and said, "I would not believe the she-warrior would want to miss the goings on."

His smile and tone indicated he was but teasing her, so she smiled back. A stiff smile because her stomach was clenched into a ball as tight as when Cathair's fist had pummeled her. Everything she'd eaten threatened to come back up her throat.

Nodding to Darragh, she said, "I will stay."

Darragh kissed her forehead lightly then turned his attention back to Francis. "He has the weapon, or so he says."

"Ye question his truthfulness?" Francis did not seem surprised.

"He claims he follows the trail of the murderers." Darragh shrugged. "For all we know, he may have even caught them."

"How many men?"

Tipping his head, Darragh offered a look of disbelief. "Seigine claims it was only one man who murdered his brother."

Brighit forced down the bile flooding her mouth.

"And Seigine has become king?"

The man's tone implied a meaning beyond the words he used. Darragh's eyes narrowed on his friend and Brighit's stomach gurgled.

"Is there a reason they should have chosen another?" Darragh asked.

"My experience with both of these men—lads—was that they do not agree on much. Both fostered with me, but I could not keep Seigine here long. He fought with my sons as well."

"Terrence didn't mention anything about knowing Seigine."

"Terrence was staying with his uncle in Alba. I do not remember the two ever meeting."

When the food began working its way up her throat, Brighit stood suddenly. "I am going to be sick."

Darragh jumped to his feet and wrapped an arm around her shoulders, taking them away from the large hall and out the side door, where she promptly emptied her stomach. She collapsed against him, her breath heaving. He brought them to a small bench set beneath a tall tree.

"Aw dear Brighit. Has the talk of murders been too much for ye? I believe 'tis too much for me most days."

Brighit hated her weakness and her tears, but she would not allow her husband to think such talk was too much for her. What weighed on her was far more serious. She was being forced to encourage her husband to support the kingship of a man who had fought with everyone. How terrible for his neighboring clans. How terrible for everyone. And yet if she did not...

"I believe the soup may not have set well with me."

He pulled her close, smoothing her hair as he stroked her like a child. "Ye have handled yerself well in all situations."

The pride in his voice forced the tears to the surface and she buried her face against his shoulder.

"Do not feel ashamed, *a ghráidh*."

"Ye call me darling only because ye do not know how I really am."

His body stiffened. "What d'ye refer to?" He hooked a finger beneath her chin to raise it up so they were eye to eye. "I know ye believe ye must be as strong as a man, but I do not agree."

"If that is what I believe, then I have fallen far short," she said.

The words burned her throat and she hid her face again. Darragh shifted slightly and halted his soothing caresses, clearly discomfited by what she was saying. Soon enough he would be confronted with her

224

misdeeds and then he would be encouraged to set her aside.

"*A ghráidh,*" he continued to soothe her, "ye have never fallen short in my eyes. Yer spirit is what intrigues me the most. I was not able to share that with my own family. They are more... traditional. But here? They knew quite well what I truly thought of ye. While I heard my father speak of the need to set away childish things, I found myself wanting to spar with ye, to test yer mettle."

Brighit cringed inside. He thought so highly of her, and yet she had agreed to extol the virtues of a man who had none. She no longer believed she could speak in Seigine's favor, even if Darragh had to pay the price for what she had done. To lie in such a way would only dishonor her husband.

"Here I can be myself and not the warrior son my father wants me to be," Darragh said, smiling at her. "Here I studied the law, learning to become a *brithem* myself. I may even be called upon for advice when the murderer is found."

Aghast, she pulled back to stare at him and covered her mouth.

"Does that displease ye? I shared with ye that I may never be king."

She shook her head. How terrible it would be for him to be the one to decide her fate *and* his own.

"Then why would ye be upset?"

Closing her eyes, she swallowed down her fears. These were the words of a man who cared for her, and she didn't want to destroy that with the truth. Not yet. Unless she was going to tell him here and now what had happened, something she was not yet ready to do, she needed to reassure him.

"I am overwrought by everything. Forgiveness please."

"If ye are overwrought, then we will go to our room." He nuzzled her hair. "I believe we have some unfinished things to see to."

Hopeless, she merely nodded. No longer able to fight against the inevitable. She would be exposed as a murderer because the price for Seigine's silence was too high.

"I would like that."

Chapter Twenty-One

The decision was made that Francis would accompany Darragh and his men back to Drogheda following the shorter coastal route. A long enough ride, but there was a sense of urgency that Brighit could not quite understand. When she awoke to an empty bed, she assumed Darragh had gone to break his fast. Instead, she found him in the entry hall. Pacing. His broad smile and gentle kiss set aside any worries that his dark mood was her doing.

"What is amiss?" she asked.

"We are ready to depart as soon as ye have broken yer fast, my love."

She dropped her gaze, not wanting any questions about the fear he might see there. "I will do so quickly."

Darragh offered her his arm and accompanied her into the hall. Many of the Meachair clan were still partaking of the meal, but the warriors who'd come with them were missing.

"Francis is excited to be a part of the group of nobles. As am I." He beamed at her, selecting food from what had been set out on the side table. "The treaty put to writing the practices carried out for generations by many of us. My father's clan. Yer father's clan." He poured her some mead and refilled his own mug, taking a deep swallow before continuing. "The treaty is a way to bring the others in line, which will be less of a challenge with everything written down for all to see. A very exciting time."

His smile couldn't be contained. She nodded, shoveling a spoonful of the porridge into her mouth to avoid speaking.

"I will be back anon." He kissed her lightly on the cheek and was gone.

"Ye haven't told him still?" Terrence spoke from just behind her, his voice only loud enough for her to hear.

She swallowed. "Of what d'ye speak?"

Turning to him, she feigned confusion at the question, but his expression never wavered.

"Ye know what I refer to. If it was not him, he needs to know who it was."

Turning back to her porridge, she closed her eyes, struggling to steady her breathing and her fears. "Ye take on too much. See to yer own duty."

Her clipped words carried enough irritation that anyone else would have taken the hint and left her alone. Not Terrence. He stood there. Unmoving.

Brighit felt the weight of his rift with Darragh. She

knew she was the cause of it, but she wanted more time with her husband.

"What d'ye want from me?" She hissed the words, glancing around to be sure no one else was watching them. "I tell ye it does not matter."

"I assure ye that it does and I will not keep the secret from him any longer. Either ye tell him or I will."

Terrence marched away without a backward glance. Brighit shoved the wooden bowl aside, her appetite gone. It was Devin who sought her out a few minutes later.

"Lady, we await ye. Darragh is seeing to yer mount."

The thought of riding side saddle the entire way rankled her last nerve, but she held her tongue and slapped a smile across her face. At least the need for speed would ensure she was not expected to ride in the carriage. "Of course. Lead the way."

The men were still preparing for the trip and she was quickly abandoned by Devin, who went to help his father load some of his belongings.

"Brighit." Darragh's excitement was obvious. "Ye have eaten?"

"I am ready."

Darragh glanced at her gown. "Did Devin not bring ye what I'd sent him with?"

Weary by now, she was in no mood for any games. "He did not, Darragh. Are we ready to leave?"

His bewilderment at her sharp tone quickly shifted into pleasure. "Wait here."

"Devin." Darragh approached the man in three strides, ripping a sack from his hands.

"Apologies." Devin called after him. "I had forgotten."

Darragh shook his head then smiled, holding out the sack. "Go get changed."

She glanced down at her green gown. "To what purpose?"

He frowned at her. "Will ye argue with me on everything?"

She ripped the sack from his hand, eyes surely aflame, and turned about to head back to her room. Once there, she ripped open the sack and dumped the contents on the bed. Her trews had been neatly folded inside along with a heavy mantle cut small enough for her petite frame but long enough to cover anything the trews may reveal. Tears filled her eyes, making it hard for her to change quickly. By the time she had clubbed her long hair back, she knew they would all be waiting for her.

Brighit's expression spoke of her gratitude when she approached Darragh. The others fell silent as they watched her cross to him.

"*A ghráidh,* ye have pleased me greatly. How blessed I am to have ye as my husband."

She kissed him, and he kissed her back just as passionately, breaking it only so that he could glare at the others who had their eyes stuck on them.

He said, "A moment to ourselves, if ye please."

As one, the others turned their horses away.

"Ye like it?"

"'Tis wonderful, Darragh. *Ye* are wonderful. Many thanks for yer thoughtfulness."

"I will admit it was for selfish reasons."

Brighit's brow furrowed.

"We will ride much faster." He put his lips to her ears. "And I will be here to see to ye if ye have any need for... release from the... sensitivity ye may experience."

"Many thanks."

In a short time, they were on their way. The others in the group were known to her. From the Meachair, Francis and his two elder sons accompanied him. The sheepish grins they directed at her were endearing. To have men so very huge duck low whenever she glanced at them made her smile.

"Brighit, is this the first time ye have been so far south?" Devin asked.

"Aye."

"I understand yer sense of adventure is greater than most women."

She paused to control the grin that threatened to erupt. "Mayhap 'tis only my husband supporting my desire for adventure that makes me appear so different."

"Ah, a wise woman, too, Darragh." Francis glanced at her husband. "A fine one to argue the points of law with before ye must confront the others."

A chill passed over her skin at the thought of Darragh discussing any punishment with her. She had lain awake most of the night considering what to do. Her thoughts continued to bring her to the same conclusion: she could do nothing to encourage Seigine's kingship. And that meant the truth would be revealed, either by her or by Seigine.

Brighit had decided to tell Darragh herself. If he wasn't too angry to speak to her, he could tell her what she should do. The hours of restlessness had taken their toll, however, and she found herself yawning now.

"Did ye not sleep well?" Darragh had ridden up alongside her. "Ye tossed about quite a bit."

"Mayhap 'twas the sudden softness of our bedding." She forced a smile.

"Ah, my thanks for not accusing me of not seeing to ye properly."

Brighit gasped with embarrassment and looked to where Francis had been a moment earlier. He had moved ahead and was riding alongside Terrence now. With a start, she realized no one was nearby. This may be her only chance to speak to him.

Darragh smiled mischievously. "Ye believe I would speak of our private moments so that all could hear? Ye think little of me."

Her eyes rounded and she reached for him.

His concern was evident in his expression as he moved in close to take her hand. "I was teasing."

"Forgiveness?" The word was heavy with meaning. When she told him what happened, could he possibly forgive her?

"Always."

She prayed that was true. "Darragh, I need to te—"

"The paths split ahead." Iain called back to Darragh. "Which way do we go?"

Darragh's look of exasperation was followed by a kiss to her hand. "A moment please."

Fear squeezed her throat as she helplessly watched him move to the front of the group.

As they neared the end of their travels, Darragh was greatly relieved that he would soon have Brighit to himself again. At least they would have their own chamber, a place that they could call their own. Though they'd stopped at various houses along the way that had opened their doors to accommodate the weary travelers, they'd had little time to be alone with many squeezed into each room. At meals he would see to her, but not as he would have liked.

Brighit seemed more comfortable with the others now that she was dressed as a lad and riding her own mount. Could her earlier discomfort have come from being around so many people she did not know? He saw Terrence and scoffed. She'd felt comfortable enough to tell him, a near stranger, what she would not share with her own husband. Even though they were getting closer, she'd still offered no explanations about what had transpired with Terrence and he refused to continue questioning her.

Terrence's cold demeanor had softened some toward him, but his old friend still refused to give any details about what he knew and, more importantly, why he continued to avoid Darragh. Mayhap if Darragh could ease his concerns about Brighit's unhappiness. After they stopped for the midday repast, he sought out his friend before everyone took to their horses again.

"Will we be home this night?" Iain called to him as he passed, his travel-weary expression lightened by the excitement in his eyes.

Darragh smiled. "Mayhap by the evening meal."

The men's excited voices carried as they mounted. Devin was to take the lead for the rest of the way with Iain alongside of him.

Darragh finally caught sight of Terrence and came up alongside him as the man pulled on his leather gloves.

"Terrence." Darragh put a hand to his arm to stop him from mounting his horse. "We will need to talk when we arrive. As my second—and my friend—there should be nothing held back from me."

The man's nostrils flared slightly before he glanced toward the others to be certain no one was listening.

"Something is not right, but I beg ye to speak to yer wife yerself." Terrence's eyes pierced his before he spoke again. "Tell me ye would never hurt the lass."

Darragh pulled back as if he'd been punched. "How could ye think that of me?"

"Just tell me." Terrence hissed the words through gritted teeth, his expression revealing the torment in his mind. "Reassure me."

Torn between relieving his friend's concerns and offense at such an accusation, Darragh didn't answer immediately. The others were mounted, patiently waiting, and glanced toward them.

"I would *never* put a hand to her in anger. I am called to protect her—to be her sole protector." He moved in closer, gripping the man's shirt. "And ye will tell me now why ye could think such a thing of me after knowing me all these years."

Terrence gulped. "She had bruises on her face."

The earth tilted beneath Darragh's feet. He could not have heard him aright. "What?"

"That was the reason she wore the powder, to cover it up."

Darragh reeled back from the man, unable to form a coherent thought. She'd finally stopped wearing the powder, but he'd believed it was at his request. With her stubborn streak, he wasn't surprised it had taken a few days for her to give in.

"Is ought amiss?" Brighit called to him, turning her courser toward them.

"We're anxious to be on our way, man." Francis's gruff voice was met with agreement by those around them. "My arse is sore as hell and I'm looking forward to a long soak. Can ye not speak to my son after we've arrived?"

"Certainly." Darragh glared at Terrence, his voice low enough for his ears only. "Do not make me find ye, Terrence. Ye will explain yerself right quick."

Darragh mounted and pressed past the others to take the lead himself. Clicking his tongue, he urged his horse into a fast gallop that left the rest struggling to keep up. At this pace, he expected to be able to question Terrence long before sunset, leaving him with enough time to confront his wife. That suited him fine.

Chapter Twenty-Two

Along the trail that followed the coast, Darragh rode as a man possessed. Terrence's words ran over and over again in his head like a monk's chant. Now that he knew about the bruises, he was struck anew by the fact that she had confided in Terrence rather than him. Darragh had unknowingly given her several opportunities to explain the powder and why she was using it. She had chosen not to.

The fact hurt him deeply. Had he ever given her any reason to believe he would not care? Never. She'd even compared him with her own father. But she had not trusted him enough to reveal someone was abusing her, and she'd gone so far as to hide the bruises from him.

Francis and Devin had tried to engage him at

different points along the route, but Darragh could not be moved to respond. When the castle was finally in sight, Francis came alongside him to pull back on his reins.

Darragh turned on him with an angry scowl. "What are ye about?"

"I'm thinking ye need to calm yerself before ye have the entire castle up in arms."

A quick glance toward Brighit showed she, too, was concerned, though she didn't speak.

"Is something amiss?" Francis's kind eyes were rounded with concern and Darragh felt chagrined by his own behavior.

He shook his head. "I have much on my mind. I need to sort out some things."

The older man glanced over his shoulder and moved closer, lowering his voice even more. "Have they to do with yer wife?"

"Why would ye ask that?"

"Of everyone here, she's the most upset by yer behavior, Darragh."

He glanced at the hands fisted in his lap. Taking a cleansing breath, he struggled to calm the demons in his mind. The feelings of inadequacy. The belief that he had been found lacking. Had he known Brighit was hurt, he would have moved heaven itself to care for her and see her avenged.

"I have too much on my mind."

"I should not have interrupted yer talk with Terrence?" Francis flattened his lips. "Forgiveness please for interrupting ye both. Please go and see him now. I will lead the rest in and see yer wife settled. Come when ye have learned what ye need to."

Brighit watched with concern as her horse was led past Darragh. He offered her not even a word and it seemed strange that he would stay behind. Impulsively, she blew him a kiss. The shadows fell away from his face and he smiled back. She released the breath that had tightened her chest. Though she'd had no chance to speak with Darragh, she'd had a lot of time to reflect on the things he'd said and the way he'd accepted her for herself. Surely those were good signs that he would not turn his back on her completely. Mayhap together they could face what was to happen.

"Well, lady Brighit," Francis said, "I have the duty to see ye inside. I'll be happy to have such a lovely lass on my arm."

She glanced at her clothing then gave him a dubious expression.

Francis laughed. "Think nothing of it. My wife dresses the same when we travel together."

Brighit's mouth opened, her gaze sharpening with incredulity. "And no one thought to share that with me?"

"Share that with ye?" The man scratched at his heavy brow in a thoughtful way. "To what purpose?"

Her nostrils flared, but she pressed her lips together and remained silent.

"Ah, I suppose I should have thought of it." Francis was clearly saying whatever he thought would get him out of her bad graces. "Let me help ye dismount."

They entered the small area alongside the castle,

equipped with a standing block of stone. Francis gallantly lifted her from the saddle as if she weighed nothing at all. Despite his age, he was as strong as he looked.

When he raised his arm to her, Brighit placed her hand on his forearm and walked with him to the entryway, only to be met by Tisa, whose expression quickly fell. "Oh my."

"Good day, Tisa." Francis dipped his head, his arm still raised for Brighit. "If ye'll allow us to pass, I believe Brighit would like to rest by the fire."

"Of course," Tisa said before she reached up to kiss him on the cheek, her eyes still rounded with obvious concern as they perused Brighit's trews.

"Come, fair Brighit," Francis said in his courtly tone.

She would admit she greatly appreciated his attendance on her as they passed through the wide opening to the great hall. Relief flooded her at finding the hall nearly empty. They'd arrived before the evening repast and only the sound of the servants moving about broke the silence.

"I must see to my horse, if ye'll excuse me," Francis said. "She is not kind to others laying hands on her... much like my wife." He grinned and was gone in a moment.

Brighit was taken aback by the sight of Tadhg at the far end of the hall. She hadn't noticed him when they'd arrived. He was in close conversation with another man, not even his voice carried. Her gaze took in the back of the large man sitting opposite him. The sight of his wolf-skin mantle sent chills through her.

No.

Tadhg shifted away and his face brightened when

his gaze landed on her. He stood. "Brighit. How lovely to welcome ye home at last."

Seigine stood as well and turned toward her, quirking a brow when her mouth dropped open. "Welcome home, Brighit."

Darragh waited until the others had passed them before confronting Terrence.

"Finish what ye started. Tell me everything ye know."

The man sighed, looking uncomfortable. "Someone took a fist to Brighit's face."

"What?" The word was more a growl. Duncan had lingered behind and revealed himself now. He was livid.

Darragh ignored the outburst and directed his question to Terrence. "Did ye ask her where the bruises came from?"

"She tried to tell me it was from hives." The man's face reddened. "And assured me ye'd never hurt her."

"Ye needed her to tell ye that?" Darragh shook his head, his hands at his waist.

"I didn't believe her since ye'd said nothing to us about it. What other reason would there be for ye not to let us know what had happened?"

Than if ye had inflicted the bruises yourself.

Darragh finished his friend's unspoken thought. If this man—whom he'd counted as his closest friend— knew him at all, he'd know there was nothing that could cause him to hurt anyone except another warrior. Damn him for keeping such a thing from him.

Clearing his mind, he tried to recall every time he'd seen Brighit prior to the wedding. If the powder was intended to hide her abuse, she had only started using the stuff that day. He had risen early that morn to watch for Brighit, and there'd been no sign of any early-morning visitors.

But he did remember the late-night revelers.

Niall.

"A group of men came late into the hall the night before the wedding. Niall may have been among them." Darragh spoke more to himself.

His jaw dropped right before he slammed it tight. "And that morning the lads were less attentive than usual and seemed tired. What was it Seigine had said? They were attacked?"

"Niall wouldn't attack the men. Even in Alba, the raids are not intended to do harm to the other clan but to steal cattle. The stories I've heard always spoke of avoiding engagement. And he certainly wouldn't dare to do so here because of our laws against it." Terrence turned a knowing eye on Darragh. "And he knows who the law is here."

Nodding in understanding, Darragh shared a possible conclusion. "But Seigine could have exaggerated. If his people were the aggressors and Niall got the upper hand, mayhap wounded pride made him tell the story the way he did."

"That still doesn't explain how the lass was harmed," Duncan said, his arms wrapped about his barrel chest. "And *she's* my only concern."

"Ah, Brighit would want to be a part of any raiding Niall had planned. I'm certain of it." He tried to ignore the raw pain at the realization she may have defied him, and after reassuring him she would not.

"The man would be daft to take her out the night before her wedding," Terrence said.

"His niece was hurt and he didn't even tell ye? Who is this man?" Duncan's fierce scowl revealed his inner rage.

"I've never considered him the sanest man alive." Darragh frowned. "But bruises on her face? Bruises on... her." He remembered the shadows beneath her gown, he'd assumed it was the lighting, but what if she'd been more thoroughly beaten? "Oh damn."

"What are ye about?" Terrence came closer to Darragh.

"The way she attacked me on our wedding night? What if it wasn't just her face that was hurt? What if I'd caused her more pain without knowing it?"

"She'd kick ye in the balls without hesitating." Duncan spoke matter-of-factly.

"Something went wrong with the raid. I do not know what, but despite what Seigine claims, it must have somehow contributed to Cathair's death." Darragh scrubbed his face. "If Brighit doesn't care to share with me, no amount of insistence will loosen her tongue. It may push her away."

And just when they were coming to terms.

"I'll approach Niall." Duncan's expression had taken on the look of a man with a duty to perform. "I'll get the details from him."

The two stood watching Darragh, the tension pouring out of them while they awaited his orders. He nodded his consent.

"Ye cannot say a word to Brighit." Darragh confronted each one of them with his fiercest scowl and they nodded, their expressions distraught.

An intense, possessive anger sparked in his gut. No one was going to get away with hurting her. No one.

"Forgive me, Darragh." Terrence's expression spoke of the guilt he felt for believing Darragh would ever hurt his wife, but he couldn't forgive him. Not yet.

"Do yer duty, Terrence. We'll speak later."

Terrence walked away to catch up with the others, but Duncan remained.

"Ye know what ye need to do, lad. She needs yer love and acceptance. Gain her trust. Then mayhap she'll share with ye what happened."

When they entered the great hall, Darragh avoided looking at her directly but kept her in his sight. He didn't want her to notice him studying her too intently. He set his troubling thoughts aside, trying to focus instead on the numerous foodstuffs being set upon the trestle table.

"Ye're busy I see." His words were for his mother, who was watching over the servants. He kissed her on the cheek.

"Welcome back, son." The source of her obvious irritation was quickly revealed when Darragh saw Brighit standing with his father.

Her proud demeanor, even dressed in trews and a man's mantle, took his breath away. She was beautiful. Her shoulders back, her chin high, her long hair hanging down her back.

"And aren't ye smitten with yer little she-warrior."

"Hush." Darragh turned an angry face at his mother, only to realize she was teasing him. "Do not call her that."

"Never. I would have thought ye'd prefer a milder woman, who ye wouldn't have a constant battle of wills with." She searched his face. "Clearly I was wrong."

Tipping her head, Tisa returned to the kitchen to check on the rest of the meal.

Darragh crossed his arms about his chest, his eyes intent on Brighit now that she no longer returned his gaze. It was as if she'd entranced him with that very first kiss. Could he have ever thought, even in passing, that a calmer woman would be more pleasing? More the fool was he.

"Father." Darragh smiled at his father, bracing himself to glance at Brighit, praying his feelings were well hidden. He needed that stoic façade now more than ever. "Brighit."

He kissed his wife's cheek, his hand lingering on her arm. She seemed to sag against him as if in relief. He lowered his voice. "How fare ye?"

Her eyes downcast, she merely shook her head that she was not well.

Darragh turned to his father, his brows lifted in supplication. "Father, I believe Brighit and I have some unpacking to do. If ye'll excuse us?"

When his eyes finally fell on the third figure who'd approached the trestle table, the realization that it was Seigine set his anger ablaze. Though he didn't understand the depth of the man's involvement, Darragh didn't trust him. He knew, at the very least, that the man had lied to him.

"Seigine." Darragh forced the acknowledgement

out between tight lips.

"Of course," Tadhg said.

Seigine paused, his eyes looking at Brighit far too intimately before he noticed Darragh's scowl. "Of course. We will speak later. Brighit?"

She mumbled something without meeting the man's eyes and turned, but Darragh quickly wrapped his arm around her so that they left together as if nothing were untoward. Brighit trembled beneath his arm.

"Did the man say something to upset ye?"

She simply shook her head, but when she finally met his eyes, his concern only increased. As soon as they reached the privacy of his room, he pulled her into his arms. She was stiff in his arms.

"Tell me what upsets ye."

She tugged away and sat on the edge of their bed, her eyes cast downward.

"Brighit. Look at me." He spoke with a coaxing tone, lifting her chin with a gentle touch. When she obeyed, her light skin was without blemish. His relief was so great, he slid the side of his finger along its softness. "What is amiss? Exhaustion again?"

She simply nodded. He carried the sack of their belongings to the bed. "Mayhap ye have the strength to help me sort through our things?"

Brighit nodded, standing beside him as it was all dumped on the bed. Folding this and shaking out that, she seemed to be far off in her thoughts. Darragh reached for the powder.

"D'ye wish to still keep this?" He held the jar up.

Brighit's eyes widened with concern and she quickly searched his expression, appearing quite afraid. His heart lurched. He didn't want to see fear on her lovely face.

"It matters little to me except that ye have no longer been wearing it, which I greatly appreciate."

He paused, but her eyes kept their roundness as if she feared what he might say.

"Ye can keep it in here if ye prefer." He put it back in the sack, keeping his eyes downcast. "I did not think ye needed it anymore."

"Darragh."

His breath shuttered and he closed his eyes, sending up a prayer that she would open her heart to him and share what had happened.

He slowly lifted his gaze to her, struggling to maintain that stoic demeanor. "What is amiss?"

Brighit nibbled at her thumb, her eyes darting away. "I do not need the powder. Ye are right. If ye did not like it, I should not wear it."

His nostrils flared, but he held back his disappointment at her lack of trust. Locking the uncomfortable feelings away, he simply nodded.

And yet she did not continue unpacking as if nothing had happened. Rather, she sat on the side of the bed, her eyes unfocused. He swallowed, trying to appear disinterested as he fiddled with this and that, waiting to see if she would speak freely at last.

"The powder came from far away, where a woman's beauty is judged by how pale she appears. It covers everything. They use powder to make themselves more beautiful." Brighit seemed to be talking to herself, so he didn't respond. "They treat the women as if they will break apart if touched too harshly." A sob brought him closer to her. "Their women would never dare to confront a man, or... try to defend herself against one bent on hurting her."

Darragh's heart broke for the pain in her scrunched-up face when she started to cry. He took her in his arms ever so gently, lifting her from the bed.

"Shhh. I have ye now. Ye're safe with me."

She pressed her face into his chest, rubbing it back and forth. "I am a stupid girl, thinking I could see to my own defense."

The tension fell away from Darragh. She had put to words what he needed to know, but a new sense of purpose rose in his gut. He would protect her. He would avenge her. "Ye are fine with me now. Ye can do more than any other women I know."

Pulling back, her tear-stained, blotchy face crushed him. "I can do very little. D'ye not see that?"

"No. I see ye can do much. Brighit?" He swallowed, attempting to pull back on the skepticism that had crept into his tone. He didn't want to offend, he wanted her to stop berating herself. "Ye are not a man, but ye have great ability and skill. 'Tis plain. No one can argue that. If a man was stronger than ye and hurt ye, 'twas not a fair fight."

She wiped at her tears. "I was wrong to think I could defeat any man."

"I've seen ye defeat many men." He wanted to shake her, make her realize how very special she was to him, but even more importantly he wanted the name of the man who'd dared to hurt her. "Tell me who bested ye?"

"He knocked me off my horse." Her eyes darted away as if again seeing the fight. "I couldn't breathe when I hit the ground. He was livid. He would have taken out his anger on me. But I couldn't let him discover I was a woman." What could have happened next hung in the air between them, each knowing what he would have done. "I couldn't let him find out."

Darragh was beside himself, struggling with what to do, what to say, how much to comfort her. He needed to hear this story in full, however, so he locked his jaw tight, his hands fisted at his sides.

She turned toward him, but not seeing him. "He was massive and his expression was so cruel. I thought—" She looked away, a great sob heaving her chest. "I could best him because I was faster but he showed me how wrong I was."

Brighit hugged her self tightly, gazing toward the ceiling as if seeing the sky. "He laughed at me and shoved me away when he could have ended me right there. A fair fight and he gave me a second chance, taunting me." She dropped her gaze to Darragh. "He knocked me down and got on top of me. He beat me with his fists and… and I could do nothing."

She covered her face, her shoulders heaving but no sound coming out of her as she broke down.

He took her in his arms while her body was wracked with sobs. Compassion for her heightened his need to defend her. So close to getting the name of the man, he smoothed down her hair as if she were a child. Brighit shook her head, defeated.

He spoke in a tight whisper. His anger barely contained. "Tell me who did this."

"It was Cathair." Her words erupted on a sob. "Cathair beat me… and I killed him for it."

Chapter Twenty-Three

Brighit could see the man again in her mind.

"D'ye seriously want to do this?"

Cathair had wanted revenge for something and he'd wanted it from her. If she had not defended herself at all, he would have found out she was a lass sooner and then... his excited expression at finding her binding and realizing she was a female flashed through her mind. She shivered.

Darragh's concerned expression broke through her thoughts right before her mind went to Seigine, mounted and watching from the crest of the hill. It suddenly struck her as odd, beyond odd, that he'd sat there waiting. Watching. Had he stayed to see if his brother needed assistance? No. He would have assumed Cathair needed no help, so why watch? Why not join the others in fighting her uncle and brothers? Had he—

It was the disbelief on Darragh's face that finally halted her tears and stiffened her spine. There was no question about what she was saying and he had to understand that. Having confessed, it was required that she be believed.

As if reading her thoughts, he said, "I do not believe ye."

She refused to respond, keeping her expression blank, and remained quiet.

"I saw the body, Brighit." Darragh shook his head as if shaking off a bad dream. "Ye could never be so vile, so cruel, so destructive."

The tears had stopped and Brighit felt an overwhelming relief in his condemnation of what she'd done. She glanced away, unable to meet his eyes.

"He was beating me, and when he felt the bindings at my breasts, his expression… changed. He became excited about discovering I was a woman because it meant he could punish me even further."

"Punish ye?"

"I shouldn't have been on their land. It was the middle of the night."

Something flickered in Darragh's eyes, and she feared that she'd somehow revealed her uncle's role.

"I had wanted to take a midnight ride. One last ride as a final goodbye to my freedom."

Darragh's brows dipped low. "And have ye found yerself truly subdued by me?"

She blew out a breath. "Ye know I have not. I was so wrong in what I thought of ye. Forgiveness, please?"

"For thinking the worst of me or for breaking our agreement?"

She winced. "Both."

He was measuring her sincerity, she knew it deep down in her gut. It was on his face. He wondered if she could ever be trusted again.

"Ye are forgiven," he said. No hesitation. No disappointment in his tone.

Brighit had not expected that. Somewhere in her thoughts she'd imagined him railing at her about her willfulness for not listening to him. And he would have been right to do so. Although breaking their agreement had not been her idea, she had gone along willingly enough. Niall had merely been looking for a way to indulge his beloved niece, but all his plans had gone awry.

"I was wrong to sneak off and to be on their land. I had thought no harm would come of it." She hadn't thought at all. Holding up her hand when he started to speak, she continued, "Do not ask more of me. I will speak only of my crime."

Darragh flattened his lips, not in the least bit happy with her. "Crime? It sounds like defense to me." He hesitated, his gaze dropping away. "I'm not certain how the *rig túaithe* will judge it."

She closed her eyes and took a calming breath. When she opened them again, Darragh was staring at her. "Tell me how it happened. Exactly."

"I do not want to relive it."

"I wouldn't ask it of ye unless I needed to hear it myself."

Brighit had gone over this so many times in her head, but where was she to start without implicating Niall?

"I was racing across the field, pushing Valiant up a hill at top speed." The sight of Cathair following her flashed through her mind. "I saw a man following me and…" The sound of the fighting that had broken out behind her filled her ears. The others had attempted to send her to safety—they'd never imagined she would be chased. "…he was relentless in his pursuit. I couldn't get away."

She took a quivering breath. "When I thought I had lost him because he was no longer behind me, he knocked me from my horse. He'd gotten the jump on me, arriving at the bottom of the hill before I could."

"Which hill?"

"What?"

"Tell me which hill ye went up?"

"The one to the east."

"That is the opposite of my *túath*. Did ye not wish to return home?"

She had been going where Niall told her to go, away from the MacNaughton so they couldn't be traced back. "I was… panicked."

Darragh watched her, his face expressionless.

"D'ye wish me to continue?"

"Not if ye continue to prevaricate."

Brighit turned away, petrified that he'd see the truth of his words, her guilt, on her face. "I cannot—"

"Ye must tell me everything, Brighit. If they find out that ye killed him—"

"Seigine knows that I killed him. He saw me. He watched from the top of the hill as I murdered his brother."

Darragh's mind reeled with the revelation. She'd

murdered a man with his brother a witness?

"Seigine watched the man beat ye?"

She nodded.

"And did nothing to help ye?" His irritated tone had Brighit pulling back, fear in her eyes.

"When he finally came closer... after I killed Cathair... I got on Valiant and I rode away from him. I was afraid of what he would do to me, but he didn't chase me."

"Were ye still dressed as a lad when Seigine saw ye?"

Brighit hesitated the slightest bit, and said, "I was still dressed as a lad."

Darragh nodded thoughtfully before asking, "Cathair used his hands to beat ye?"

Brighit nodded. Swallowing, she opened her mouth to continue but nothing came out, her eyes were wide with fear. Chagrined, Darragh poured her some mead from the carafe left for them on the chest. "Mayhap this will help ye."

After one sip, she got up and ran behind the single screen to the chamber pot, retching loudly. The sweetness of the drink must have sickened her. In two strides, he was beside her, pulling the loose hairs away from her face and rubbing her back. "*A ghráidh.* Ye have been through much."

"I will be fine."

He heard the tears in her throat, but her face remained dry. He eased her back to sit down and brought her some water. "Mayhap this will be better, but drink it slowly."

Settling down beside her, Darragh took her hand. "If this was something that could wait, I would say we could discuss it later but..." He turned wide eyes on her. "…ye have kept it to yerself for so long. 'Tis best ye tell yer story." He kissed her forehead before looking into her eyes. "I believe ye will feel better after ye tell me what happened."

Brighit nodded. "Cathair engaged me with his sword, laughing when I thought to fight back, but he quickly got the upper hand. I had no chance against him."

"I was a lad he needed to put in his place. I didn't think about how fast he could be, then he knocked me down and got on top of me. I couldn't breathe."

Darragh's breath stilled, his mind imagining the scene as she described it. Her delicate body subdued by the huge warrior. No wonder she'd been afraid of Darragh. Mayhap it wasn't even pain from her bruises that first night that had caused her to lash out, mayhap his size had simply reminded her of the beating and fearing for her life.

"He backhanded me. He wanted to know who had sent me."

"He asked who *sent* ye?" The man believed she had intentionally intruded on his land.

She nodded. "He wanted the name of my leader and said he wouldn't get away again."

Brighit sat gazing into the distance as if not seeing anything.

Darragh assessed her condition before he spoke, giving her his back. "Why would a single lad on Cathair's land be of such great concern to him, Brighit?"

"I do not know."

"A group of lads on his land could be cause for worry, and he would demand the name of *their* leader."

She said nothing.

He closed his eyes to rid them of their moisture before facing her. "When ye feel ye can trust me with everything, we can talk. I will await ye below."

"Darragh, I—"

"Do not." He gave her his most scathing expression. "I made my decision about ye a long while ago. It is up to ye now to make yers about me."

Once in the hall, he leaned back against the wall, feeling as if he'd been in a terrible battle. His insides ached and his eyes burned. How could he reach his wife if she refused to show herself to him?

The door was suddenly yanked open, and Brighit appeared in the frame, looking down the hall toward the stairs before turning to find him there beside her door. "I have made my decision. May I tell ye what I've done? And mayhap ye can help me know what I need to do?"

Chapter Twenty-Four

Darragh sighed out his relief as he followed her back into their room. He helped himself to the mead and swallowed down the contents before facing her again.

She looked at him and dropped the thumb she'd been absently nibbling. "Ye know, don't ye?"

She said it like a statement and Darragh was not about to argue with the truth.

"If ye refer to the fact that Niall took ye out with the other lads, including yer brothers, then aye, I had my suspicions."

"Do not be vexed with them. Niall was hoping we would have a memorable adventure. Nothing more."

"He was not being protective of ye."

"I did not want his protection!" She put a hand to

her mouth again and turned away. The silence lasted but a moment before she spoke again. "We all thought we would just be traipsing across open land, imagining the enemy all around us."

Brighit turned to him, her tight control slipping as a single tear slid down her cheek. "He was indulging me as he always did. As soon as we crossed onto their land, they attacked us. Niall ordered me to head east, alone, rather than be caught with them."

"He was trying to protect ye and instead made ye an easy target." Darragh's mind had a hard time moving beyond the careless treatment Brighit had received from her uncle and brothers. "Does Niall know what happened to ye?"

She shook her head. "There was no time to tell him. When I returned…" Glancing down, she wrung her hands. "I washed the blood off me and snuck back into the hall. There was no sign of any of them."

"Does Seigine know that *ye* are the lad who killed his brother?"

A strangled sound escaped her, and Brighit got up to pace the small area, keeping her gaze averted. He watched her with narrowed eyes, emotions flitting across her face as she considered how best to proceed.

Darragh crossed his arms about his chest. "Brighit?"

"I know. I know. A moment please."

He cleared his throat. "Ye cannot keep anything back from me."

Halting suddenly, Brighit turned to face him. "Seigine has my weapon and he will give it to yer father tonight if I do not do as he ordered." Her eyes widened with fear. "He didn't just threaten me. He threatened ye and my father. I never wanted to take ye down with me."

The other words sunk into his brain. Slowly. "How long has he had yer weapon?"

"From the first. I left it when I ran away from Cathair's body."

"And how long has he known it was *yer* weapon?"

"He's known all along." Her throat constricted. "I have done so many things wrong, Darragh. I do not know how to make any of it right."

His mind went back to the night of their wedding. When he'd returned from inspecting the body, Seigine had been left in the hall with Brighit. Everyone else in his party had gone outside with them. Then he remembered how Seigine had arranged for some time alone with her at the camp. Darragh had been called away to examine some blood that had turned out to be from an animal.

"Has Seigine been threatening ye all along?"

She nodded.

"And what is it he has asked ye to do?"

"I must get ye and yer father to side with him against the Dubhshláine. He wants to become their new king."

Darragh's amazement at the man's audacity held him speechless. He turned from her, running his hand through his hair and shaking his head in disbelief.

"I am sorry, Darragh."

He turned to her. "Ye have done nothing wrong."

"What? I've murdered a man."

"Because ye had no other choice." Darragh did not doubt her instincts were correct about Cathair and what he was willing to do to her. "When Francis spoke of Seigine, he spoke of a man who would do anything to get what he wanted."

"But he had no way of knowing I would kill Cathair."

Darragh shrugged. "And mayhap he watched merely to be entertained, but when ye stabbed him—" He'd seen the body, and there was no denying the man had died a brutal death. "Brighit, ye stabbed the man? Where?"

"In his side. It was the only target I had."

"Then what?"

Her face scrunched up and the tears returned. "I couldn't get him off of me. He was as heavy as a horse. I pushed and pushed but he wouldn't budge. I couldn't breathe."

Darragh took her into a close embrace. "Shh. Ye're fine now. And ye did get out from under him."

"Aye, and that was when I saw Seigine watching me."

He pulled back to look her in the eye. "So ye stabbed the man and he stilled right away?"

"No. He pulled back to glare down at me as if he couldn't believe I had stabbed him. He was about to cut my bindings and I was so afeared of what he might do to me if he realized I was a woman."

"And when he looked at ye, what did ye do?"

"I jabbed the dagger deeper into his side, until I came up against his ribs and it would go no further." She covered her mouth. "His blood leaked down my hand and the disgusting sound of his flesh being severed filled the air."

"One wound? That was all?"

She nodded, dropping her hand, a curious expression on her face. "I must have injured an organ. He died quickly."

Darragh walked toward the single arrow slit that

showed the night sky outside his room. The crickets sang their farewell song in the distance, and the music carried to him from below. The feast to celebrate their return had commenced.

With a wide smile, he turned to face her. "Cathair was stabbed fourteen times."

Her mouth dropped open before slamming shut. "I do not understand."

"The wound ye inflicted was not mortal, but he may have passed out from the pain." He closed the distance, taking her hands in his. "It was Seigine who stabbed him the other thirteen times. My guess is that he watched to see what would happen. Mayhap he even believed ye had managed to kill him. When the man came to, Seigine was so incensed to find he wasn't dead, he took the knife to him in a rage."

She moved closer. "Then I did not kill him."

"It does not appear so to me."

Brighit eyes glistened with unshed tears, but she remained quiet, no doubt thinking through the implications.

"Now all we have to do is prove it."

Tadhg was seated beside his wife, the music filled the great hall, and Brighit's hands were damp with sweat as she stood in the threshold with her husband.

"I do not know if I can do this."

Darragh turned to her and they locked eyes. "I know that ye can."

"Ye know that I can sit there and lie through my teeth?"

"Through yer teeth, around yer teeth, and out yer ear if need be."

She dropped her brows for a fierce frown. "'Tis not humorous."

Darragh kissed the tip of her nose. "It is. Relax. Work yer wiles."

She pursed her lips as they entered the hall, her hand resting on his arm as he led the way to the head table. No applause but an appreciative smile from Tisa since Brighit had taken the time to change into an acceptable gown.

"Tisa." Brighit inclined her head to the woman as she passed in front of her to sit on the opposite side of her husband. Tadhg leaned in to kiss his daughter-in-law's cheek once she was seated beside him. Darragh took his place next to her, nodding his greetings.

"Now Darragh," Tisa's scolding tone grated on Brighit's raw nerves, "have I taught ye nothing about a proper greeting?"

Brighit dropped her hand into his lap and squeezed his thigh, which caused him to smile.

"Forgiveness. Good eve, Mother, Father, Seigine."

The odious man sat on the far side of Tisa as if he were a favored guest.

"Darragh." Seigine turned a bitter smile toward Brighit. "Brighit."

Straightening her back, Brighit smiled brightly when she turned toward the man. He was not quick enough to hide his look of surprise. Good. She had him off balance, mayhap now he wouldn't notice if she was less than convincing.

The food was promptly served to their table and the ale flowed without restraint. Seigine quickly asked for a refill. Tisa didn't appear to notice, but she knew

Darragh's mother—she noticed everything.

"Seigine has been very busy with his hunt for his brother's killer, Darragh," Tadhg said.

"Oh has he?" Darragh broke the crusty bread with his bare hands and handed a portion to her. "I would expect no less from him. He was deeply saddened by Cathair's death."

"He mentioned seeing yer party."

"We did cross paths," Darragh said.

Brighit held her breath as she brought the goblet to her lips, hoping to stop the shaking of her hands. The liquid was cool and refreshing. Darragh was quick to offer her a bite of the duck that had been prepared in his honor. "Be sure to eat, my love, ye may even now be eating for more than just yerself."

"What? Did I hear ye aright?" Tisa's excited proclamation rippled across the hall until every eye was on them and all talking had ceased.

Brighit beamed, nodding enthusiastically.

"Well done, Darragh." Tadhg slapped his son on the back before standing, his goblet in his hand.

"Waiting to be certain…"

"Hah, a toast to my son."

"…might be wise."

Shouts of congratulations and encouragement erupted while everyone followed their king in drinking to his son. When Tadhg sat back down, he wrapped an arm around his wife's shoulders. "I am quite pleased and ye?"

"I am beside myself with happiness."

Seigine cleared his throat. "Congratulations indeed." He raised his cup to Brighit before throwing back the contents. "Did I mention I have brought the murder weapon with me?"

"Aye, ye did mention that." Tadhg responded, clearly irritated at the turn of the conversation. "What say ye we wait until after our meal to discuss things."

"Mayhap we need to discuss it before we eat." Seigine's irritation was growing.

Swallowing the food, he'd just placed in his mouth, Darragh smiled awkwardly. "Too late?"

"When will the other nobles be arriving?" Seigine emptied his mug for the third time. The young lad was quick to refill it.

"We should have our panel by the morrow. First, they would consider the murder charges," Tadhg said. "Has yer search turned over anyone?"

"It has." Seigine was not touching his food, but the liberal amount of ale was affecting him, his words slurring.

Tisa shifted beside him, unnoticed by the man.

"A few possibilities," he added.

When he turned his intimidating gaze toward Brighit, he stilled. She was prepared with a smile. Seigine's mouth tightened slightly, and he quickly glanced away. As she'd hoped, he'd accepted the gesture as confirmation that she had been successful with what he had ordered her to do.

"And what is yer hope for yer clan now? Have ye given yer brother's plans any further consideration?" Tadhg asked Seigine directly.

Openly smiling, Seigine appeared barely able to contain himself. He hesitated as if to gather his thoughts back together. "My brother had decided nothing. It was merely talk."

Tadhg lifted his goblet, resting it from his raised hand. "I'm certain he intended to move forward with it."

"And when did ye speak of this?"

"When we discussed the destruction being visited on both our lands." Tadhg turned to watch Seigine's expression. "He said he had a good idea who the culprit might be."

The large man laughed. "And did he say who he thought it was?"

"He did not, but he promised me it would stop."

"A king who cannot keep peace on his own land is not much of a king at all."

"Are ye insulting my father?" Darragh sat up and narrowed his eyes at the man. "Or are ye speaking of yer brother?"

"Cathair." Seigine burped. "My brother could do little to protect the small bit of land that was his. To offer help to a neighbor is merely talk. Nothing more."

"Then ye must have been pleased with his decision to join with Dubhshláine."

"There was no decision." He barked the words loudly enough that some of the others in the hall stopped talking to glance at the head table.

Seigine's eyes were wide with anger, but when he caught Brighit watching him, a sickening smile lightened his face. He opened his mouth to speak, but the sound of the entryway doors bursting open distracted him for whatever he'd planned to say. A gust of wind came into the hall, along with Francis, flanked by his eldest sons. All eyes turned in the same direction.

Seigine raised partly from his chair as if in awe of the sight, whispering, "*Datan.*"

Tisa turned a sharp gaze to Seigine. "*Datan?* Ye fostered with the man?"

He didn't respond but kept his eyes fixed on the man he held in such high regard, he still referred to him with the endearing title.

"Apologies for our tardiness." Francis bellowed as he crossed the hall to the head table.

"Welcome." Tadhg offered, standing to greet the large man.

"I did not realize ye would be joining us for the meal." Tisa's agitation was sincere. "We would have awaited yer arrival. Something about a soak…?"

Devin settled beside Seigine, wrapping an arm around the man whose eyes darted around as if looking for a way out. Brighit scooted away from Tadhg, creating room for the other *ri*.

"Ah, a bit indelicate of me," Francis said.

"When have ye ever been accused of being delicate?" Tadhg asked.

Francis's laughter bellowed across the hall, the others joining in as they resumed their eating. He settled in the spot Brighit had made for him.

"Have I missed anything of importance?" Francis asked, helping himself to a generous portion from the platter brought to him.

"Not at all." Tadhg nodded toward Darragh and Brighit. "We were just discussing the importance of having good neighbors."

"From what I remember of my father's advice…" Brighit tried for an easy tone, doing her utmost to ignore the lump half way down her throat, "'tis better to be an ally than an enemy to yer neighbor."

She had Seigine's total attention. His body was rigid while his eyes seemed to bore into her. The tension pouring off him was intense. Darragh's hand against her back encouraged her to continue.

"Certainly, Seigine has demonstrated his belief in the same approach."

Chapter Twenty-Five

Darragh seethed inside at the look of appreciation Seigine now bestowed on his wife, but he averted his gaze.

"Ye have enemies, Tadhg?" Francis wiped his sleeve across his face.

Tadhg sighed. "Someone has been poaching my deer, which I find far less offensive than the poacher's habit of also ripping open its guts and leaving it to waste."

Francis paused, his food halfway to his mouth, and sat back. "Ripped across its belly? Like this?" He demonstrated the unusual cut.

"The same. Have ye had a similar experience?"

Someone shifted near the end of the table, but Darragh couldn't be certain who it was.

"I have." Francis looked straight ahead, raising his goblet to his mouth. "D'ye remember, Devin?"

"I do, Father."

Darragh leaned forward to take in the strikingly ominous expressions of the Meachair, all three of them.

"A long time back now." Devin continued. "After Liam had nearly had his head split open with a rock."

Tisa gasped. "How terrible."

Francis turned toward the other end of the table, and though Darragh couldn't see his expression, the tightness of his body reminded him of an arrow about to be let lose.

"D'ye remember the time, Seigine? Ye were fostering with me."

The man's face was suffused with anger. "Are ye still claiming I'm the one who tried to hurt yer lad? Ye couldn't prove it then and ye cannot prove it now."

Liam sat on the far side of Seigine. "But I remembered, despite yer claim of innocence. 'Twas ye who hefted the boulder over me, barely missing my skull."

Shaking his head, Seigine tried to make light of it. "We were children. I had no reason to want to cause ye harm."

Francis continued with the same hard tone. "And at the time, we'd several animals that had been savaged and left for dead."

"A hard winter, too, and with the extra mouths to feed…" Devin's voice dropped off.

"A decision was made to quit the fostering and ye were returned to yer clan." Francis faced front again, his lips flat against his teeth.

The people seated in front of them continued their

conversations, eating and drinking, oblivious to the sudden tension at the head table.

Brighit swallowed loudly beside Darragh and he clasped her hand that rested on her lap. He offered her a smile of encouragement and removed his hand before giving her a gentle nod. She stood beside him, a tight smile on her face.

"If ye'll excuse me, I need to check on my father's arrival. I expect him anytime."

"Of course, dear." Tisa said. "Ye may check with the guards at the gate. Word may have come after we sat down to dinner."

"Would the guard not have brought us the information?" Tadhg asked.

Darragh tensed as did Brighit. If she wasn't able to leave the hall, there would be no opportunity for Seigine to speak to her. Their plan would be stalled.

Tisa shrugged. "He does not always deem it necessary."

Tadhg's expression of surprise was followed by a loudly exhaled breath, and Darragh felt certain he was about to defend his men.

"Father, allow my wife to see to whatever she needs to." He widened his eyes, hoping to instill the slightest question in his father's mind about her reasons for needing to leave.

Tadhg merely nodded, no doubt catching his meaning. "Certainly."

Devin stood on cue as soon as Brighit disappeared into the entry hall. "Calum."

A man turned toward him with a look of surprise before glancing around to be sure he was the Calum who'd been named.

"Calum." Devin laughed and stepped away from

the table, clasping the man's arm in a tight grip. "Do not tell me ye do not remember me."

The man smiled and nodded and those at the head table quickly lost interest.

"Did ye enjoy yer duck, Darragh?" Tisa asked, dabbing at her lips with a cloth.

"Certainly. My favorite."

Tadhg turned his back to the others at the table. "And when ye return, we always eat well."

Darragh smiled, answering absentmindedly while his eyes followed Seigine, who also left the table. Stretching, he went toward the side table covered with pitchers of ale and mead. Reaching toward a tall clay pitcher, he glanced around. Darragh turned to his father, Seigine still in his sights as the man left by way of the entry hall.

"Is something amiss?" Tadhg asked, his stoic expression intact.

"What d'ye mean?"

He glanced at Francis. "Are we laying a trap for anyone in particular?"

"Indeed we are," Darragh said.

Darragh stood, tipping his head toward Francis, who also stood. "And we'll know soon enough if we were successful."

Brighit had waited at the door until she saw Seigine leave the table. Her hand gripping the latch, she counted to five before opening the door leading outside.

"Brighit." A sense of satisfaction flowed through

her when Seigine called her name. In a flash, she forced her expression to collapse into a frown as she turned toward the man.

He glanced around to see no one was near. "Little one, ye surprised me."

She swallowed. "I did as ye demanded. If ye are not given the kingship, 'twill be because of yer own foolishness and not for lack of trying on my part."

The man stopped close enough that she had to tilt her head back to look into his face, his heated anger pouring off of him. "Ye insult me and yet I am well pleased by the attempt."

When he touched her cheek, she cringed. His hand stilled.

"But that is not the game ye will play now, certainly. Not when I wish to show my appreciation for yer efforts."

He moved forward, trapping her between the wall and his huge body. "We have other things to see to now."

"I will not be yer whore." She spat the words at him. If this was the direction of his thoughts, it would be difficult to turn the conversation toward his brother. She prayed Darragh and the others were within hearing of the man—his voice was so low, it was nearly a whisper. When he pressed his hips against her, she tried to shove him away.

"Ho ho." Seigine grabbed her hands, glanced behind him, and pushed her through the door into the outside. The pitch dark enveloped them as he dragged her into the shadow of the castle. She cried out in pain when he shoved her against the wall.

"I will see to *this* now."

He pulled at the ties of his trews, glancing over his

shoulder into the darkness. Brighit did the same, her ears straining to hear anything. They would never find them here. Nothing was going as planned.

"Stop this at—." She cried out and his large hand covered her mouth, strangling her words.

Seigine's eyes rounded, his face so close she could smell the sour ale on his breathe. "When I was so looking forward to ravaging ye? Will this be the way of it?"

She held his gaze, his meaty fingers squeezing her mouth tight. There was no chance of her getting him to talk like this. It took all her will power to shake her head knowing it would be a sign of her acquiescence. He beamed, stroking her cheek as if he were petting a cat.

He reached beneath his mantle and withdrew the serpent-headed *miodóg*, holding it up to her face. "This is the very weapon ye used. Shall I show it to yer lusty husband?"

"I know I did not kill yer brother." Brighit blurted it out, hoping to redirect his thoughts. "I stabbed him only once. *Ye* murdered him in a rage."

He smiled. "Ah, very good, little one. I told ye that ye intrigued me."

She held her breath and prayed his arrogance would make him want to tell her the rest.

"Ye did disappoint me in not killing him. I had such high hopes, but when I went to check on him, he was coming to even then. He shook his head, searching for ye. So I took the knife out and shoved him down. I stabbed him until he stopped struggling against the inevitable."

"And ye say this is the dagger that killed yer brother?" Tadhg stepped away from the building, his hands at his waist.

Seigine didn't move, his widening eyes remaining on Brighit. A panicked expression. "It is." His voice louder now. "And I certainly should have mentioned that I personally witnessed the brutal attack. I was unable to stop it, but when I came to my brother's aid it was too late to save him and the murderer had ridden off."

"Unhand my wife." The demand was delivered in a low, unyielding tone, Darragh's voice as sharp as a shard of glass. "Immediately."

"I cannot, my friend. She murdered my brother and she must face her punishment."

It was Francis who broke out in applause, his slow, steady clap accelerating. "Well done, Seigine. Well done indeed."

"*Datan*, ye misunderstand—"

When Seigine would have turned toward his one-time mentor, Francis took the opportunity to shove him face first against the stone wall to the side of Brighit, a knife to his back.

"Remove yerself," he said to Brighit, jerking his head toward Darragh. "We've got the man we want."

She collapsed in her husband's welcoming arms while her knees trembled beneath her, threatening to give way.

He held her tight against him, supporting her. "Ye did very well."

"It did not go as we had planned." Her sobs were taking hold of her and she fought to steady her breathing.

"It did not," Darragh chuckled, "but ye kept yer head."

Devin secured Seigine's hands behind his back

with the length of rope he'd brought. Francis all but growled when he yanked the huge man away from the wall, dragging him toward the heavy wooden door, and turned back to Darragh. "Ye've a wise one there, lad."

Darragh nodded over her head, where her face was buried against his chest, fighting back sobs.

A firm hand on her shoulder squeezed gently. "Well done, daughter," Tadhg said.

The men spoke around her, but she couldn't pay attention. She fumed at how afraid she'd been. How she wished she'd stood up to him. Dropping her hand, she felt for Darragh's dagger, which she kept strapped to her waist.

"My dagger." Brighit pulled her head up, looking around. Seigine was gone, led away by Francis and his sons. Only Darragh and Tadhg remained with her. "May I have my weapon back?"

Her husband handed it to her. "Do not tell me ye thought I wouldn't realize the importance of ye having this."

Brighit ducked her head, her hand rubbing the hilt. Though flashes of the serpent's head dripping with blood went through her mind, she was determined to reclaim the weapon. It was a good dagger and had served its purpose. It had protected her.

"I will see ye within." Tadhg spoke to Darragh before turning to her, kissing her gently on the top of the head and disappearing through the doors.

She took a deep, shaky breath, forcing a genuine smile for her husband.

"I shall be fine."

"Are ye certain?" His eyes rounded with his concern, and his hand made a gentle sweep of her

273

cheek as he pushed her hair back. "Any other lass would have trouble recovering... but ye are not any lass."

"And glad I am that ye know it." Sifting through the many thoughts, regrets, and hopes running around her mind, she closed her eyes to gather her wits before speaking. "I have been more unlike myself these past few weeks than ever before."

"But I know who I married, and I would be greatly saddened if my feisty love were to never show her face again." He moved closer, their foreheads almost touching. "Mayhap I believed ye might be too much for me at one time, but now I know without any doubt that I want nothing less than all of ye."

His kiss was gentle, considerate, as if testing how she felt about everything. She returned the kiss just as tentatively, his words having touched her deeply. Never before had she been totally accepted. Mayhap once, when she was young, her father had enjoyed her skill, but that had changed the moment she'd revealed her vulnerability. Darragh had chosen to prepare her to confront the man who would take her down, even arming her with a weapon.

Brighit pulled her lips away, her gaze unable to meet his. "Darragh, I want ye to know how much I love ye."

Finally looking at him, she saw a stillness on his face she hadn't expected. Fear bit into her, but she did not regret her words. Even if he didn't love her back, her love was enough for both of them.

The moisture gathering in his eyes caught her by surprise. Darragh cleared his throat, glancing at the castle behind them before returning her gaze.

"To be loved by a woman as passionate and loyal

as ye is all I could have ever hoped for... especially since I love ye, too."

Epilogue

Brighit and Darragh met Sean in the bailey when he arrived bright and early the next day. Her father pulled her away from Darragh and embraced her as if he'd not seen her for years rather than a mere few weeks.

"How have ye fared?"

Her face nearly buried in her father's burly chest, she managed to say, "I am fine, Father."

He pulled back to look her in the face, a hand on each shoulder. "And ye'd tell me if ye weren't?"

The cough behind him certainly sounded forced, but neither Sean nor Brighit turned to Darragh.

"I am well cared for by both my husband and my new clan."

Sean's expression relaxed into a beaming smile.

"And that's what I wanted to hear." He finally reached out to take Darragh's hand. "How have ye fared, son? My daughter not too much for ye?"

There was the slightest hint of a challenge in the question and Brighit turned to hide her grin.

"I find her just enough for me. Kind of ye to ask."

"Sean." Tadhg crossed the open bailey to his friend, whom he embraced. "Glad I am ye're the first to arrive."

"And why would that be?"

Brighit's heart started racing. Would he insist that she and Darragh tell the story of how she'd put herself in harm's way to reveal Seigine? But Tadhg wrapped a firm hand around Sean's shoulders, turning him toward the castle and away from the couple. "We've a few things to discuss."

Brighit and Darragh exchanged a relieved look. She had not looked forward to breaking the news to her father and it was clear her husband felt the same way.

"WHAT?"

As one, they turned toward Sean and Tadhg. Her father's outrage was not something she'd seen very often. He was level-headed and seldom became this irate, but the look he sent her way made it difficult to swallow.

"Should I speak to him?" Darragh spoke quietly to her, neither of them daring to move.

"Probably not." Brighit had no idea what to do, but she was thankful Tadhg was still leading him toward the castle. If anyone could get through to her father, it was his oldest friend. Though he seemed reluctant, Sean eventually allowed himself to be herded within.

"Praise God I did not have to explain how it all came to pass," Darragh said.

Brighit turned her wide eyes on him. "Are ye that intimidated by my father?"

"When it comes to his only daughter, Sean is not reasonable."

From the way he averted his eyes, Brighit knew there was something he was not sharing with her.

"He is an extremely reasonable man," she said, countering his assertion in the hopes she'd convince him to talk.

Darragh threw his hands up in surrender. "Shall I share with ye how I was to take ye the first time?"

Her eyes widened, and her mouth dropped open.

"Aye, he was extremely concerned that ye experience no pain."

Brighit reddened. "Oh my."

"He explained his first time with yer mother."

Brighit covered her mouth.

"And had some very specific pointers for me."

"Oh, Darragh, I am very sorry."

Darragh shrugged. "It may have been intended only as a man-to-man talk but being that he is yer father… ye understand."

She nodded, her lips pressed tight to keep from smiling.

"Besides—" Darragh wrapped his arms about her, pulling her into his warm embrace, "—it made me more determined to be sure our joining was without witnesses, making my bride very happy."

"Very happy indeed." Brighit offered her lips to his, still amazed at his ability to make her feel safe and secure when everything around them was dangerous and unknown. "Forgiveness please for hurting ye."

He tipped her chin up with a gentle touch, looking into her eyes. "My love, ye had been through a horrible ordeal. I wish only that ye could have shared it with me."

"I should have trusted ye." She nodded. "I did not trust Terrence over ye. Some of the powder had rubbed off. He saw the bruises."

"Thank ye for that. Terrence told me ye refused to give him any details. I am pleased ye've decided ye could trust me." He brushed her cheek. "We have come a long way with trust, have we not?"

"Indeed."

"Good." Darragh bent over to lift her from the ground, tossing her over his shoulder.

"What are ye about?" she squealed.

Heading to the left of the main entrance, where Tadhg was no doubt still soothing her father's temper, Darragh climbed the steps that ran along the outside of the building, taking them two at a time.

"I've a powerful need for my wife."

"Now?" Brighit gripped his body as she tried to pick her head up, forcing herself to resist any thrashing about or loud carrying on despite her desire to be put down.

"I can think of no better time."

"But my father is here," she said, and even to her ears it sounded like a lame excuse.

"And he'll have to wait."

She refused to laugh. "But—"

He halted whatever she was about to say with a firm slap to her bottom, his hand remaining where it fell. When he started caressing her lightly, setting off her own need, Brighit decided there were definitely worst ways they could spend this time.

The council convened, and the proof brought forth before the panel of nobles included the testimony of the three witnesses who had heard everything Seigine had said to Brighit—Darragh, Tadhg, and Francis. Since Seigine himself confessed what he had done, there was little need for more discussion. The kings and others from the line of kings deemed worthy to be on this council were not insensitive to her plight, but it did become necessary for Brighit to tell her side of what had happened.

As was the custom, the meeting was held outside in plain view of any who wished to come and bear witness and most did. Brighit handled herself with a dignity rarely seen in any of the warriors who addressed the council. Although Sean's outrage was barely contained as she told her story with little emotion, Darragh could only feel an amazing sense of pride in his wife.

Seigine was determined to be guilty of murdering his own brother. The condition of the body, stabbed repeatedly by an enraged man, brought him little sympathy. The fact that he had killed the very man he had pledged to protect only made it a more horrific crime, requiring nothing less than Seigine's death.

Cathair had believed the warriors sneaking onto MacCochlain land that night were the ones who'd killed their livestock, ruined their grain, and mayhap even attacked their women. The warriors had lain in wait to defend what was theirs. The sorrow of the rest of the MacCochlain warriors was only deepened by the realization that Seigine had been murdering their leader while they were off fighting the intruders.

These same warriors had traveled with Seigine because they'd believed he wished to find his brother's murderer. Cathair's closest friend, Garbhán, had stepped up to promise personal protection to Seigine. As a sign of his commitment, he'd added a braided lock of the man's hair to his black arm band, which all of the warriors wore as a symbol of mourning for the loss of their king.

Once he had heard the witnesses, including Brighit? Garbhán stepped out from the crowd, ripped the lock of hair from his arm to drop it on the ground and crushed it beneath his heal. Seigine averted his eyes when the men who had served him lined up beside Garbhán and turned their back to him.

The execution of Seigine was to take place in a fortnight, giving enough time for his entire clan to be present to witness the punishment. At the urging of the council, and with the agreement of the other warriors including Garbhán, the joining of Clan MacCochlain to Clan Dubhshláine was completed as Cathair had planned. It was the very thing that had enraged Seigine enough to murder his own brother. Prayers were offered for Cathair.

Darragh considered this a good time to take Brighit on a trek back to visit their friends, Gwen and William. He did not want her to have to see the man chained in the bailey every day or to have to witness his execution. It would be too much. And if the weather was rough as they traveled, he felt certain they would manage.

The couple took the news about their nephews very hard. They'd never had their own children and the brothers had been like sons to them. Gwen was beside herself to learn how Seigine had threatened

Brighit, especially since she herself had unknowingly played a part in it. William privately admitted to Darragh that he'd always had his own concerns about the rivalry between the boys.

The parting was hard for both couples, but Brighit and Darragh promised to come visit again in the spring.

"Ye've been very quiet." Darragh glanced at Brighit riding beside him, dressed in her trews and tunic. "Do ye have concerns about the council's declaration?"

"Oh no, I believe they were more than fair."

"Difficult decisions to make."

And selecting who would live and who would die was the hardest duty for any leader. Battle required a warrior be put in harm's way. Some survived and some did not. Darragh had faced his fair share of such choices.

"Is that one of the reasons ye'd prefer not to be named *ri*?"

His perceptive wife.

"I would prefer not to have to leave ye and our children as my father always did. He could be gone for years. A warrior does battle, sometimes long, drawn-out battles, but then he returns home. It is the king who stays behind after the fighting is done to settle things." Dreading her answer a lot less than he had earlier, he asked, "Does this change yer opinion of me?"

"It does not. I will always hold ye in the highest regard whatever ye choose for us."

"Did ye see yer uncle when they described what had transpired? He was unable to remain present."

"I did speak with him." She turned to him, her

eyes rounded with concern. "I did not want him to feel guilty."

"So ye did not tell him everything?"

"I tried to tell him." She frowned, glancing away. "Lachlann finally had to spit it out in that way that only my brother has."

"Brighit. It was his fault ye were there at all. His and yer brothers'."

"I know ye feel that way, but mayhap ye do not understand exactly how persuasive I can be."

"Ye say this to me?" Darragh put his hands to his hips and quirked a brow. "So ye believe ye bullied them into allowing ye to come?"

"No." She had the grace to blush. "Mayhap ye do know, but my uncle has been through so much. He just lost his wife."

"I understand that and I have great sympathy for the man, but he put *my* wife in harm's way and I do not take that lightly. I had trusted him to protect ye, not drag ye into the dark of night where ye—"

"I know what happened, Darragh, I was there."

He slammed his mouth shut. She had been correct to not allow him to come with her when she spoke to Niall. Darragh would not have been able to hide his irritation with the man, even though he would have been right.

"He offered to pay his honor price to Clan Dubhshláine for his part in the untimely raid. They refused him." Brighit sighed. "My uncle is a good man."

"I do not dispute that."

"Clan Dubhshláine wants only good will with their neighbors, including yer clan and my father's clan."

"It did help clear the tension when Seigine admitted he was the one killing the deer on our land and his own." Darragh rubbed at his face. "A tiresome ordeal, this whole thing."

"And it was that outlaw Black Oengus who attacked the women in his clan, did my father tell ye that?"

Darragh nodded.

"Seigine's wife was so damaged from the attack, she is no longer right in the head."

"Garbhán assured me the man was a cruel husband even before that." He pulled back on his horse's reins, stopping just within the tree line near a small clearing. "This seems like a good place to rest for the night."

Brighit dismounted and pulled her bag down with her as she came toward Darragh. He took the sack and dropped it on the ground beside them to take her in his arms. "Have I told ye how pleased I am with ye as my wife?"

"I believe ye show me every night."

"Ah, our passion is indisputable, but do not underestimate how much ye impress me with yer bravery and intelligence."

She held his gaze for a long moment before she finally answered. "No other man would have accepted me just as I am. They would have needed to break me to their will."

"And it would have been their loss."

Brighit swallowed, her gaze intense. "That ye do accept me as I am means everything to me."

"My she-warrior." He kissed her again then nuzzled into the crook of her neck. "I have married a warrior who also pleasures me in bed."

"Have I told ye how pleased I am with ye as my husband?"

"I believe ye have shown me as much." He tugged at the opening of her tunic to nip at her shoulder.

"And is that yer appreciation pressing against me now?"

"Hmm, appreciation for all that ye are. Now let us see to these trews and tunics."

He reached to assist her, but she stepped out of his arms. "Ye said ye liked me in these."

"Ah, but I like ye without them even better."

She smiled and moved closer. "Ah, then I give ye permission to have yer way with me."

And he did.

THE END

GLOSSARY

Kingship in Éire:

rí means "king" (plural is *ríg*)

ri túaithe – The king of a *túath* (small territory)

ri túath – The overking of several *túatha* (several small territories)

ri rúirech – The king of a *rúirech* (lordship, a huge territory)

árd rí – The high king

Definitions:

a grádh – sweetling
a thighearna – oh lord
báirseach – termagant
brithem – an attorney
Datan – affectionate term for a fostering father
derb fine – council that advises the king
fili – a member of an elite class of poets
grádh – darling
mamaídh – mama
miodóg – dagger
mo mhíle stór – my love

Pronunciation of Names:

Aednat – Ain-it
Darragh – Die-ruh
Diarmuid – Deer-mid
Lorcánn – Lurk-an

Seigine – Say-ghine
Garbhán – Gar-ven

Clan Name Translations taken from *Clans and Families of Ireland* by John Grenham:

Cruadhlaoch – Crowley
Dubhshláine – Delaney
Meachair – Maher

ABOUT THE AUTHOR

Aside from two years spent in the wilds of the Colorado mountains, Ashley York is a proud life-long New Englander and a hardcore romantic. She has an MA in History which brings with it, through many years of research, a love for primary documents and the smell of musty old libraries. With her author's imagination, she likes to write about people who could have lived alongside those well-known giants from the past.

Connect with her online at:

Website: www.ashleyyorkauthor.com
Email: ashleyyork1066@gmail.com
Twitter: @ashleyyork1066

The Warrior Kings Series starts with *Curse of the Healer*, Diarmuid and Aednat's story.

After the death of Brian Boru in 1014, a legend arose of a healer so great she could raise a man from the dead, with a power so strong it could make any warrior the next high king of Ireland... and to steal it away from her, he need only possess her.

Fated to be a healer…

Aednat has spent her entire life training to be the Great Healer, knowing she must remain alone and untouched. When she meets Diarmuid, the intense attraction she feels toward him shakes her resolve to believe in such a legend. If she gives in to the passion he ignites in her, can she settle for being less?

Destined to be his…

Diarmuid of Clonascra is renowned for his bravery in battle. Only one thing daunts him: the prospect of taking a wife. The safest course would be to keep his distance from Aednat, the bold, headstrong healer who's far too tempting for his peace of mind. But his overking orders him to protect her from a group of craven warriors intent on kidnapping her to steal her power.

What starts as duty for Diarmuid quickly transforms into something more. Aednat's power might be at risk, but so is his closed-off heart.

www.ingramcontent.com/pod-product-compliance
Lightning Source LLC
Chambersburg PA
CBHW031222120726
47905CB00002B/430